"Don't make a sound. . . ."

Then the room thundered with hoofbeats; the windows and walls and the doors rattled with a gale force. Buffy bit her lower lip to keep from shouting out; it wasn't her way to cower, and everything in her longed to jump up and face this Wild Hunt.

The hoofbeats came louder, louder still. Buffy braced herself to be trampled. She was shaking with cold; it was as if she had been plunged into a sea of ice.

"Their leader wears the horns of a buck. He's shaggy and no man can see his face and live," Angel whispered. "All heads must turn away when the Hunt goes by."

"Angel . . ."

"Hush, Buffy. My soul is my curse, they can't take it away," he said. "But they can take yours."

The room resounded with howls and thunder and Buffy's own heartbeat roaring in her ears. Her body ached with cold. Pinned beneath Angel, she could barely breathe. . .

Buffy the Vampire Slayer™

Child of the Hunt

Available from POCKET BOOKS

Buffy the Vampire Slayer young adult books

Buffy the Vampire Slayer (movie tie-in)
The Harvest
Halloween Rain
Coyote Moon
Night of the Living Rerun
The Angel Chronicles, Vol. 1
Blooded

Available from ARCHWAY Paperbacks

BUFFY
THE VAMPIRE
SLAYER™

CHILD of the HUNT

CHRISTOPHER GOLDEN and NANCY HOLDER

POCKET BOOKS
New York   London   Toronto   Sydney   Tokyo   Singapore

An *Original* Publication of POCKET BOOKS

POCKET BOOKS, a division of Simon & Schuster Inc.
1230 Avenue of the Americas, New York, NY 10020

ISBN: 0-671-02135-4

First Pocket Books printing October 1998

10 9 8 7 6 5 4 3 2 1

POCKET and colophon are registered trademarks of
Simon & Schuster Inc.

Printed in the U.S.A.

The authors would like to thank their agents, Lori Perkins and Howard Morhaim, and Howard's assistant, Lindsay Sagnette; their editor, Lisa Clancy, and her assistant, Liz Shiflett; Caroline Kallas, Jennifer Sarbacker, and their spouses, Connic and Wayne.

Prologue

THOUGH SHE HAD YET TO TURN EIGHTEEN, BUFFY Summers was intimate with death. In some ways, death was her life.

The wind had shifted just right, and she could smell the salty tang of the ocean on the night breeze. It should have been a pleasure, but Buffy ignored it. Leaves rustled in the trees above her head, and somewhere off to the north, on one of the typically tidy suburban streets that lined Weatherly Park, a woman shouted at her dog to stop barking.

Buffy wondered what the dog was barking at.

In any other town it might have been something no more threatening than a neighbor kid on his bike. In Sunnydale, the thing that set the dog off might well be something horrible that had crept from the darkness out into the glow of the streetlamps.

If so, it would be Buffy's responsibility to find it and destroy it. That was her calling. She was the Chosen

One. She was the Slayer. Sunnydale, California, was a magnet for the unnameable horrors of the world, things the rational human mind insisted did not truly exist. But, oh, they did exist.

The dead. The undead. The Slayer spent far too much time with them, lurking in cemeteries to await their predatory resurrection; stalking parks and playgrounds in search of the tribes of the night— vampires, demons, werewolves. She had died once herself, actually. For a moment. Before she was resuscitated.

Resurrected.

Buffy Summers was, to her own mind, far too intimate with death. But in some ways, it was her life.

She crouched in the darkness among the trees that lined the western fence of Weatherly Park and listened. Not for barking dogs, blaring car radios, or the wind in the trees. Buffy listened for the sounds that would reveal the presence of the dead.

The presence of a vampire.

Something had been stalking people in the park, yet again. If Sunnydale was the Hellmouth, then the park was one of its hunting grounds. It was a regular stop on Buffy's usual patrol. But lately, patrolling hadn't been enough. In the last week, six people had been slaughtered in the park. The sign on the gate said the park was closed at ten, but that didn't matter. The rules were regularly ignored, the fence frequently vaulted by teens looking for a place to party or be alone with their boyfriends or girlfriends.

The bodies had been savaged more brutally than was common even for a vampire. There was anger in those killings, and neither Buffy nor her Watcher, Giles, had been able to determine the source of it.

Now, she sat and waited. Giles had told her she ought to be able to sense when a vampire was near. It might be her imagination, but she was certain that she did sense something. Evil. Danger. Bloodlust. Whatever it was she felt out there, she couldn't focus on it, couldn't narrow it down. She had been in the park nearly two hours and hadn't seen anything more than a few guys she recognized from school drinking too much warm beer.

Buffy was getting anxious. Angry with herself. While she was sitting there, the vamp could be killing again. Waiting just wasn't good enough. She should be out looking for it, hunting it the way it was hunting fresh human prey.

The waiting was driving her a little crazy.

She promised herself she'd give it to the count of one hundred.

At seventy-nine, she heard a scream.

"About time," Buffy snarled, and sprinted across the park in the direction of the scream.

She vaulted a park bench, trampled a patch of yellow flowers she couldn't name if her biology grade depended upon it, and angled toward a copse of trees next to the duck pond at the center of the park.

Another scream shredded the night air; a male voice, terrified beyond any concern for masculinity. The scream of someone being murdered.

Branches whipped past her face. Buffy dodged around the wide trunk of an ancient oak. Then it was there, in front of her, lips stretched wide over the pale, blood-spattered throat of a homeless man whose eyes were already glazed with death. The corpse was sprawled on the ground in the midst of a clearing. The vampire crouched over it, like a dog worrying a bone.

3

Before it had died, the vampire had been a boy, not more than eleven or twelve years old. Buffy thought she recognized him, in fact. Maybe she'd seen him, walking to the middle school.

For once, Buffy Summers had nothing to say.

It turned on her, wide yellow eyes blazing bright in the darkness. Bloody fangs flashed in the dim moonlight that streamed through the trees. Then it was rushing at her, fingers curled into talons.

Buffy reached inside her leather jacket and withdrew a stake she had slid into the long pocket there.

"Come on, then, kiddo," she whispered. "Mommy's calling you. Time to go home."

Though Buffy had never asked to be the Slayer, nor wanted to be, she had found to her surprise that she was quite adept at it. Once upon a time, the idea that she might have some kind of talent for violence, for murder, would have horrified her. But that was before she knew there were things in the world which deserved nothing but death. The world needed a Slayer. And Buffy was Chosen.

It was a concept that her mother was having a great deal of difficulty dealing with. Buffy had hidden the truth from her mom for as long as she was able, and truth be told, she thought that Joyce Summers had been working very hard not to see the clues that might have led her to that truth.

Eventually, however, all hell had broken loose. Pretty much literally. And then Buffy had no choice. Her mother had to know. In some ways, it was a relief not to need excuses. At least her mother could stop wondering how a girl could get as much "tutoring" as Buffy supposedly did and still barely squeak by in the grades department. But in other ways, it was a disaster. Joyce did not handle the truth very well at all.

For a while after that horrible night, Buffy had left town. She just couldn't take it anymore. But she was back now, and back to stay, and she and her mother would just have to deal with the awkwardness between them.

They avoided the subject whenever possible. Purely to avoid having to talk to her mother about where she was going, what horrors she might face, Buffy still snuck in and out her window a lot of the time. It was just easier that way.

Up the tree, then through the open window. The climb only got easier every time she did it.

Buffy slipped into her darkened bedroom, and her mother was sitting there on the edge of her bed, holding something in her hands. For a moment Buffy was reminded of the horrible night when she'd entered this room to find her mother's late boyfriend, Ted, waiting for her—it was a night that had ended violently. For him. Then the memory was washed away as she saw the sadness on her mother's face, and recognized what she held in her hands. It was a small trophy Buffy had won for figure skating when she was nine years old.

"Hello, Buffy," her mother said.

"Mom," Buffy said, trying not to meet the woman's gaze. "Y'know, I've been meaning to pick up my room for days. I promise I'll take care of it tomorrow . . ."

Buffy swallowed as her mother rose and flicked on a light.

Joyce's face was streaked with tears.

"All I asked was that you show," she said quietly. "I didn't tell you what to wear. I didn't ask if you might bring a date with pierced eyelids and tattoos . . . somewhere. I just wanted you to come."

Once again I fail Daughter 101, Buffy thought sadly. She looked down, and wished she hadn't. On the edge of the bed was a flyer for the benefit at her mother's art gallery. SAVE THE LOST, it said in bold letters. Beneath that, it read:

> *In these troubled times, so many of our young people don't know where to turn. Too many of them turn to the streets.*
>
> *Join us for a special showing of a private collection of paintings by Mary Cassatt, followed by a silent auction of a few select works to raise operating funds for the Sunnydale Runaway Project.*

Buffy swallowed hard. She knew all about running away.

Mary Cassatt was known for her paintings of mothers and their children. When a wealthy L.A. couple had donated a group of Cassatt paintings for the auction, Buffy's mom had been ecstatic. Joyce had lovingly shown the pieces to Buffy, each one depicting a mother with her child or children, holding them, bathing them, rocking them to sleep.

"Look at the tenderness. The love," her mother had said, eyes moist. And her smile as she gazed at her own daughter had made Buffy ashamed. Because she didn't deserve a mother like hers. She so constantly let her down.

Like tonight.

Joyce gazed levelly at her. "A lot of people came tonight. We made a lot of money for the project." Her voice cracked. "And a lot of people asked me where my daughter was. Oh, I smiled and said you were studying at the library. Buffy, I know you have your . . . obligations, but you promised you would be there."

Buffy looked down at her hands.

"Mom," she said again. But there was nothing more to say. Nothing more she could say.

"Just go to bed," Joyce said wearily, and turned to go to the door.

Defeated, Buffy sat down on her bed, hating her life.

"Sometimes I just wish . . ." Joyce murmured as she stood in the open doorway, and the hair stood up on the back of Buffy's neck.

She wished what?

That Buffy had never come back?

Her mother walked into the hall, then stopped, half-turned, but did not turn. Almost as if she couldn't quite look at Buffy again.

"A couple came to talk to the representatives from the runaway project," she said softly. "Their little boy has been missing for almost a week. His name is Timmy. He's in the seventh grade. They're frantic. Have you any idea what it's like to wonder, night after night, where your child is?"

Tears rolled down Buffy's cheeks.

Timmy.

Little Timmy Stagnatowski. Now she remembered that face. She had seen the flyers at the grocery store: *Missing. Please help us find him.*

Buffy knew exactly where he was. Or rather, where

7

he last had been: earlier tonight, she had driven a stake through his heart.

Her mother reached behind herself and closed the door to her room.

It was a long time before Buffy managed to get up to turn out the light. She undressed and then crawled beneath the bedclothes.

It was after two in the morning before she finally drifted off to sleep.

It was three in the morning. The hour of the wolf.

Down at the Sunnydale bus depot, Connie De-Marco hunkered against the wall and watched in silence as the ladies passed out pamphlets about the new Sunnydale runaway shelter. One of the women wore an out-of-date lavender coat with padded shoulders. The other was trying to go for hip or whatever in overalls and a stretchy polyester jacket. They were both old enough to be Connie's mother.

In fact, one of them *was* Connie's mother.

Her mom's name was Liz, and she looked old. Her black curly hair was shot through with gray. Connie grimaced with distaste. Her mother could at least dye it. And put on some makeup and dress better. She wished she had a cool mom, a mom who tried to look good, like Cordelia Chase's mother. She wished she had Cordelia's life. The DeMarcos had been poor and low class all Connie's life. They were trailer-park trash who lived in a cheap apartment that smelled like oil all the time because Connie's dad worked in an auto shop.

Connie figured that was why Cordelia had so thoroughly trashed her in front of all her friends at school.

Cordelia knew class, and she knew Connie didn't have it. Willow Rosenberg was the only girl who had ever been nice to her. In computer lab, she had told Connie she had an aptitude for programming. Connie had been so surprised and pleased that she went mute, hadn't been able to say a word. After that, Willow probably thought she was a moron.

Then Willow sort of started hanging around Cordelia. So Connie couldn't ever go up to her and say thanks. She'd never even have the chance now.

Now that she had run away.

Connie fingered the locket that hung on a gold chain around her neck. It read, CONNY, because Bobby hadn't known how to spell her name. It was the only thing she had taken from home besides the clothes on her back. Bobby had given it to her for her birthday. That and a wonderful kiss, which her mother had seen.

The things Mom had said about Bobby . . .

She touched the locket and swallowed.

Liz DeMarco and her best friend, Lesley Jones, were passing out flyers about how safe the shelter was, and how you could go in there without telling anybody your name. No hassles, guaranteed.

Maybe Connie's mom believed that, hoped that, but it wasn't true. If Connie walked in there right now, there would be a million judgmental remarks about drugs and all kinds of things. *All* kinds. Accusatory questions about what she had been doing all the months she'd been living on the streets. They judged you, those stupid social workers and oh-so-liberal and cool Runaway Project volunteers. Especially the old church ladies who brought the blankets and the sandwiches. The Blue Hair Brigade. Before they even knew a thing about you, they had already decided you ran away from a great home and a wonderful, loving family. That *you* were the freak. The problem.

They pretty much believed your family would be better off without you, and that you had done the right thing running away. But something in them, some guilt impulse or something, made them try to help you.

It was such a steaming load.

"Hey, Treasure."

Connie's heart skipped a beat as she turned and low-fived the guy in the black duster. It was Shock, so named because of the streak of white in his hair. He claimed to have seen a dead man rise out of his grave in the Sunnydale Cemetery, claw his way right out and then run at Shock with a mouthful of big, sharp teeth. Connie wasn't sure if she bought his story, but something had put that white streak in his hair.

Shock was the one who had named her Treasure. He was at least nineteen—she was sixteen—and he was her partner on the streets. They stole stuff together. Little stuff. It kept them going. They never took anything from poor people. They took things from people who looked like Cordelia Chase. Or even from people who looked like her mom, she had to admit. And her mom's stupid best friend from church, the one in the out-of-date coat, Lesley. Liz and Lesley. It was so cute how their names both started with *L*.

Connie wanted to vomit.

"What's the haps?" she asked Shock.

"Something's going on, man," he told her. Whenever he called her "man" it reminded her that they were just friends. Sometimes it made her a little sad but it also helped her remember that he had promised to stick by her. If he ever told her he loved her, she would get scared, because then he would be much more likely to leave her. That's what love did to people. You just had to look around and you knew it was true.

Her mother had succeeded in getting Bobby Lopez to leave her.

Shock went on, "Everybody's freaking out down at the park."

Most nights they slept in Weatherly Park. Every once in a while they found an alley or an abandoned building, but the park was okay and a lot of the street community hung there at night.

"Freaking out how? Why?" she asked, smiling as he slid his hand into her back jeans pocket and kissed her forehead. Maybe they weren't boyfriend and girlfriend exactly, but they were a team. She really liked him, and that was one reason she wouldn't come in from the streets. Her parents hadn't liked Bobby, and they would hate Shock. And she would never leave him out here alone.

"They say some more bodies turned up." He clicked his teeth together like he was eating something. "Some perv was nibbling at them again."

"Gross." She shook her head.

"I'm thinking maybe we should move on."

She flared with panic. Shock had left Sunnydale and traveled for years. He'd only been back a week or so when they'd hooked up. She didn't know why the thought of crossing the town border made her so nervous, but it did. Kind of like she was almost back home if she stayed in town.

Not that she wanted to go back home. But the

world, she had discovered, was not all that much better than her own backyard.

"But we've still never seen anything. I think it's all a crock. Something the police made up to keep us out of there," she said anxiously.

Something rippled across his face—pain, a bad memory, she didn't know what. Then it was gone, hidden away like most of Shock was hidden away from her. He might not be her honey, but she was the only person in the world he could open up to, share with. He had confessed that to her the first time they'd met, when both of them were going through the dumpster behind the Sunnydale High cafeteria, gathering up the leftovers. She'd only been a runaway for two nights, and doing such a bad job of it she was thinking about going back home.

Standing behind her now, he tugged on her hair, jerking her head back slightly. She didn't know what to say, because maybe that was like, flirting with her, and she wasn't sure what to do if he did flirt with her. They had been on the streets together for six months, and he had never tried anything. He said he called her Treasure because he found her in a dumpster like a buried treasure. He said she was "a find." He was the nicest guy she had ever met, and after a while she relaxed around him.

He tugged harder on her hair, hard enough to pull out a few strands. Mostly out of reflex, she shouted, "Hey!" Then she quickly added, "Sorry, it hurt," because she was always very polite to Shock. He didn't have to hang with someone as young as she was—even though she was very mature for her age—she often passed at the Bronze for much older—and she was grateful beyond words that he did. If she'd been out here all alone, she would have been dead by now. Of that she had no doubt.

Behind her, he said, "What?"

"Ow!" This time it was like someone had nicked her scalp. She half-turned and gently batted his arm. "Stop pulling my hair, Shock."

He cocked his head. "You're tripping, Treasure." He held up his free hand. His other was still in her back pocket. "I'm not touching you."

"Well, you were—ouch!" She clutched the back of her head. "Something's in my hair!" she cried hysterically. "Something's biting me!" She started screaming and lowered her head for Shock to see. "There's something in my hair!"

"Stand still!" Shock ordered her.

"Connie?" Liz said, her voice high and stunned. "Connie, is that you?"

That voice. That nasally, whiny voice.

"Run," Connie said to Shock. "Get me the hell out of here."

"Connie!" Liz shouted. She ran after them. "Connie!"

Her mother's voice became a wail on the wind as Connie and Shock flew into the night like ghostly kites, his duster streaming out behind them.

As they rounded a corner, tears dripped down Connie's face. Then, panting, she stopped beneath a streetlight and bent her head forward. "Maybe it's a big spider," she said. "Find it. Ow! It's biting me!"

"Hold still." He started combing through her hair. There was a rumble in the distance.

"Rain tonight," he grumbled. "Great."

"Ow!" she shrieked, wagging her head as the pain seared her scalp. "Hurry up!"

"I don't see . . ." Shock said. "Hey, wait!"

In a blind panic, Connie ran from him, clutching at her head.

Just off the main drag, in a condo complex with a quaint Spanish motif, Jamie Anderson surfed his entire Mega-Gold cable package, but nothing grabbed his attention long enough to make him stop switching channels. He pretended not to realize it when his left hand grazed the bottle of Scotch on the end table beside his recliner. He didn't let himself register the act of bringing the bottle to his lips. But nothing could hide the hot, burning sensation of the whiskey tearing down his throat.

He knew how much was left in the bottle—about a third of it. He also knew how much more he could drink and still be able to function at work: none.

So he took one more swig for the road, then resolutely put the bottle back down.

A few months ago he had met his neighbor, Rupert Giles, on a Saturday morning while they were collecting their mail from the boxes in the foyer of their building. Jamie knew he smelled boozy and looked terrible and made some offhand, joking remarks about having had a bit too much the night before. A typical Californian would have brushed it off, said something innocuous—not for nothing were there fences between every single house in your typical southern Californian suburb—but Rupert Giles had surprised him.

The Englishman had leaned against the wall for a moment, regarding Jamie with genuine sympathy. He'd said, "Recently, I found myself escaping into the bottle. Not to imply, of course, that you're doing anything of the sort. It's merely that . . . well, I found no genie at the bottom of a bottle. Only a demon I thought I'd escaped."

Jamie had almost told him then of the struggle each day had become. No, it was not the days that were impossible. It was the nights. The nights of tossing and turning, of taking things to knock himself out so that he could perform at work. Of drinking to stop feeling. Of searching for anything to escape the constant, relentless worry.

But then the fear would close in. The fear that he would be too far gone to hear the phone if Brian called. He would wake up in a sweat, calling for his son, his wife, and check the phone machine again and again and again.

And scream into his pillow.

Four years of living hell, night after night.

But he was a man in a hard line of work, and crying in your beer didn't cut it. So even though he had wanted like anything to tell this virtual stranger the whole sad story, Jamie had muttered something about not having demons, just missing his son. Then he'd averted his eyes, pretending that he didn't want to talk about it.

But he did. He really did.

He had turned to go, quickly, so that the other man wouldn't see the tears.

It wasn't until their second encounter, at the high school, that they'd really connected. Once a semester or so, the police sent somebody over to the high school to talk to the kids about suicide, running away from home, and the ways to get help before getting that desperate. Jamie knew the Chamber of Commerce didn't want the stats publicized, but Sunnydale had an alarming truancy, runaway, and mortality rate among its young-adult population.

This semester, he was the one who had drawn what he and his buddies on the force called "Downer Duty"—insisting that yes, of course he could handle it; no, it wasn't too close to home. All day he had stood at the front of classroom after classroom. (An assembly, it had been decided, was too large and impersonal. The kids might want to ask questions.) He had dutifully passed out the info sheets about national hotlines and the new runaway shelter set up by Liz DeMarco—a local woman whose own daughter was a runaway. High time for something like that, too. Maybe if that shelter had been around when Brian ran . . .

Out of the blue, some girl had raised her hand, asked, "Have you heard from Brian?"

The pain and, yes, the shame, had flooded through Jamie like a double shot of Scotch. For a moment, he had been speechless. He fumbled and stammered, unwilling—and unable—to share his private agony with this sweet young kid.

But Rupert Giles, seated in the back of the room (the librarian, having no actual class of his own, had come in to listen), cleared his throat and said, "It's my understanding the shelter is looking for donations, yes? Perhaps a fundraiser might be arranged by the Key Club. Or some such, ah, benevolent organization. It's quite a worthy cause."

The conversation was deflected away from Brian, but the girl continued to look troubled. Maybe she'd had a crush on him. Jamie decided to talk to her after the class let out, but he lost track of her in the swirl of departing students when the bell rang.

Rupert had come up to him, said, "Are you all right, old man?" and invited him for some tea in the library.

They had talked, venturing into dangerous territory, although the Englishman was very English, indirect and a bit guarded. Protective of his own privacy. That was okay. Jamie had never been very good at speaking about how he felt anyway. Maybe that was why Brian had left.

That was when Jamie figured out where he'd heard Giles's name before. Or, rather, read it. On a case file. About the Sunnydale High teacher who had been murdered and her corpse left in her boyfriend's bed. Giles had been the boyfriend.

Rough stuff.

It hadn't been his case, but once he knew Rupert's connection, Jamie poked around a bit. So far, nothing had turned up. Didn't look like anything would. He never mentioned his inquiry to Giles, but the man had extended the hand of friendship to him, and Jamie wanted to return the gesture in his own way. No. He wouldn't mention it—except to comfort the man on the rare occasion when he might bring it up—until he found some new information that might help. He also never bothered to tell Giles exactly how long after his girlfriend's murder the librarian himself had remained the prime suspect.

Now—as he remembered the man's kindnesses, and realized that he had too few friends since his own family had fallen apart—Jamie thought briefly about taking Rupert up on his offer to call whenever he needed to talk. He glanced at the clock. It was nearly four in the morning. Even British librarians had a limit to their benevolence.

Rupert had been the school librarian going on three years. He'd never met Jamie's son. The man had still lived in England when Brian had left. Giles couldn't know what a terrific kid Brian had been.

It was Brian's birthday. He was nineteen tonight.

If he was still alive.

Praying that he was, Jamie Anderson toasted his son's birth with the good stuff, keeping the rotgut hooch for the other three hundred sixty-four nights of the year. Praying that he would hear from his son. Praying Brian would call again.

Once. Just one phone call, in the last four years. Six weeks after Brian had run, the phone had rung, just once.

Sarah had glanced at Jamie and caught her breath. Staring at him, she had picked it up, cleared her throat, and rasped, "Hello?"

Afterward she managed to tell Jamie Brian's entire conversation, word for word, before she collapsed: "Mom, I'm okay. I'm alive. I'll call again soon."

Jamie had not gotten to hear Brian's voice. He had never felt so cheated in his life.

Brian had never called again.

Now Sarah was gone, too, from an inoperable tumor, and Jamie still waited by the phone to hear his boy's voice.

He took another swig of Scotch, mentally calibrating just how drunk he was. If he took something in the morning to perk himself up, he might be okay.

Well. Not okay. He would never be okay. But he might be able to work.

He put the bottle back down and changed the channels four times, five, seven. Every program was the same. They were always the same.

Everything was always the same.

He thought about his gun.

He thought about the bottle.

He thought about his child.

He picked up the phone and dialed the number, which was handwritten on the back of one of Jamie's own business cards. It had sat by the phone so long that it was coated with a layer of dust.

The connection was made. The phone was picked up on the first ring, almost as if the other party had been waiting for his call.

"Giles, ah, Rupert?" Jamie said softly. "I'm sorry. It's late—"

"Not at all," said the British man, very politely. "I'll just put on a pot of coffee."

Chapter 1

LOST . . . BUT NOT FORGOTTEN. LOST . . . BUT NOT forgotten.

Buffy woke with tears sliding down her face. Had she been dreaming again about being on the road?

She lay very still and closed her eyes tightly, feeling the pain, just giving in to it, just for one moment longer, letting it sear like a cauterizing blade. Then she deliberately wiped the tears away. If she could be very honest with herself—and these last few months had made her nothing if not honest—she knew she hadn't been dreaming at all.

What she hoped was that the tears were healing a very deep wound, the one that cut right through to her soul. The pain that lingered even when she smiled.

So many friends lost. Ford. Kendra. Ms. Calendar. Love lost. Angel's face filled her mind.

Even now, her mom was trying desperately to cling to the idea that Buffy had done something that had made her the Chosen One. It was like Joyce was blaming her for making some mistake—like the punishment for shoplifting that tube of lipstick from Macy's back in L.A. freshman year was a lifetime of battling the forces of darkness. Because if you got handed the Slayer rap because you were bad, maybe you could make up for it and get the sentence reduced.

So very untrue.

Buffy knew now that some people never got touched by all the bad juju. When you didn't expect much, you got what you wanted: a husband or wife, a good job, some kids. At the mall, they bought happy little magnetic plaques they put on their refrigerators: *Take time to smell the flowers. Kiss the cook. What you believe, you can achieve.* Maybe they went to church, or did crafts, like Mrs. Calhoun, two doors down, who spent half the day doing paint-by-numbers. She was so proud of the finished pictures, but really, all she had to do was make sure she painted inside the preprinted lines on the cardboard. She didn't even have to pick out what colors to use. They came in little containers with numbers on them.

There was nothing about Buffy's life that was like that. Not a single place where all she had to do was stay inside the lines.

There were also people whose lives were full of joy. People like that artist, Mary Cassatt, who must have been a very happy mom to paint all those pictures of mothers and children. Buffy could just imagine her washing a chubby little baby or tenderly rocking a child to sleep.

Then the image of Timmy Stagnatowski exploding into dust blotted out the picture.

No, it was not self-pity that made Buffy cry in her sleep. She was the Slayer, the one in all her generation who stood between the forces of darkness and the rest of humanity. She had accepted that, moved forward with that.

She believed it was a personal exorcism to let herself feel this much pain, and try to find a way to let it out. Let it go. But sometimes she felt that with each tear, she was losing more than the pain. A memory. The ability to care so deeply, want so terribly . . .

She caught her breath and stopped her tears. She could take no more, not now. It was just that it was always darkest before the dawn. That's what people like Mrs. Calhoun or the famous baby-painter would say, anyway. But for Buffy, the world kept getting darker, and dawn seemed further and further away all the time.

Outside, clouds were rumbling, threatening a downpour, and the sound echoed inside her room. In the back of her mind, she was always wondering, *Was that really thunder?* Or was it actually a portent of some as-yet-unknown evil about to descend, one she'd have to fight, to her death, if need be?

But that didn't make her cry. It honestly didn't. She had accepted her duty as the Slayer. It wasn't that she was looking for a way out.

She wasn't trying to run away.

Not anymore.

She silently gazed at what was left of being a normal teenager: Mr. Gordo, her stuffed pig, and all her stuffed animals. The butterflies on her door and her Japanese umbrellas. Some friend of her mom's had said this was such a sweet room. Never guessing, of course, that in the false-bottomed trunk in the closet were hidden vials of holy water, bulbs of garlic, and lots of very sharp, pointed stakes.

So sweet.

There was her picture of Xander and Will on the nightstand. She smiled faintly. There weren't two of Willow in the world, and Xander was likewise unclonable. Sweet friends. Good to her.

She heard talking and frowned slightly. Did her mom have company at this hour? Or was there something in this house that shouldn't be?

Moving with Slayer's reflexes, she jumped out of bed, put on her robe, and slipped a stake into her pocket. Stealthily, she hurried down the hall and headed for the stairs, pausing to assess any and all possible dangers.

She heard crying, heaving, bone-deep. She knew that kind of crying. Was . . . friends with it.

"Mom?" she called softly.

She hurried down the stairs, then passed from the front room into the kitchen.

In her pleated bathrobe, her hair frowsy from sleep, Joyce Summers stood facing Buffy. In her arms, a woman in a black raincoat sobbed desperately. As Buffy stood watching, the woman clung to Buffy's mom, barely able to stand.

"They'll find him, Anne," Joyce said. She lifted her eyes toward Buffy. Locked gazes with her. Buffy didn't know what to do. She stood awkwardly for a moment, then tiptoed out of the room and paused on the stairs.

"Joyce, he's so little. He's too little to run away. Something's happened to him. Something bad. I just know it. I know it!" The woman almost screamed. "Oh, my God, Timmy!"

Buffy was frozen to the spot. Guilt drenched her. There was no reason to feel guilty, she reminded herself. The boy who had been Timmy Stagnatowski had been dead before she staked his walking corpse. It was not this woman's child she had destroyed.

But she knew what had happened to him, and she could never tell his mother. Mrs. Stagnatowski would go to her grave wondering what had become of her happy little boy. Every night, she would wander to the window and look out, praying that he would run up the walkway. When the phone rang, she would jump. For the rest of her life.

Buffy could save her from that pain. She could stop the wondering right now.

Her heart thundering, she descended one stair. She was not supposed to tell anyone about the Hellmouth, about the terrors and dangers she fought to save them from. Would it be better for Mrs. Stagnatowski to know the truth? Would she even believe Buffy? Or would she assume—as her mother once had—that she was crazy?

"We'll put up some more flyers," Joyce said gently. "And I'll call Liz DeMarco at the shelter. If he comes in, they'll ask him to contact you."

"But what if he doesn't?" Mrs. Stagnatowski asked dully. "What if he doesn't understand how much we love him and miss him?"

Were they always missed, the ones who ran away? Buffy felt fresh tears welling in her eyes. With effort, she swallowed them down and stared into the distance, remembering the road and the way back home.

She looked at the panes in the front door.

The sun had risen.

It was time to go to school.

Buffy sprinted through a vicious downpour across the lawn of Sunnydale High, her laced ankle-boots sliding on grass that had quickly become more mud than green. She muttered curses the whole way. Her Chinese embroidered blouse was spattered and clammy. Her long skirt, muddy at the hem.

Barely managing to keep hold of a bag filled with books she hadn't so much as glanced at in days, she wrenched open the front door to the school and squished inside. She ran her fingers through her ruined hair and started along the corridor toward the library.

"Hey, Buffy!"

She turned to see Willow and Xander coming toward her. Willow, of course, had come prepared with a hooded yellow slicker, while Xander's only concession to the weather was a battered baseball cap. Which might be good for keeping the rain off but really didn't do anything for him. His just wasn't a hat kind of head. He looked a little goofy in his typically oversize shirt, the sleeves hanging over his wrists, but that was standard Xander gear. She had pretty much decided it was a rebellion thing for him: *Yeah, I'm a geek, so what?*

"Good morning to the seriously umbrella-challenged girl clad in the latest fashion in spongewear," Xander teased, obviously having no notion that she had been equally harsh about his fashion challenge but hadn't felt the need to mention it.

Tired, frustrated, she glared at him. "Yes," she said. "I'm wet. Any other brilliant observations this morning? And by the way, the cap looks way past stupid."

"Ooh," Willow said gently. "Down, girl. Bad morning, huh?"

Buffy took a breath and tried to calm down. Xander was acting like he wasn't hurt, but she knew him better than that. She saw how his hand went halfway to the cap, as if he were about to take it off, then hang at his side, as if he'd rather not bring attention to it.

"And bad night, and bad everything," she admitted. "At least one of our recent runaways wasn't exactly a runaway. And Mom was less than pleased that I completely forgot her benefit last night." She couldn't tell them about the rest. It hurt too much.

"Running away," Willow said, sighing. "Sounds good to me."

Buffy paused, narrowing her eyes.

"No," she said bluntly. "Good it is not. Trust me on this one, Will."

Willow looked abashed. "Sorry, Buffy."

Xander turned to Willow and said, "Plus, you're a senior. Which, y'know, automatically means that running away would be kind of childish. Unless you were running away to join the circus, which would be cool. High wire, Will. You'd be good with that. No clowns, though."

"Clowns are evil," Willow noted, smiling a little.

"All of them," Xander confirmed, smiling back.

"So spill, Willow," Buffy demanded. "Otherwise I'm just going to keep complaining about my problems, and yours will be summarily ignored."

Willow shrugged, letting her hands flop loudly against her hips.

"My parents think Oz has no ambition."

Buffy and Xander stared at her, waiting for the rest.

"That's it," Willow added, raising her eyebrows. "They like him, y'know. Even though they want him to pay a little more attention to the clock when we go out. But they think he has no ambition, no goals."

"Well that's just riddichio," Xander said. "Oz has plenty of ambitions. . . ."

Xander's words trailed off and he looked at Buffy with a little nod, a hint that she was supposed to pick it up from there because he couldn't come up with anything. Buffy thought for a moment. Oz was a majorly laid back guy. He just kind of took things in. Oz smiled a lot. Waited to see what would happen next. Not that he wouldn't pitch in when the situation called for it. Just the other night, he had tripped a vampire so Buffy could stake it. He'd also worked pretty hard to steal Willow away from Xander. Okay, not steal. Like, all he had to do was offer her some animal crackers. Treat her like she was interesting. And pretty.

All the things Xander had so not done.

"Yeah," Buffy said lamely. "Oz has plenty of ambition. With . . . the band and all. And, y'know . . ."

Willow shook her head. "Don't even bother, guys. You both get A's for effort . . . well, maybe C's, but Oz's ambitions in life just aren't the kinds of things that parents can understand. It's just a whole other world of priorities that will never be their priorities and . . . well, they'll get over it when I go to college."

"Ah, yes." Xander nodded sagely. "Higher education heals all wounds. Or so I'm told."

And so he wondered. He wasn't even sure he was going to college. His grades sucked, and nobody had really talked to him about going. Oh, sure, they dragged *Will* out of classes to see the guidance counselor about this scholarship or that one. And Cordy, well, she kept making noises about expensive private schools where you could buy your way in if your SATs just laid there and died. So where did all the Xanders go? To the Air Force, every one?

Still, he didn't have it as bad as Buffy. He supposed she could go to Yale if she wanted to—well, maybe not, because her grades sucked, too—but she was smart enough to go to Yale. Maybe not in the book-learning department. But in a bad, sad, so not fair way, it didn't really matter what she wanted to be when she grew up. All that mattered was that she got to grow up. Because in the Slaying business, that was not a given.

He turned his attention back to the girls—his girls, his very special pals, one a girl he had wanted to date, and one a girl he should have wanted to date—too late for that now—and smiled his best Xander smile. He was da man for the riffs and the one-liners, and he wasn't about to let his vixens down now, when they obviously needed some cheering up. It was his job in their little social circle. Willow made the brilliant observations, Buffy killed bad guys, and he told jokes.

Even if it cost him a little something in the let's-share department. Heck with it, he was tough guy. He could handle his own problems.

Buffy shook her arms, sending droplets of rain flying. "Am I the only one who thinks that when you live in a place called Sunnydale, there ought to be some kind of rule against rain?"

"Unless you're Giles, and then you think there should be a rule *for* rain. Like that line in Camelot." Xander paused, trying to remember the lyrics.

"Y'know. 'It really rains a lot, here in Camelot.' Whatever."

When neither Willow nor Buffy so much as cracked a smile, he grimaced and mock-shuddered. "Ouch. Tough crowd. A little too much rain on everyone's parade this morning. So smart Xanders everywhere creep off the stage."

"Sorry, Xander," Willow said. "I'm just not used to having problems with my parents. I've always been the *good* daughter." She thought for a moment. "As opposed to the bad daughter. That they don't have." Willow being the only daughter, of course.

Buffy nodded sympathetically. "I used to get in trouble for being a flaky daughter, maybe, but not for being a terrible daughter. You're about six degrees of evil away from that, Will, but I know it must be a shock."

"A shock," Willow said slowly, as if testing the words. "Yeah. You could say that." She nodded back.

"Which I just did," Buffy replied, giving her a grin. "So, Xander," she went on, "obviously I had one of those nights that reminds us all that parents are from Mars and teenagers are from Venus, and Willow's mom and dad may have finally realized that she's not nine anymore. How about the Harris household? Have you been getting any hassle for coming in late all the time?"

"Not really," Xander admitted with a shrug. "My parents have sort of rediscovered dating. Each other, of course. They go out a lot after dinner. Come back all mussed and flushed. It's really, um, 'shocking' is our *word du jour,* yes? Otherwise, they just figure I'm out with Cordy."

"Until way too late on a school night, and this doesn't bother them?" Buffy said, frowning.

He was the one it bothered a little, if truth be told. He kind of wished they would notice that he wasn't doing the study thing and all like that. Like the girls' parents. Which was childish, he knew, but all this parental angsting everybody else was kvetching about was, frankly, something he had no experience with. Rules and regs? Not so many for the Harrises. Just like conventional mealtimes. Which might explain his passion for junk food. Or not.

"Well, I can't say they haven't chastised me for lateness now and again, but as long as I get my homework done, and I'm in before the news comes on, they pretty much leave me alone."

And if I ran away, would they notice? he thought. Then he edited himself: *Too bitter, Harris. Way too bitter.*

Things are not that bad.

It was just that in his house, there were not a whole lot of . . . things.

Buffy and Willow scowled at each other. "Total double standard," Buffy said, sighing, and turned to start walking toward the library.

Willow fell into step at her side. "Completely unfair. By the way, you and I were studying at Cordelia's last night . . ."

"At Cordelia's?" Buffy asked, astonished, almost tripping over her own feet.

"It was all I could think of on short notice." Willow shrugged sheepishly. "Besides, my mom doesn't know Cordelia. She won't really get how ridiculous a concept it is."

Buffy considered. "True. Of course, you'll have to tell Cordelia."

"She'll go along with it," Xander assured them. "She's been trying to find a good excuse for being out late all the time too." He rolled his eyes. "Looks like we're doomed to be rebellious teens for the rest of . . . well, at least for the rest of high school."

"We're just born to be wild," Buffy said, sighing as she pushed open the library doors.

"Bad to the bone," Willow concurred.

"I'm not bad," Xander protested. "I'm just drawn that way."

The girls both chuckled faintly. Xander brightened. Mission accomplished.

The library was incredibly dreary. Dank and shadowed, it made Buffy think of a shipwreck, of diving on the sunken remains of some old galleon or something. With the wan light and the dust, the brown and faded books . . . it was like peering through a lot of murky water to make out books, tables, chairs. No sunken treasure, though.

Sigh.

Since moving to Sunnydale, Buffy guessed she had spent more time in this one place than she had anywhere else, including her bed, yet there was nothing welcoming about it. Maybe she should ask Giles to wallpaper it. Get some stuffed animals.

Make it more homey and sweet.

"Ah, there you are," Giles said as they entered the library. He looked a little tired, or maybe that was how people looked when they were creeping toward the notion of old. There were dark, puffy circles under his eyes. "Horrible storm, isn't it? Reminds me a bit of home, actually."

Despite looking tired, or perhaps slightly less than young, Giles was smiling. Buffy didn't know why he was smiling, but she did know that as far as she was concerned, he shouldn't be.

"You have a completely perverse appreciation of weather, Giles," she said. "For once it actually looks like we live in the Hellmouth outside, and you're grinning."

"Hmm? Yes, well, the storm is supposed to be over quickly," Giles replied. "And tomorrow night the Renaissance Faire opens to the public. They'll be here for several weeks, and I hope you'll all avail yourselves of both the amusement and the educational experience of a visit to the Faire."

"Fair?" Xander asked.

"Renaissance Faire," Willow said. "Kind of a carnival if they'd had one during the Dark Ages. Knights. Ladies in waiting. Hunchbacks. Jousting. Eating with your hands."

"I'm for eating with your hands," Xander said quickly. "Utensils are grossly overrated."

"Speaking of gross . . ." Buffy murmured.

"It has nothing to do with the Dark Ages, Willow." Giles cocked an amused though disapproving eyebrow in her general direction. "As I'm certain you know, considering that you tutor Buffy in history. The Renaissance began in Italy and spread throughout Europe. It reached its height in Italy in the fifteenth century, spread through Europe in the sixteenth and seventeenth centuries, and it is largely considered to be the end of the Middle Ages and the beginning of what we would call the modern world. It signified a new idea of humanity's place in the universe, and a new respect for art and education."

Giles looked at the three students expectantly. They stared back at him, waiting for him to say more.

"And the part that we love is?" Xander asked at last.

"The part somebody thought would be cool to make into a fair?" Buffy added.

Willow considered. "Actually, jousting sounds like fun." She assumed a fencer's stance. *"En garde."*

Buffy raised an eyebrow at her Watcher. "Moving on, I'll take 'Creatures of the Night' for five hundred, Alex."

"Very well, then," Giles said, sorting through a small pile of paperwork. Finally he found what he'd apparently been looking for and glanced up at them.

"These are the autopsy reports for the various Weatherly Park victims from the past week or so," he explained. "Willow was able to . . . *appropriate* them from the computer at the coroner's office."

Willow grinned proudly. "You can call me Webmistress. If you want."

"You *hacker,*" Xander teased her.

Buffy started to reach for the autopsy reports. "Why the extra research? I thought you said we were dealing with slightly extra-savage vamp attacks?"

Giles pointed a finger at the photos. "Yes, well, that's what I had assumed. However, after a bit of consideration and a review of the wording of the articles on the killings in the Sunnydale Press, I decided a closer look was warranted.

"It's fortunate that I did," he added, and the last trace of the smile he'd worn when they entered was now gone from the Watcher's face. "It appears as though only one of those victims showed the usual signs of vampiric attack. The other five had been . . . eaten. At least partially. And not by any animal familiar to the coroner's office."

Buffy took a look. Wished she hadn't. Silently she gave them back to Giles and thought, mournfully, of little Timmy and his mother. Her flesh prickled and she shivered with a chill that had nothing to do with temperature.

Xander looked at Willow. "Any chance Oz slipped his leash?"

Willow whacked him on the arm.

"Oh, what?" Xander asked indignantly. "Ask the question everybody's thinking, and get physical punishment in return."

"I wasn't thinking that," Buffy said in a low, sad voice.

Xander wagged a finger at her. "Fibber. You're just afraid she'll hit you."

"Actually," Giles said, putting the reports facedown on the table, "the coroner's office postulates it's a very small animal, something with a bite radius no larger than that of a raccoon's. But no raccoon did this."

"So what did?" Willow asked, turning her head quickly in Xander's direction, as if daring him to say anything snide about her boyfriend again.

"I've no idea," Giles replied. "And until I do, Buffy, you'd best take extra care. Be on guard for something small and quick. It's small enough that you might not see it coming before it's too late."

"Okay. Rabid raccoons. I'll keep a lookout."

Giles sighed and began to sort through a pile of his

latest research books, moving a stack of green paper. "Now then," he said after a moment, "how did you fare last night?"

She glanced down at the stack. They were flyers for the runaway shelter. Her mom's art gallery was listed at the bottom. Her mother must have given them out at the benefit last night. Which meant Giles must have gone. She felt even guiltier that she hadn't shown.

But then who would have destroyed Timmy?

"Buffy?" Giles prodded.

"Oh, last night? Just super," Buffy said harshly.

Xander stared at her. "Super?"

"Should I have said 'swell'?" she retorted, glaring at him.

"No. Please." Xander held up his hands. "I just figured anybody in a mood like yours . . . would be, um, looking for someone to hit a lot harder than Willow hit me. That's not what we call a super mood, at least among my people."

Buffy raised her chin. She did not want to tell them, felt unaccountably ashamed. "My people do."

"Super," Giles repeated, and looked at her expectantly.

"Okay," she caved. "I staked a twelve-year-old boy, but not before somebody else died in Weatherly Park. His mother was at my house this morning sobbing in my mother's arms because she has no idea that he's dead. Isn't that super enough for everyone?" she asked.

All three of them seemed momentarily uncomfortable.

"Yes, well," Giles said finally, clearing his throat, "I know it's difficult for your mother these days . . ."

36

"For my *mother?*" Buffy echoed, astounded. "My mother?"

"Buffy," Willow said gently, touching her friend's arm, "if there's anything we can do . . ."

"Yeah, maybe you should take a little R and R," Xander said. "Leave the staking to us."

Giles cleared his throat. "Yes, well, that brings us to a topic I believe we need to address. I'm not sure now is the time, but I suppose one must confront these things head on."

Buffy cocked her head and looked at Giles more closely. He did seem agitated, but as far as she knew, nothing had happened the night before that ought to concern him. Concern her, yes.

"Buffy," he said, and then hesitated, pushing his glasses up on his face. The library was dingy gray with the rainstorm outside, only the dimmest of light filtering in. It seemed to have made everyone a little sad today. And a little slow-brained.

"Giles," she prompted.

"Yes, well, regardless of the tragic nature of your accomplishment last night, it docs seem to me that you found this . . . vampire because you were able to focus. This is but one example of an issue that has begun to concern me of late. I think we may be getting a bit carried away with this whole business of 'Slayer-ettes.' "

"Uno minuto, Señor Libro," Xander said, raising his hand. "The family that slays together . . ."

"Not now, Xander," Giles warned.

Xander lowered his hand and looked at Buffy and Willow. Willow bit her lower lip and frowned nervously, clearly waiting for the next part.

Giles perched on the edge of the study table and crossed his arms. It was weird, but sometimes Buffy almost forgot that he had come to Sunnydale specifically to be her Watcher. Hers. As in Buffy. There he was in England, filing things—bones—whatever—in the British Museum, then . . . what? He gets a call from HQ and grabs a jet to California? *Giles, old man, the Slayah's relocating. See to it.*

It still wigged her that she and her mother had assumed their move here was through random chance, and not because this cursed town sat atop a mystical convergence swirling and whirling with every kind of evil thing you could possibly think of, both generic nasties and the name brands.

"As you know, traditionally the Chosen One works alone," Giles continued. "In fact, there is a school of thought that says that the Slayer should be required to work alone. I don't adhere to this theory, of course."

"Of course," Xander said urgently.

"As your Watcher, I have accompanied you on an irregular basis," Giles persisted. "And, given their enthusiasm and the fact that they came into the knowledge of your true identity and your obligation through a threat to their own lives, I was content to allow Willow and Xander to join you when the threat seemed to warrant that risk."

"Yes, and that was a *good* thing," Xander said. Moving beside him, Willow nodded earnestly.

"But now that Cordelia and Oz have also begun to participate, it all seems a bit much," Giles concluded. "I know that it is rare for your entire group to be on patrol together, but we may have to begin weighing each crisis in order to determine if the risk is great enough to involve your friends."

Xander leaned back in his chair. "Giles, in case you haven't realized it yet, it isn't as though Buffy invites us along for kicks. Or even invites us at all."

"Right," Willow said, looking slightly hurt. "We help because . . . well, I know I couldn't sleep at night, knowing what goes on in this town, if I wasn't doing something to help. If that means research, then research. But if that means going after the bad guys, well, I'll do that too."

Buffy had heard enough. She stood, walked over to Giles, and snatched from his hands the book he was glancing at. He looked up at her in surprise.

"You know what, Giles, you're right," she said. "Most nights, I should be on my own. Or maybe just with Angel." She caught the flicker of unease on his face and decided to ignore it for now. She knew he had mixed feelings about Angel. Who didn't?

"And you know I don't want anything nasty to happen to my friends. But when it starts raining vamps and demons, I'm the first one to admit I might not be able to do it all myself."

Her gaze took in her friends and a dozen images flashed through her mind, each one of a time when one or several of them had come to her aid and saved the day. Even though they had no special obligation to patrol and fight, as she did. Even though they had no sacred duty.

They did it simply because they were her friends. And because somebody had to do it. In that way, Buffy often felt they were far more heroic than she was. If she wasn't the Slayer, she might not even . . . but she was the Slayer. It wasn't healthy to wonder what might have been.

"It's not like we're having beach parties when we

work together," she went on, feeling a little angry. "We do what we have to do because we have to do it. Don't give us a hard time about it."

Giles didn't respond at first, but Buffy could see that he wasn't finished. That there was something still on his mind. He began to glance at the books stacked on the table and kept flipping at the cover of the one on top until Buffy couldn't stand it anymore.

"Spit it out, Giles!" she snapped. "You're making me a little edgy, here."

"Actually, you were edgy when you got here," Xander ventured. "You remember, the rain, your mom, and all?"

Buffy shot him a withering look.

"Not now, Xander," Xander said to himself.

"Well," Giles said, "several nights ago, it seemed to me that we were, all of us, having a bit too good a time at this. It's no game, you know. What you do is horrifying. Dreadful. The things we face are evil incarnate, and well, the kind of caprice evident during the hunt the other night could get you all killed."

Buffy knew exactly which night he was talking about. It seemed there was a strange little group of vampires who were into numerology or something, or maybe they watched too much *Star Trek*, but they had given each other wanky names like "Seven" and "Twelve B Two." They had somehow decided that the seventh of the month was the perfect time to make a sweep of the beach and chomp on kids partying around the fire rings. After the first time, Buffy and Giles probably would have passed it off as a particularly hellish night on the Hellmouth, but Angel had heard about this latest little sub-cult, and Angel had told Buffy.

So the next month, they had all saddled up and headed for the beach, Xander mangling ancient Beach Boys lyrics while the rest of them just generally made far too many jokes. Maybe because they'd known one of the girls who'd died the night before. That was what the gallows humor was all about, wasn't it? Laughing so you didn't cry?

Giles knew it, but it had been obvious that even with that understanding, he'd still thought they were going too far. His facial expressions and his reserved commentary had made that abundantly clear. But Buffy hadn't expected any long-term repercussions. Not like this.

After all he'd been through himself, all the pain he'd suffered, Buffy would have thought Giles would understand. Even a little bit.

"How dare you?" Buffy asked, offended not only for herself, but for all of them and all that they did.

Giles seemed taken aback. "I'm your Watcher, Buffy. It isn't a matter of daring at all. I have an obligation to . . ."

Buffy angrily slapped her palms on the big study table in the library.

"That's it!" she said. "I'm done for today."

He reached out a hand. "Buffy—"

She whirled on Giles. "I can't believe you!" she cried. "Never once did you get one of those little light-bulbs over your head that told you that maybe we're just blowing off steam? Maybe this whole thing is so disgusting and awful that the only way we can deal with what really goes on in our lives is to laugh about it? To make the kind of jokes you're always giving Xander a hard time about? Maybe that's how we make it from one day to the next, Giles. Because it isn't by hanging out at the Bronze or the mall or gossiping about what you-know-who wore to the dance!

"We . . . no, let me just speak for myself. I, Giles, . . . I don't go to the dances! How many times do we have to go over this? If it helps me be the Slayer, helps me get through the night—and my nights are very, very long—to have my friends around and to make jokes, why can't you just leave it alone?

"If you want to wallow in your own pain, to . . . savor every moment of suffering, hey, crunch all you want, we'll make more! But don't get all pissy if the rest of us want to run away to the Bahamas for a few seconds. Don't try dragging us down to your level of misery, Giles. I think you'll find that, speaking just for myself, I'm already soaking in it!"

Buffy stood glaring at Giles, breathing heavily from her tirade and waiting for a response.

Giles blinked several times. "It was merely an observation," he said at last.

"Well, stop with the observations. You're as bad as my mother half the time." She flushed, feeling guilty again, but she stood her ground. She had a point. That she was making.

Now it was Giles's turn. He took his glasses off, which usually meant he was getting serious.

"Well, Buffy, if you want to see it that way, that is your prerogative," he told her crisply. "In fact, when you compare me to your mother, you're not far off in some ways. As the only adult among you, and as your Watcher, I am in many ways responsible for your well-being."

Buffy turned and walked to the door in a huff. "You

know what, Giles? My dad is gone. Absentee father. I've adjusted, and I don't need you to take his place. You want to be my Watcher, fine! You want to be my friend? Okay. But do not try to be a parent to me!"

Then she stormed out.

When Buffy was gone, all Giles could do was stare after her.

"I didn't say anything, didn't voice any concerns I haven't brought up in the past," he said, after a few seconds had ticked by.

"Today just isn't the day for it, Giles," Willow explained.

"Yeah," Xander agreed. "Parents are from Mars. Teenagers are from Venus."

At that, Giles was truly speechless. A rare and wondrous thing.

"So, Giles was talking about this Renaissance Faire thingy," Buffy whispered.

She crept across Mrs. Calhoun's backyard, feet squishing in the damp ground, hoping the lady's yippy dog wouldn't start barking like crazy. At least it had stopped raining. But it was cold and damp, and it occurred to her to wonder—not for the first time—if she would ever make it to a fine old age where she could complain about rheumatism, arthritis, or— worst on her list—have to start wearing glasses.

Angel was at her side, hidden in the night, as she was, in all black clothing. Both of them were keeping their eyes peeled for vampires. The bad kind.

"Before my time," Angel replied. "The Renaissance."

"Wow."

"Yeah," Angel admitted. "Wow."

"I teased him about it—before I yelled at him for something else—but I don't know. Knights and swords and ladies in those beautiful gowns, it does have a certain appeal," Buffy admitted. "I thought maybe we could go."

"I don't know," Angel replied softly. "I try not to think much about the past, even if it's further in the past than I can personally remember."

Buffy paused. Glanced at him. Noted briefly the glint of moonlight on his hair and pale features, framed in blackness. Like Angel's life: washes of light, and so much dark.

"I guess I don't blame you," she said.

And she didn't. But she did wish that he'd go with her to the Faire. She'd thought it would be very romantic, after she'd cooled down from her argument with Giles long enough to give it some consideration. Not that romance and Angel made a comfortable pair these days. But she'd kind of thought Angel would like it, to remember another time like that. A time that was probably a lot more like the era he grew up in than Sunnydale was at the turn of the millenium.

"Maybe we can hit the museum?" Angel suggested.

"I think I'd like to stay away from the museum for a while," Buffy replied. That was where Angel had stolen the statue of Acathla, back when he had not been . . . himself.

Angel looked at her. "Yeah," he said. "I see your point."

Willow hung up from her conversation with Oz and lay on her back, angling her legs so that her bunny slippers hung over the edge of her bed. She wore an oversized T-shirt, and her red hair hung freely down her back. Oz had told her he liked the color of her hair.

Her stuffed animals lounged in their places on her bedspread. Her fish burbled in their tank. Life was good.

Well, except for the part of the phone conversation where Oz realized he would have to cancel out of the next Dingoes gig at the Bronze because he would be a werewolf that night. That kinda sucked.

"Willow?" her mother called from the hall. "It's a little late for phone calls, don't you think?"

Willow sighed. She got calls from Buffy and Xander much later than this, and on a regular basis, too. She wondered if her mom had picked up the extension and listened in. If she was doing stuff like that, they would have to be careful with what they talked about. Willow tried to think if she'd said anything tonight that might have freaked out her mom.

She winced.

Oz, you're such an animal, she'd said. He'd chuckled and replied, *Only sometimes.* Her mother would definitely misinterpret that kind of thing. Great, Willow thought. Something else to worry about.

"Willow?"

Willow sighed. "Sorry, Mom."

Her mother moved on.

"College," Willow reminded herself, setting her jaw. "One that's far, far away."

Flipping open Cordelia's cell phone, Xander waited for the connection and said, "Hi, it's me."

Queen C herself was at the wheel. At the corner of Bartholomew, Cordelia made a sharp left, tires squealing. They were late for her curfew, as usual. And she had made a big deal about the fact that he lived awfully far away from her—translation: not in the snooty part of town, where Rapunzel here dwelled—so much so that he had suggested she just let him out so he could hitch home.

"Maybe not a good idea," she had said tentatively.

So he was already in the not very best of moods when his mom said, distractedly, "Yes?" with no obvious notion of who "me" was.

"Xander." He exhaled. "Your son."

"Hi, honey."

She was watching TV. He could always tell. Sometimes when he thought of it, he made sure he called her during the commercials. Only she liked to watch some of those. At least she had some outside interests.

"I have a terminal illness and I have decided to end my life by jumping off a train," he said.

Cordelia rolled her eyes. She narrowly missed a Miata as she zoomed around to pass, pointing frantically at the digital readout on the instrument panel. As if his talking on the phone were going to slow her down.

"Are you on something?" Mrs. Harris asked suspiciously.

"No, Ma, just high on life," he quipped.

"Okay. Well, be home soon."

She disconnected.

"And so, we will not be taping the news for tough guy," Xander said, flicking the phone shut.

"What?" Cordelia took her eyes off the road. Not a good thing. "Why didn't you just come right out and ask her?"

He shrugged. "Willow will tape it."

There was a slight chance they were going to run a piece about the escalating runaway situation in Sunnydale. Giles had suggested they all watch it, and Xander, eager to remind the Watcher that he and the Slayerettes were useful and productive citizens of the Hellmouth, had wanted very badly to comply.

Well, so much for that. It wasn't his mom's fault, not really. He could have made sure he and Cordy knocked off the smootchin' a little earlier.

"We could catch it at my house," Cordelia suggested. "I'm closer."

"Oh, right. You're coming in late again and I'm walking through the front door? And I still need a ride? Not the best plan."

"Yeah." She sighed and checked her makeup in the mirror for telltale smears. "I wish you'd move."

He looked out the window. "Yeah, well, we can all dream."

"Whazzat?"

Bernie Sayre sat upright in the bed he had once shared with his wife, long gone, and frowned in the darkness. Was Simon pawing through the trash again?

"Dang cat."

He yawned and climbed out of bed with a groan. His hip was acting up—don't tell the manager of the Sunnydale S&L, he might fire ol' Bernie, and him so close to retirement—and he favored it as he limped down the hall.

"Simon, dang it," he called.

Back when Vera was alive, the kitchen was always spotless. But with his job and his hip and all . . . well,

47

who was he kidding? He just wasn't the housekeeper she'd been. Not that it mattered too much. He didn't get a lot of company, and the cat didn't seem to mind.

There was a clatter, like a cat food tin falling to the ground. Bernie grunted, envisioning a pile of garbage on the floor—coffee grounds, banana peel, wadded up circulars and junk mail—and he said, "Simon, stop it!"

Another clatter.

He sped up, and nearly fell over the lump in the middle of the hall.

The lump gave a meow of displeasure and cocked his head at Bernie. It was Simon, who got up, stretched, and deigned to saunter out of Bernie's way.

Bernie was not very glad to see him.

"If you're out here, what the heck is in the kitchen?" he demanded.

Simon said, "Meow."

Chapter 2

SUNNYDALE HIGH WAS CONSIDERED AN AFFLUENT school district. Though boisterous, the students were, as a rule, well-behaved. The Mediterranean-style main building never bore unsightly graffiti for more than a few hours—and there was never much of it in the first place. No one put Kool-Aid in the Olympic-size swimming pool. Classrooms were not locked between classes, as was the case in many southern California schools, and teachers still welcomed their charges alone into their offices for conferences.

So the fact that Sunnydale's escalating runaway problem was put down to bad kids, and that the more numerous and escalating acts of vandalism were laid on the shoulders of "teenagers," seemed patently unfair. That the principal felt the need to discuss it over the P.A. system for half of first period might have been a puzzle to some. But to others, they figured he was just covering his . . . reputation. He had a very small, toadlike reputation.

The principal droned on about respect for property, zero tolerance, yada yada yada, taking so long that the history test was postponed until Monday. At least until the student uproar brought the teacher's attention to the concept that Monday exams tended to put a damper on weekends. And they were seniors, after all. They felt they deserved a little slack.

The teacher didn't seem to agree.

"If you can tell me one thing you'll spend time doing this weekend that will teach you something," she said, "I'll postpone the test until Tuesday."

Willow raised her hand.

"Miss Rosenberg?"

"Well, there's a Renaissance Faire in town," she said brightly. "Which should be cool."

From the expressions on their faces, some of the other students were dubious. But when the test was postponed, Willow received a resounding round of applause.

Oz met her after class, and they caught up with Cordelia and Xander in the hall. They were quite the mismatch, those two, Xander in Xander clothes (which Willow thought were just fine) and Cordelia so dressed up you'd have thought she was a French fashion model on assignment. Short plaid jumper, very crisp white blouse. Willow was glad she and Oz both did the cazh thing together, she in cords and a brown sweater, he in one of his many very cool bowling shirts. This one was green and brown, so they kind of matched.

* * *

Cordelia and Xander were in the middle of one of their frequent arguments, as the four elbowed their way through the between-bells mosh pit that was the halls of Sunnydale High. Finally Cordelia scowled at Xander.

"Stop walking so close to me," she snarled through gritted teeth. "You're invading my space."

What is this thing called lust? Xander wondered, *that I put up with this woman?* But to the object of that lust, he said, "Yes, majesty," and very purposefully took several longer strides so that he moved slightly ahead of her. Then he said over his shoulder, "Not that you complained about that last night. Or this morning."

Oz chuckled as Cordelia huffed.

She said after a beat, "You weren't, like, bashing into me then."

"I sure was."

"Shut up."

Now it was Willow's turn to chuckle.

"Cordy, honey, sweetie." Xander slowed so that Cordelia either had to stop walking or run right into him. He made a show of taking her hand as she sighed and rolled her eyes. He pointed to a girl who was walking past them with a blank, almost zombie-like expression.

"A quick look around, and one might notice the many students who have nothing in common with each other, but are forced to trudge these halls like cattle."

Cordelia jerked on her hand. "Xander—"

He slipped her hand around his arm and patted it in a fatherly way. "Upperclass moos, sophomore veal

calves, trudging into the slaughterhouses of indepen-
dent thought also known as classrooms. And since
this rampant stampeding might—just might—
account for the fact that I am actually—gasp—in
your vicinity, and yet you still live, guess what, Cor,
no one notices, and no one cares."

Cordelia shook his hand away as if he had rabies.
Oz may be the man with that problem—who
knew?—but thus far, Willow had not accused her
sweetie of all the terrible offenses Xander had apparently committed in his important new role as Cordelia's official doormat. Tops of course was his bad
fashion sense. Okay, he could cop to that.

On the other hand, if that was all Cordelia could
really find wrong with him—even though she gave it
her all—somewhere in the recesses of her mind, she
must actually find him . . . not despicable.

When they were alone, she most definitely did not
find him despicable. All this schizophrenia was making him dizzy. And very confused. And everyone said
Angel and Buffy had the weird relationship. . . .

"As if no one cares. You know gossip follows my
every move." Cordelia stopped walking and threw
back her hair.

Oz chuckled and Xander's grin widened. He
couldn't help it. Schizo or not, sometimes there was
something so darn cute about his imperious girlfriend. He was about to shoot something back at her
when a clap of thunder boomed overhead and everybody around them in the hall whooped and applauded. A few seconds later, rain clattered on the
roof.

"Oh, great, what about the Renaissance Faire?"
Willow said gloomily.

"It'll clear up," Oz assured her. Then, as the rain intensified, he added, "Mmm. Or not."

"Not works for me." Cordelia made a face. "I'm not tramping around in the mud looking at dueling midgets or whatever." She caught her breath.

Above, the rain spattered like buckshot. Xander shrugged as Cordelia gave him her heavily mascared evil eye. Like they said, a day without sunshine was like a day with Cordy.

Though she was loath to admit it, Willow felt a little sorry for Cordelia. Perfect clothes, perfect hair, perfect body; add it all up and it still didn't mean she had a perfect life. Willow was still baffled by the fact that Xander and Cordy had gotten together at all—they'd despised each other since kindergarten—and there was still some jealousy there of course. Willow and Xander had been best friends almost since diapers, and Willow had always secretly hoped that she and Xander . . . well, that he would notice her as a girl, instead of just his friend.

But since that seemed about as likely as Giles watching MTV, Willow wasn't holding her breath. Once she had acknowledged that, she was willing to give Cordelia the benefit of the doubt. After all, shallow as the girl might seem, she had risked her life with them time and again. Had to give her points for that. So when Xander went a little too far with his barbs, Willow felt bad for Cordy. Other than Oz, he was the nicest guy she knew, but his wit was sharp—sharp enough to cut sometimes. Willow knew that from experience.

"If it will make you feel better," Willow offered, smiling helpfully at Cordelia as she and Oz caught up to her in the crush, "Oz and I will move away from you."

"No," Cordelia said quickly. "It's okay. Oz is cool and you're with him. Just don't, like, talk to me a lot, okay?"

Oz slid an amused glance at Willow, took her hand, and gave it a squeeze.

"You're nice," he said quietly. "I like that in a person."

Willow shrugged shyly, but her heart was thundering. Oz could do that to her so easily.

"So, moving right along," Xander said happily, clapping his hands and rubbing them together as they all slowed once more to a crawl. "The Renaissance Faire. Tomorrow afternoon. Dueling mud midgets for milady's pleasure. Show of hands?"

Willow raised hers. Oz shrugged and said, "Eating without utensils for a day? Sure, why not? Besides, I always wanted to know what knights did when they had to pee."

"Well, at the Faire they have those porta-potties," Willow observed. "But I don't think there was, y'know, a Middle Ages equivalent."

Cordelia stared at them all in amazement. "Are you kidding?" She shook her head. "Absolutely no way."

"Too tragically unhip, eh?" Xander asked.

"Well, yes, since you put it that way. The only people who will be going to that are boring adults and role-playing tweekos."

"Cor, you'll be missing out," Xander said. "You can buy these really cool costumes there. They make your waist really tiny and your, ah, other attributes look really, really big. It would make a great Halloween getup for a stupendous babe such as yourself."

"Please, Xander," Cordelia said wearily. And then she cocked her head. Willow could actually see the wheels turning as Cordelia imagined herself in a sexy Renaissance costume.

"Also, they sell lots of jewelry," Xander went on, tempting her. "Sparkly jewelry."

"And they have Shakespeare plays and lute concerts," Willow added enthusiastically, but then fell silent as Xander flashed her a don't-go-there look.

"Maybe if we just meet there," Cordelia said slowly. "Then if I see anyone I know—which isn't very likely—I could say my mom made me go. Or something."

Giles sat in his office with a cup of cold tea at his elbow. Ostensibly, he was looking though a forensics reference manual on bite marks, but in reality, he was staring at a strip of pictures of himself with Jenny Calendar. They had been taken in one of those booth affairs when they'd gone to see the funny cars. Despite his sorrow, he was smiling faintly to himself. He had been grinning like a fool; she making silly faces. He remembered the thrill even now as she had told him to sit as far back on the stool as possible, then wedged herself half on his lap, half on the stool.

"Don't move," she'd said fiercely, and then the first flash had gone off. "You'll blur."

"Good heavens, can't have that," he'd shot back. "No blurring, no indeed."

"No talking, English. And sit still!" she'd commanded.

He had tried to sit still. Oh, how he'd tried.

He sighed. A happier time. Simpler? Perhaps.

Memento mori, Jenny, sweet Jenny.

He opened the top right drawer to put the treasured pictures back. His hand brushed the stack of sympathy cards tied with a black ribbon. His heart caught. The one on top was a proper condolence card, simple, elegant paper lined in black. From his father, who had once warned him that as a Watcher, falling in love could be a risky proposition. He had not elaborated, and Giles had not pressed.

Jenny . . .

He lowered his head to compose himself.

"Hello?"

Realized, with a flash of resentment, that someone was actually looking for him. May actually wish to check out a book in this godforsaken land of theme parks and strip malls.

"Yes," he said gruffly, then tried to sound more friendly. "May I help you?"

It was a young, gangly boy with a fashionable haircut. "Um, I'm looking for something about . . ." He squinted up his face. "Um, some dude named after that guy in *Titanic?* An inventor dude?"

Giles sighed. "Leonardo da Vinci?"

"Yeah." The boy nodded eagerly. "How'd you know?"

Sometimes, Buffy wondered how Giles managed to keep his job. Sure, he was well-liked by the students and the faculty. But anyone who'd ever been into the library at Sunnydale High School would have to admit that he hadn't exactly created an environment conducive to learning.

The place was dark, dreary, and not terribly well organized. The magazines Giles subscribed to for the school, oddities ranging from *Bon Appetit* to *The*

Fortean Times, weren't things that immediately came to mind when one considered the needs and interests of high school students. In fact, it was rare that students actually attempted to use the high school library. It was far more likely that anybody with a research project due would head over to the town library instead.

This, of course, suited Giles just fine. It also worked out well for Buffy and her friends, who used the library as their de facto base camp. Still, it baffled Buffy that Giles was still employed by the school. Granted, other faculty visited the library as infrequently as students, but it had to be more than that. In the end, she was forced to simply chalk it up to his Britishness. After all, he'd previously been a curator at the British Museum. For the school board, that was probably enough.

Whatever the reason, Buffy was grateful. Though he could be infuriating at times, she didn't know what she would do without Giles. Considering that, Buffy sat on the edge of the study table and watched him stamp "returned" without much enthusiasm on the few books that students had actually bothered to check out.

After her outburst yesterday, things were a bit tense between them, and Buffy didn't know how to fix that. Or if she should even try. But she hated not getting along with Giles. After all, he was her Watcher. And her friend.

But not my father, she reminded herself firmly. And he had to learn to back off sometimes.

"Giles, I'm sor—" she began in a rush.

But she realized he hadn't heard her as he said crisply, "So, no Slaying last night?"

"Um, no." She flared with guilt. "We, that is, I looked and looked, but no one wanted to poof! go up in smoke, I guess. Or ashes."

He looked intently at her, a familiar emerging-from-the-fog-of-my-own-mental-wanderings expression on his face. "I'm sorry, Buffy. You were about to say something?"

"No, no," she said quickly. She was hurt by his distant tone. "I was just wondering, um, if the Renaissance Faire thing is a thing that you would like to go to with other people."

Whoa. She had no idea where that had come from. But not a bad idea if she wanted to repair the bridge she'd played arsonist with yesterday.

"People like me and other . . . people you know." Buffy moved her shoulders—not quite a shrug. She'd started this. She'd finish it. "I mean, the other kids. That we hang with. I hang with."

Giles's cool expression slightly defrosted. "Why, Buffy, how lovely." He blinked at her. "I had assumed the Faire held no appeal for any of you."

"Well, surprise." She swung her legs where she perched on the counter. "There's just the Bronze and a theater that shows movies we've already seen on Pay-Per-View. And there's Pay-Per-View. So." She smiled hopefully. "Maybe it won't be too dorky."

"I should think a bit dorky," he said agreeably. "The people who put these things together mean well, of course, but they frequently make historical errors. Elaborate ruffs in the wrong decades, smooth-faced men when beards were in fashion, that sort of thing. But if one can suspend one's disbelief, it can be quite entertaining."

"Oh, I believe that . . . you believe that," she said with all sincerity.

"Indeed." His faraway look was back. "However, I did have some pertinent business to discuss with you. I'm afraid I have rather distressing new information about these 'raccoon' incidents," he said.

She groaned.

On Saturday morning the sky was overcast with heavy, gray clouds, threatening downpour. The ocean breeze was strong, however, and just before noon, the last of the storm that had been brewing blew inland, and the sky was a magnificent clear blue, as if there had never been a single cloud up there at all.

By dusk, when they had all agreed to meet at the Faire, Buffy had passed a long afternoon helping her mother uncrate the pieces of a new gallery exhibit before the two of them shared sugar-overloaded iced tea in the backyard. They didn't talk about Timmy or any of the other runaways in town, but Joyce took several calls on the portable that were obviously coming from the shelter. Buffy squirmed with each call.

"So, uh, Oz," Ira Rosenberg said. He always stumbled over Oz's name.

Oz was cool with it. It was an unusual name.

"Your plans for after graduation, do they include . . . anything?"

They were sitting at the kitchen table. Willow's mother was puttering around making grilled cheese sandwiches. She'd gone off on a tangent about not keeping an absolutely kosher kitchen, then let it go at a look from her husband.

Mr. Rosenberg, Willow, and Oz were drinking iced

tea. Willow looked not exactly scared to death, but not about to jump up and dance either.

Oz wanted to tell her to be cool with it, too. They were her parents. They loved her. That was what all this was about. Not what kind of name Oz was and what he was planning to do post cap and gown.

"Oz was the only other student recruited by that computer firm at Career Week," Willow said eagerly. She'd told them that before. Maybe she was so nervous she didn't remember.

"Computers," Mr. Rosenberg said expansively. "There's always going to be good money there, don't you think?"

"Yes, sir." Oz sipped his tea. "This is great tea, Mrs. Rosenberg. Those sandwiches. Do you need any help?"

She half-turned with a surprised smile on her face, which she directed first at Oz and then at Willow's dad, as if to say, *See? He's a nice boy after all, Ira.*

Mr. Rosenberg grunted. "Have you applied to very many colleges? Willow's being recruited from all over." He clapped a hand on Willow's back. She gulped down the tea she'd had in her mouth and smiled earnestly.

"I'm trying to keep my options open." Now was not the time to announce that the Dingoes were working on getting signed to a label.

"Options." Mr. Rosenberg's voice dropped a few octaves, as if he were saying a dirty word. "Willow knows she's too young for options."

Willow kept smiling.

Oz said, "Mrs. Rosenberg, would you like help setting the table?"

* * *

"This is so strange," Cordelia said to Xander. They were sitting under a tree in Weatherly Park—one not occupied by some homeless man enjoying a nice Saturday afternoon nap beneath a shopping cart—with the contents of a large bag from Subway Sandwiches spread between them. It was the fastest food Cordelia would eat, and even there, she was stretching it to accommodate Xander—a strange notion, true. But one did have to make sacrifices in a relationship. Or so she'd read.

Although she wasn't sure what the point of that was.

"What is so strange?" Xander asked.

Cordelia smiled at him. He looked nervous. She was a pain, she knew she was. Oh, well.

She was worth it.

"We're not fighting," she told him.

He shrugged. "The day is only half over."

"True."

Under the spreading eucalyptus tree, they dined.

The normally punctual Giles was last to arrive at their agreed-upon rendezvous, most likely due, Buffy thought, to the ancient transport he continued to refer to as a "car." To the astonishment of everyone—and to the cheering-up of one bummed-out Slayer—the Watcher arrived wearing what Xander called a "puffy beret," a brown velvet hat, which Giles informed them was called a "porkpie," a reference which, of course, sent Xander off on a riff about the value of snack food.

Giles began to launch into a lecture on the history of the porkpie hat, complete with footnotes, but Buffy tuned him out the moment a familiar hand gently touched her shoulder.

Angel said, "Hi."

"Hey," Buffy replied, half-turning. She couldn't help the skip of her heartbeat, although she struggled to hide her feelings from everyone, including herself. Angel and she could no longer be together, and that was that. But he was dressed in a black silk shirt and black leather pants, and his eyes shone as he smiled at her. She was suddenly very glad she had tried Cordelia's guaranteed method to get rid of puffy eyes, which was slices of cucumbers followed by a hot, steamy shower.

"Thanks for coming." She wondered if he would notice that her double-strap red velvet tank top was new. And that she, too, had on black leather pants. And boots, like his. That they looked like they might be a couple, sort of.

Angel smiled that lopsided smile of his, and Buffy sighed to herself. They were not a couple, not in the usual sense.

But then, when had they ever been one in the usual sense?

Angel nodded to the others, who all nodded back. Even Giles, though it took him a beat longer than the others. Not that Buffy blamed him. Angel's . . . return had probably been the most upsetting for her Watcher. He had loved Jenny Calendar very much.

As much as Buffy had loved . . . still loved . . . Angel.

"It looks like fun, huh," Willow offered.

"Wouldn't have missed it," Angel said.

"Unless we went during the *day*," Xander noted. "Which would have been a much better idea."

Angel shot him an annoyed look, which was probably mostly out of habit, then turned to smile at Buffy again.

"Shall we?" he asked, holding his arm out for her in old-fashioned chivalrous style.

"We shall," she replied, and together they walked into the Faire, leaving the others to bring up the rear.

The entrance to the Faire was an ornate wooden sign that read, KING RICHARD'S FAIRE, decorated with real flowers. There were several lanes of booths that looked like cottages and little castles, and tents for Gypsies. The air was redolent with the odors of barbecued poultry and fire-baked meat pies. Small carts sold everything from full period costumes to handmade jewelry, from chain mail to fantasy chess sets.

"Behold, ye olde mall," Xander said. "We paid to come in here? It's all a scam to get us to buy ye olde and useless trinkets."

"Oh, Xander, don't be such a downer," Cordelia said, her eyes shining as she took in the vast array of merchandise. "This looks like fun!" Then she must have caught herself, because she murmured, "And if you ever tell anyone I said that, I'll have to kill you."

She flounced away from him, not an easy thing in tight black jeans, and walked up to a nearby tent. As Buffy and the others followed, a sound like tiny cymbals filled the air.

"What's in here?" Willow asked, as they reached the entrance.

"Oh, yeah," Xander said.

It was a belly-dancing show. Behind the tent flap, people sat on large decorative pillows as three women in spangled tops and silk skirts with tiny bells sewn on them gyrated and shimmied on a stage. Two men in cone-shaped red hats with flat tops sat to one side of the platform, one playing some kind of flute and the other beating a drum.

Cordelia yanked on his arm. "Oh, no," she said. "No, no, no."

"We can meet up later," Xander pleaded.

"What ho, gentles!" boomed a voice.

Buffy jumped and turned around, semi-pulling Angel with her.

A man dressed in a green shirt and leggings, with a bow slung over his shoulder and a quiver of arrows strapped to his back, stood next to a hugely rotund man who wore a long, gold robe. A purple cape trimmed in white fur was slung over the fat man's shoulders and two small boys in tights and blousy shirts carried the ends. A heavy, dark gold crown set with chunks of colored glass sat on his long, brown hair.

"Bow in the presence of Richard the Lion Heart!" the green man bellowed.

The surrounding onlookers began to applaud, and some bowed, laughing.

"You see," Giles began, "this is precisely the kind of thing I was talking about. This is Robin Hood, and that man is King Richard the Lion Heart. Actually, Richard was king of England during the Crusades, that is to say, during the twelfth century. So his presence here is not at all historically correct, although he was a symbol of English pride by then. And Robin Hood, though usually associated with him, has also been connected to the—"

"Art thou deaf, villain?" Robin Hood shouted. He reached out and pushed Giles's arm. "Kneel!"

Caught off guard, Giles half-bent his left knee and said angrily, "I beg your pardon!" His porkpie hat fell to the ground.

"Granted!" boomed the king. He lifted a sword and pointed it at Giles. "Be ye forewarned, however, that we require deference in our presence."

Saying that, his majesty swept away, snootier than Cordelia at her worst. Robin Hood moved ahead of him, crying, "Make way for the king!"

The little boys—they were twins—scooted along behind with his cape.

"Good Lord, that's taking things a bit far." Giles straightened and looked after the little group. He replaced his hat and smoothed his tweedy tweed-clothes. "He actually hit me."

"Then you can sue him," Cordelia told him.

"No," Giles said slowly. "We British are not as litigious as you Americans."

"Which is why you lost the war," Xander offered.

Giles glanced at him. "Which war?"

"The one . . . that you lost."

Giles looked very sad. "Come along, my lost ones," he murmured.

"We're not lost," Xander insisted. He looked around himself. "Just misplaced."

The incident with Robin Hood tarnished the glow of the Faire, but just a bit. Soon Buffy and Cordelia were trying on wench costumes with low, ruffled blouses, tightly cinched waistcoats, and yards of skirts, and Buffy saw the look of admiration in Angel's eyes as she pushed back the dressing-room curtain and curtsied to him. It still hurt when she thought about everything they'd been through, but she was adjusting. It seemed that as the Slayer, she was always adjusting. Wouldn't it have been fun to live in this time period for real, wearing pretty clothes and what, baking bread or something?

"You should buy it," Angel urged her. "Blue's your color." He grinned. "Also black. And white." She was swathed in blue. Cordelia wore red, looking very gypsy-dramatic with her dark hair and eyes.

Cordelia posed and said to Xander, "What do you think?"

"I'm thinking things I shouldn't be thinking," Xander rasped. "Or at least, shouldn't be admitting I'm thinking."

"Well, I'm buying mine," Cordelia announced, brandishing her American Express card. "Don't leave home without it."

"Not me." Buffy sighed and gave herself one last glance in the mirror. "It's too expensive."

Willow looked pensive. She had demurred at trying something on, to the slight disappointment of Oz, Buffy thought, but you could never be sure with Oz. He was so laid back. Also, totally without judgment. Buffy couldn't have hoped for a better boyfriend for her best friend . . . unless it had been Xander. But that just didn't seem meant to be.

She paused a moment. Over her shoulder she caught a glimpse of a guy about her age dressed in a red and blue patchwork jester costume, bells jingling from the points of his hat. He was watching her, a little too intently. She frowned, and was about to tell him off when he ducked behind a curtain.

Grimacing slightly, she turned to Cordelia as they headed back to their makeshift dressing rooms and said, "Make sure your curtain is shut, okay?"

"Xander's not *that* freaky," Cordelia muttered,

then grinned at Buffy. "Unfortunately." Buffy had to laugh.

After they changed and Cordelia bought her outfit, Willow, keeper of the guidebook, announced that there would be a joust in ten minutes.

"Hel-lo! Priorities!" Xander pointed to a stall sign that read, YE RIBS OF PIG. YE LEG OF TURKEY. Women in low-cut, ruffled blouses and billowing skirts handed out Styrofoam plates heaped with steaming food as fast as they could. "Enough time to grab an authentic Renaissance turkey leg and gawk at yon serving wenches."

"I don't suppose you're hungry," Buffy said quietly to Angel. She sipped on the straw of her authentic cup of Diet Coke.

Angel smiled and walked to the line at the booth. "I'm a leg man, myself. " He took her cup and drew Diet Coke up the straw, swallowing it. "What would you like?"

Buffy smiled back at him. Sometimes she still forgot that he could eat and drink if he wanted to. It didn't do anything life-sustaining for him, but he could do it. It was like being a social smoker. Which she wasn't. But she could relate.

"I'm a leg girl myself. Turkey leg, I mean," she amended, a little embarrassed. She shook her head. "Anyway, thanks."

"You know, it's a shame we don't see more serving wenches," Xander said in a loud voice behind her. "It's a lost art."

Then there was the sound of a smack, and Cordelia snapping, "Shut up, Xander!"

"Now, kids," Oz drawled, then murmured, "Whoa. Check it out."

They all turned.

On a cart pulled by a huge thug in a black leather hood, stood a man with his head and hands stuck through a padlocked wooden stockade. He was hunched painfully over, his legs bent and trembling.

"Water," he begged in a dry, raspy voice as the hooded man stopped and dropped the handle of the cart.

Some of the other fairgoers pointed at the man and laughed. A boy and a girl applauded. The girl took a picture; her flash lit up the man's face. It was cracked and peeling—or made to look that way with makeup.

"Water," he begged again.

Buffy cocked her head and wrinkled her nose. "That isn't very funny."

"Well, it is accurate," Giles offered. "The Renaissance, for all of its flowering of scientific inquiry and rebirth of art and culture, was still rooted in the Middle Ages, which were quite barbaric."

"Please," the man said.

Buffy moved from the crowd and ripped the lid off her Diet Coke. She lifted it to his mouth.

The other spectators burst into a chorus of both booing and cheering. Buffy looked up at the man and squinted. He looked terrible.

He didn't look like he was wearing makeup.

"Come on, Buffy," Xander called from the food line. "We're going to miss the joust! Giles's pal King Richard will be there. With his fool and everything."

"Yeah, with *his* fool," Cordelia said pointedly.

"Bless you, miss," the man whispered to Buffy.

The hooded man wheeled on her and waved her away with an imperious flick of his hand. "Get away from him!"

The other man stared at her. His glance never wavering, a single tear coursed down his cheek.

"Away, girl, now!" the hooded man boomed.

With an uncertain glance over her shoulder, Buffy rejoined Angel in line.

"Wow, you're really getting into this," he said, amused.

"I guess." She frowned. "But I don't know." She looked around at the booths and the people in them. There was nothing wrong, nothing different, that she could see, anyway. "I'm getting a little creeped out."

"You're just hungry. Once you feed . . . I mean, eat, you'll feel better." He put an arm around her and gave her a little squeeze.

That made her feel better. It also made her sad for a time when things between them were so much simpler.

The hooded man picked up the cart handle and began to drag his prisoner away.

"Wow, check out that serving wench!" Xander said in line behind Buffy. "Now those are ruffles!"

Angel chuckled. "Xander's getting into this, too."

"Yeah." Buffy sighed and tried to focus her attention on her friends. But just like in math, things were not adding up too well.

"Two legs," Angel said to the serving wench in the booth.

"One for you, and one for my mistress meddler?" The wench's tone was sharp, her scowl sharper as she flicked open a money box and held out her hand.

Angel looked surprised. "Excuse me?"

"Two it is," the wench said in a more pleasant voice. "That'll be eight dollars."

"Whoa," Oz said. "Pricey eats. Good thing Din-

goes are getting regular work these days." He sighed.
"That I can perform, most of the time."

"Good thing I have a date with yon princess of
American Express," Xander piped up.

Willow touched Buffy's shoulder. "Are you okay?"

"That whole thing was pretty freaky," Buffy admitted.

Willow nodded. "It was kind of weird." She smiled
hopefully. "But, y'know, as Giles said, historically
accurate."

Buffy nodded slowly.

Chapter 3

THE JOUSTING ARENA WAS LOCATED AT THE FAR END OF the rows of shops and eateries. Surrounded on all four sides by bleachers, with brightly painted wooden fences running down the middle of the dirt, it was actually the staging area for the Sunnydale Rodeo and the livestock shows which took place during Sunnydale Days, a sort of county fair held in July.

Buffy had yet to pass a summer in Sunnydale, but if the rodeo was the best the town had to offer during that time, she wasn't all that broken up about missing it.

"What ho, gentles!" cried a hawker with a big case of sodas suspended from a thick leather strap looped behind his neck. "Quench thy thirst!"

"You see, more of what I was talking about," Giles said, as the seven of them scooted onto an empty row of bleacher seats. "Quenching one's thirst on carbonated beverages. The spectators at a joust were far more likely to drink mead or ale." He smiled at the group. "One imagines that for most of the Renaissance, everybody went about in a minor alcoholic stupor."

"Is that fancy talk for, 'I'm buying a brewski, kids, don't be shocked'?" Xander teased.

Giles considered. "Well, now that you mention it . . ."

"Please, don't let us stop you," Buffy said. "Your role model shift stopped when the school bell rang yesterday."

"Plus, you're over twenty-one," Xander added helpfully, "so we won't judge you." He rubbed his hands. "So, jousting. Do the ah, ladies-in-waiting joust? And what are they waiting for, anyway?"

"You to shut up," Cordelia said.

"Yes, majesty," Xander replied.

The platform beneath them was made up of lengths of wood, not unlike the run-down bleachers at the old field behind Sunnydale Junior High. Across from where they sat, there was a stage. Up on the stage, backless wooden chairs—not much better than stools, really—were arranged on either side of a small riser, and on that sat an ornate golden throne. Banners hung from a wire suspended between two of the massive spotlights that illuminated the area.

The paper bag that contained Cordelia's new Renaissance costume was bunched on her lap. She bent sideways and said, "I want to put this under my seat, but I'm afraid it will fall through the cracks in the floor."

"It'll be okay," Xander assured her, taking the bag from her and sliding it underneath his own seat. He smiled at Cordelia and put an arm around her shoulder. "There," he said.

"Stop that," she hissed, quickly scoping the area to see if any damage had been done to her public persona.

Buffy caught his hurt look as he took his arm away. She wanted to say to him, *What did you expect when you started dating her?*

Well, what had she expected when she'd gotten involved with Angel? Meanwhile, Oz and Willow cuddled up. Willow looked ecstatic.

Wedged between Giles and Angel, Buffy silently hoped Angel would take her hand, and when he did, she was surprised at just how cold his skin was. There had been a time she had stopped noticing. She had stopped seeing his vamp face when she was in his arms. She had no longer realized his lips were chilly when he kissed her. She had not prepared herself for any of that to matter again, once they had fallen in love.

If only she had prepared herself for the worst . . .

"Oh." Giles suddenly sat up a little straighter and half-raised a hand in greeting to someone across the arena. "Damn it." He lowered his hand and sighed heavily.

Buffy looked along his line of vision. Giles was intently watching a middle-aged man with sandy hair who was swigging back a paper cup of what must be beer. It was splashing the woman beside him and he didn't even seem to notice. Behind the man, another man sat forward and tapped the first one on the shoulder. The sandy-haired man sprang to his feet and nearly toppled over.

"Damn it," Giles said again. He turned to Buffy. "Ah, I must . . . use the loo," he said in a rush. "That is, the ah—"

"Please, Giles, just go," Buffy said. "I know what a loo is."

He raised his brows. "Indeed."

"Yeah, it's like a guitar," she said, feigning ignorance, and snickered at his crestfallen expression. "You really do think I'm a bimbo, don't you? The most air-headed Slayer in all of southern California."

"No, not at all." He was all earnestness, pushing up his glasses as his voice moved down to a lower gear, as if he were about to go up a very steep grade. "I know you possess a powerful mind. Although I must admit that upon occasion, I wish you'd think to activate it."

"Gee, thanks, Giles." She sighed. "Just go get your beer or whatever. Hey." She brightened. "If you're going to stand in line, do you think you could get some popcorn?"

"I'm not going for beer," he said with asperity. Then he started edging down the rest of the row, murmuring his excuse-me's and thank-you's in a harried, rather unGiles-like way.

Angel looked at her questioningly. Buffy shrugged. "Don't look at me. I don't have the slightest notion what he's doing." She grinned. "Something about a guy named Lou?"

Angel grinned. "Buffy, 'loo' is British slang for 'bathroom.' Giles has to use the facilities."

"No kidding. My God, does everyone around here think I'm Rain Man?"

Angel grinned again, a bit lopsided, and a little thrill ran through Buffy. Why did he have to be so charming? So unbelievably . . . unbelievable. When she'd lived in L.A., her friend Hilly used to say that she liked guys who had a certain something she could never quite put into words. She just called it 'Grrrrr.' Angel had lots and lots of Grrrrr. Sometimes—hell, most of the time—it made their new 'un-relationship' pretty difficult to bear.

Buffy gave him a mocking pout and leaned forward to survey her row of friends. Ladies and gents, on one end of this group, you have a nice boy who turns into a werewolf. On the other you have a vampire slayer. Beside her, an actual vampire. And then we have Morticia and Gomez, only not . . .

"Tomatoes! Rotten tomatoes!" cried a vendor. "Cabbages! Overripe fruit."

"Yum," Xander said. "I feel a snack attack coming on."

"Guess there weren't any hot dogs in the Renaissance." Buffy wrinkled her nose in distaste and looked at Angel.

But Angel himself looked puzzled.

"Oh, wow," Willow said. "Look, you guys."

"Tomatoes!" the huckster cried.

Just then, the hooded man Buffy had tangled with earlier entered the arena, pulling the man in the cart behind him. The man was doubled over, his knees buckling, making it look as though he might well strangle if he lost his balance.

"Make way for the prisoner!" the hooded man shouted. "Make way for one who would insult our king!"

Taking their cue, some of the audience began to boo. Someone hurled a tomato at the man, and it smacked against the side of his head and burst like a water balloon. Another one hit. And then another.

"I don't like this," Willow said to Oz. "This is *too* historically accurate for me."

Buffy set her jaw, watching a small boy two rows over clap his hands with glee.

Angel's body had only the remnant warmth of the day and the earth and the air, and whatever blood he'd ingested, blood that didn't belong to him. But somehow, the sight before them now was enough to chill even him.

"It was like this in my time," he said quietly, without realizing he was going to speak. "Once, back in Galway, they thought an old woman had caused the Lord Mayor's wife to give birth to a stillborn babe. They dragged poor Mistress McIntosh through the streets . . ."

His voice grew hoarse. "I was just a little boy. I like to tell myself I didn't know better, but I . . ." He trailed off. "I was very unkind to her," he finished.

And for a moment he was back in Galway, a little boy who had no notion of the hellish existence he was about to embark upon, a wee lad who did not understand that you do suffer in the hereafter for each sin you commit.

Then he looked to either side of himself, to Xander, whose mostly unstated distrust of him Angel completely understood. Part of him even appreciated it, for he knew that if . . . something . . . ever happened again, Xander would do his best to protect the others from him.

He looked hard at Willow, marveling at the generosity of her nature. After he had changed back into Angelus, she was the first person he had tried to kill. He, or rather, the thing within him, had understood at the deepest level that her death would have hurt Buffy terribly. Remorse washed over him in waves as he remembered the glee with which he anticipated either snapping her neck or draining her of every drop of blood.

But Willow, though perhaps a little nervous around him, seemed to be nervous mostly for Buffy's sake. They all were. And yet, because Buffy accepted him once again, they all did their best. For Willow, it must have been awfully hard.

For Giles, it must be almost impossible.

"I'm going to stop this," Buffy said, startling him out of his reverie.

"Buffy, relax. It's just a show." Cordelia waved at her to sit back down. "Pretend, ya know?"

"Just faking it?" Xander asked in a loud voice. "Well, you should know, Cor."

"That's right, Xander. I should."

Xander looked perturbed. Then a little worried. He fell silent and sipped on his authentic lemonade.

Buffy winced as she watched the poor man held prisoner at center stage. Something else hit the man—it looked to be a beer can—and he shouted with pain, then went limp. His head was bent back in the wooden stockade, giving every appearance that he had broken his neck.

The audience howled with laughter.

"Okay, that's it," Buffy announced, jumping to her feet.

"Down in front," someone bellowed at her.

She started to climb over the legs of the person on the other side of Giles's empty spot.

"Long live the king!" came a booming voice over

the loudspeakers. "Long live King Richard the Lion Heart!"

With that, a dozen riders resplendent in velvet cloaks and helmets topped with plumes thundered around the cart and into the arena on enormous, chestnut-colored horses. Huge clots of dirt and dust kicked up behind them like a wake of choking fog, completely enveloping the man and the cart.

"Make way for the king!" cried another voice, one which she recognized: it was Robin Hood's.

"Sit down!" someone shouted at Buffy.

Angel tugged on Buffy's hand. "The cart's gone," he pointed out. "They're probably taking him out of his harness backstage."

"Sit down!"

She took a deep breath and sat back down again. "It was a beer can. For all we know, it was full."

"He was probably padded. I'm sure they were prepared for something like that."

Trumpets blared as the riders raced to the four corners of the arena, then joined in a circle and galloped hard.

"Now I know what the guys who work at Medieval Times do on their vacations," Xander said. "Or maybe these knightly dudes are off-duty cowboys."

The riders made two rows facing inward. The trumpets sounded again, and a knight dressed in brilliant silver armor, a golden crown atop his helmet, trotted into the arena. He was surrounded by young boys and girls on ponies who tossed rose petals in the air.

The trumpets pealed. Then men in blue and red shirts and leggings started walking in front of each block of arena seats, waving their arms and encouraging the audience to shout, "Long live the king!"

"Long live the king!" Xander shouted. "Elvis, we love you!"

On the field, the entourage led King Richard toward the stage on the other side of the arena. Then the helmeted figure made a show of turning in his saddle and looking back in the direction from which he'd come.

From the gates, a donkey poked its nose and scrutinized the crowd. Then it minced timidly into the arena.

Atop it sat a guy about sixteen or seventeen, dressed in a red and blue patchwork jester costume, bells jingling from the points of his hat.

Buffy caught her breath. It was the boy who had spied on her and Cordelia. Well, not actually spied.

The little donkey picked up speed, then jerked to a halt, dipped its head, and kicked its back legs as hard as it could. The sudden movements must have caught the boy off guard, for he sailed over the donkey's head and landed hard in the dirt.

The crowd roared with delight. A volley of tomatoes and rotten fruit arced toward him.

Buffy felt sick. She glanced at Willow, who shook her head and grimaced in disgust. She was not enjoying this. Neither was Oz. Cordelia was doing something with her shopping bag, but Xander slowly put his lemonade cup in his lap and grimaced.

The jester got up and hobbled slowly toward the stage, where the riders were dismounting and climbing onto the platform. Each knight stood before one of the backless chairs. They all bowed as King Richard joined them.

"Where is Roland, my useless fool?" Richard demanded. He was wearing a body mike.

"Anon, my king, I come," answered the jester, also wearing a mike.

"See? It's just for show," Angel assured Buffy.

"Thou villain. Thou slaggard!" the king flung at him.

On foot, Roland was too short to climb onto the stage. He attempted to sling his leg onto the dais but got nowhere. As the spectators laughed, he tried again.

"Get thee up, or I warn thee, it's the stocks for thee!" Richard cried.

"Socks?" Buffy asked Angel.

"Stocks. That's what the man on the cart was in. It's an ancient punishment." He rubbed the back of his neck. "Painful."

Buffy's eyes widened. "You?"

"Public drunkenness," he said sheepishly.

"Speaking of, where's my Watcher?" Buffy asked, looking around.

The Faire swirled about Giles and his companion. Squealing with delight, children in Peter Pan caps and flower headdresses darted among the legs of the adults. Well-developed young women in a sort of barbarian style of dress—chain mail bikini tops, fur sarongs—that sort of thing, strutted past. Someone was playing the recorder. Someone else, a harp. In the distance came the rhythmic jingle of Morris dancers. Another time, it might have instilled a bit of home-sickness in Giles.

But not now. At the moment Giles scarcely noticed

the pandemonium surrounding them. As Jamie Anderson walked hunched and weaving beside him, Giles wondered vaguely what it was like to lose a child. Worse, to have that child choose to leave, to run away, and then to live on, never knowing if the child had survived the streets, or died alone.

Giles had no children, but he thought he had some idea of the pain Jamie was experiencing. A part of him was perversely glad he couldn't understand it any better.

"It's over, Rupert," the man was saying, as they moved gingerly away from a food stall, Anderson with a cup of coffee and Giles with some truly abominable spiced tea. Its pungent odor reminded him of the lavender bath salts his grandmother had kept in a cut-crystal jar in the bathroom. "I'm three sheets to the wind. Come Monday, they'll fire me."

"All may not be lost," Giles said. But he was not at all certain of that.

Perhaps it was the timing of their meeting that created a sort of friendship between them. Jenny Calendar had only been dead a short while, and Giles had been lost in private, deeply hidden grief. As Giles listened to the police officer's shaking voice, he thought of Jamie's missing son. He considered how much worse it could have been, not to know if Jenny was dead or alive. If she had simply disappeared one day without a trace.

And yet, even now, Giles would have preferred that to knowing for certain that she would never be back. At least, that was what he told himself. It was easy to tell oneself many things when one was certain they couldn't come true. Except that he lived on the

Hellmouth, and Jenny had died here. One could hope. Pray. Be tempted and lonely enough to contemplate casting runes and spells.

Drink.

But Giles had put drinking behind him. The one and only time he had gotten drunk in Sunnydale, he had so badly frightened Buffy that he had vowed never to be so self-indulgent again. A Watcher did not have the luxury of seeking escape through oblivion.

One would assume an off-duty police officer did. In Britain, Anderson's superiors would have looked the other way, knowing what he had endured in his personal life. At least, in the Britain that Giles knew, loved, and sorely missed.

"Are you sure you're up to walking about?" Giles inquired.

"No, but I've got to sober up." Anderson looked wretched. He reeked of beer. "I can't believe I did this. I ordered a Coke with my food, but they accidentally gave me the beer. I figured, 'Okay, why not?'" He threw back the coffee and grimaced. Perhaps it was as undrinkable as the tea. "Three beers later, I may be losing my badge."

"You asked for Coke and got beer?" Giles asked, cocking his head.

Anderson laughed hollowly. "Yeah. Some nineteen-year-old's idea of heaven, huh. I've got fifteen years on the force. I throw it away because I'm scamming a discount on a lousy paper cup of beer. And let me tell you, it wasn't even good beer."

"No?" Giles gestured toward the dirt lot that served as the parking area. Anderson had already agreed that Giles would drive him home. He'd have someone help with getting Anderson's vehicle back to his house later. Perhaps Cordelia or Oz. "That's a pity." He poured his tea into the dirt with a grim smile of satisfaction.

As they passed through the exit, the ticket-taker stuck his head out of his stall and gave Giles a long, hard, silent look. It unnerved the Watcher, and made him wonder if it was a good thing leaving Buffy here alone. Well, not exactly alone. She was with her friends.

And she was with Angel.

Which should be all right, he told himself firmly. Perhaps he, of all of them, understood that Angel was Angel, and Angelus was the demon who had possessed him. It was to Angelus, not Angel, that Giles had lost the first love of his life. Not Angel.

Giles reminded himself over and over that he was not there to be Buffy's father, as she had so tartly informed him. But despite her physical strength and her, well, her spine, she nevertheless was a young girl who had lived through more tragedy than other children of her generation could ever conceive of. Giles would never forget her plaintive cry to him outside the burning warehouse where he had gone in such unreasoning fury, determined to destroy Angelus for killing Jenny:

"Don't leave me. I can't do this alone."

So much hurt. His poor, dear Buffy. No wonder she had left Sunnydale last year.

What a tremendous act of courage that she had returned.

The man beside him needed some of her courage if he had any hopes of surviving his own nightmare.

The ticket-taker never stopped his staring. There was something a little off about him. Giles wondered if he was wearing makeup, or had on some kind of mask. He didn't look . . . right.

Jamie sighed heavily, and Giles returned his attention to his friend. In silence, they reached the dusty lot. It was packed with automobiles of all stripes, pickup trucks to a really lovely Jaguar XKE he wouldn't mind taking a spin in. The people of Sunnydale seemed almost desperate for fun . . . or perhaps they sought distraction from the obvious problems of their town. A belief in the supernatural aside, it didn't take much to realize that Sunnydale had more than its share of problems. But most of the adults turned a blind eye.

He thought of Joyce Summers and the Runaway Project. He wasn't sure it was appropriate for her to get involved. She knew things she couldn't tell the other parents. And yet, she had confessed her rather unfocused hope that some kind of "ripple effect" would extend from her efforts.

"At the very least, these parents should be aware that the world is a dangerous place," she'd told him at her charity benefit. "More dangerous than most people realize, but we just don't keep tabs on our kids the way we should."

They reached his Citroën and Giles fished out his keys. He unlocked Anderson's door first. The man grunted his thanks.

Then Giles went around to the other side and climbed in.

"You know, I find the people at this Faire rather odd," he began, then looked up as the other man chuckled.

"You ever been ticketed in this thing?" Anderson asked, staring out the passenger window.

"For speeding, you mean?" Giles queried politely, although the question took him slightly aback.

"Well, no. Because it's a safety hazard," Anderson replied. He turned his head and grinned at Giles. "I'm teasing you, Rupe."

"Indeed," Giles bit off, somewhat miffed.

The car ground on and jerked into drive. It lurched forward as if it, too, were drunk.

"It's less responsive than usual," Giles observed, puzzled, as he glanced at his gear shift.

Anderson guffawed. "Why do I doubt that?"

At the joust.

Two of the knights had hold of Roland's arms and legs and were preparing to fling him onto the stage while the audience chanted, "Heave! Heave!"

No one in Buffy's group was chanting. They were all looking very uncomfortable.

Finally Xander said, "I think some sparkly jewelry is calling my name."

"Yeah." Willow looked at Oz. "Me, too."

"So, we book." Oz looked to Buffy. In fact, they all did, waiting expectantly for her to give the word. She wasn't sure if they even knew they were doing it, but it bugged her a little whenever they put her in the fearless leader position during a non-Slaying event.

"We book," she said.

To the howls of protest around them, they left the joust.

Chapter 4

THE CRYSTALS CAUGHT THE LIGHT OF THE HALF-MOON and cast reflections across a draped panel of blue velvet. Wind chimes caught the night breeze. Incense burned in a brazier. In the distance, an owl hooted.

For a moment, Angel was transported back in time to the Romanian gypsy camp where he had first regained his soul. He felt a wave of vertigo, panic, really, and held tightly to Buffy's shoulder without realizing it. He remembered a line from a book his father had once read aloud to the family, for such was the custom in those days: *"There are more things in heaven and earth than are dreamt of in your philosophy."* He believed an Englishman had written those words, but he couldn't recall.

The truth, though. He knew that when he heard it.

He closed his eyes, listening to the wind chimes.

The group, minus Giles, had been strolling down the rows of shop stalls, stopping to browse, stopping to chat. Now they stood at a jewelry counter, but for all that, Angel felt himself to be in another world. An older world. The scents of roasting beef and poultry, spiced and charred, merged with the sweet smells of cotton candy and the unmistakable aroma of fresh popcorn. The odors were almost enough to make Angel nostalgic for hunger. Would have been enough, if it weren't for the fact that he could still remember what real hunger felt like.

His memory of appetite faded slightly when he caught another scent. The light breeze carried just a hint of the stench of human waste from the line of portable toilets on the other side of the fairgrounds. But even that had its share of nostalgia. Modern plumbing was a miracle not merely of convenience, but of health and clean air as well.

He had lived long after the Renaissance, true enough. But during his time in Eastern Europe, that part of the world was not very different from the history this Faire was supposed to represent. Romania again.

"Angel?" Buffy asked quietly. "What is it?"

"Nothing." He forced his eyes open and smiled at her. "I—I'm just . . ." What could he say to her?

Willow took a step closer to Buffy. She looked concerned and glanced quickly at both of them. "Hi," she said. "Ah, everything okay, Angel?"

"Will," Buffy remonstrated, but Angel touched Buffy's hand to quiet her.

"Yes, Willow. I'm okay. Everything's fine."

But Willow had on her resolve face and was not to be deterred from asking questions that, posed on anyone else's behalf besides Buffy, she might not be able to ask. "You're not hungry, are you?"

Buffy frowned. "Willow Rosenberg!"

"No, I'm fine, Willow." Angel gestured to their surroundings. "I guess this back-in-time thing is having a greater effect on me than I assumed it would. I mean, I never lived in these days, but . . ." He shrugged.

"I know what you mean," Willow said. "I'm feeling off-balance, too."

At that, Oz stepped over, looking concerned.

Angel was moved. These were good people, kind people. They cared so much for one another.

They cared so much for Buffy.

"It's this place," Buffy said. "It's weird. It's wrong."

Angel frowned. It wasn't what he'd been thinking, at least, not on the surface. But he felt it, too. There was a malevolence that radiated from this place that he couldn't put his finger on. Something sinister, as though even the air had a darker purpose.

He only wished he knew what that purpose was.

"Look, it's so sparkly," Cordelia said with delight, as she held up a crystal necklace. "Kind of Lori Lori, only . . . newer."

"Or older," Xander said, "sort of Merlinish."

They were all trying to have a good time, but the Faire had by now succeeded in losing almost all of its charm for everyone. It would be a far nobler thing to admit defeat and go home.

Buffy was keenly disappointed. As lame as she had expected the Faire to be, she had looked forward to spending some time with Angel somewhere besides on patrol, at a time when he wasn't only around to watch out for her. She had wanted to be a regular kid, poking fun at the crowds and spending too much money on stuff she didn't really want in the first place.

But this place was past weird and it was beyond wrong. And with each passing moment, her sense of the wrongness and weirdness was growing.

It was the Faire people. Something about the way their eyes moved. Something about not really being able to see their faces as she turned to look at them. She felt disoriented, as if she had fallen asleep and been startled awake. Off-balance, as Willow had said.

"Look, a human chess match," Angel said, pointing. "They had those back in my day."

Buffy looked. On a huge board drawn in the grass, thirty-two people stood statue-still on the back two rows of each side. One side was dressed in red, the other in black. The back row of each side were dressed in fancy robes, some with crowns, others with tall, curved hats, and some dressed like the knights in the joust. The front row were dressed like peasants in rough clothes. Buffy looked for the court jester and didn't see him. She was embarrassed to admit she didn't know anything about chess, didn't know if they had court jesters or what.

"Whoa. Cool." Oz smiled at Willow. "Will you be my queen?"

"If you'll be my bishop," Willow replied fondly, and Buffy had to crack a smile. She was sure that meant something in chess talk . . . and obviously in Oz and Willow talk. Oz leaned forward and kissed Willow lightly on the lips.

"Be my deputy!" Xander drawled to Cordelia.

Willow grinned over at Buffy, who smiled back. Willow had clearly forgotten that Buffy had not grown up with her, Xander, and Cordelia, and though Willow and Xander had laughed over this phrase in reference to Cordelia before, Buffy still had no idea what it meant.

Angel looked at her questioningly, as if to ask if she wanted to watch. Buffy shrugged. If someone moved wrong, she wondered, were they beheaded? She didn't think she wanted to do anything but get far, far away from this place.

And then she saw something that made her go limp with relief: the man who had been in the stocks, the man who had begged for water, stood on the chessboard. He was dressed in red robes with a curved hat and held a staff, and he looked great. He wore a wide smile and his eyes twinkled with mischief.

He saw her and gave a cheery wave. She waved back. He made a gesture of drinking something, and she nodded. "Look, Angel, it's my thirsty guy," she said happily.

But Angel wasn't paying attention. He was looking over her head, his arm half-raised in greeting.

Giles strode up. "Thank goodness," he said, without preamble. "Buffy, I'm afraid I have work for you."

"What, is that darn bat signal broken again?" There was an edge to her voice that she knew no Slayer's voice should have. Saving the world from the forces of darkness—over and over again—was her sacred duty, yada yada yada, her special treat, her so-impossible mission. "Well, what's up, Alfred?"

Giles looked mildly confused, but then he was all business. "Someone's tampered with my hydraulics."

Buffy blinked at him.

"My car," he supplied.

She blinked again. When he said nothing more, she

tapped her chin and said, "Let's spin again before we attempt to solve the puzzle, shall we?"

"There are bite marks on my brakes, the same as in those autopsy reports. And while it's problematic to have a chance to look at the corpses, Jamie told me about some other things the police have kept quiet."

Xander said harshly, "Those nutty police, that's why I love 'em."

"Other things," Buffy prompted.

Giles observed the chess match. As a piece moved, with stately grace, he murmured, "Ah, the Immortal Game," Giles said, nodding. "1851. Adolf Anderssen won it in London."

"And you were there," Buffy chided. "Still are, apparently."

"What?" Giles blinked. "Sorry. Other things such as ritualistic mutilations of small animals. That showed up first. Next, unexplainable but extremely destructive acts of vandalism—pipes twisted, electric lines cut, not at all childish pranks. I'd almost think we were dealing with gremlins if not for the murders. And tonight, cattle mutilations," Giles said. "Such as one finds accompanied by UFO sightings, very stylized, with viscera missing—"

"Wow, cool!" Willow cried. When everyone stared at her, she said, "Well, the viscera, no, because that means . . . organs. But it would be cool, to meet creatures from another world . . . unlike the creatures from other worlds we have met." She stood up straighter. "Okay, not worlds. Dimensions, then. Raccoons from another dimension."

"Please, all of you," Giles said. "My patience is truly at its limit."

"His outer limit." Xander nodded wisely.

"I didn't know you were dating," Buffy added, more gently. "I think that's . . . good. How did you meet her?"

Giles frowned at her. "What?"

"Jamie."

"He's a man." Giles rubbed his forehead. "But that doesn't matter, because—"

"You're right, Giles, it doesn't." Buffy nodded. "We don't care, right?" Her expression took in the entire group. "We're really happy for you." Everybody else nodded.

For a moment, Giles just stared at her. Then his lips parted. "Oh, good Lord, is that all you people think about? Buffy, this man is a police officer and his son is a runaway. It's a terribly stressful situation for him, which is why he . . . wanted to speak to me in private."

"Oh. And not because he was spilling beer on the people around him in the bleachers," Buffy said archly.

Giles continued without responding. "He played back a message for me he's just received from the woman who runs the shelter. She's been searching for her daughter, and caught a glimpse of her recently with a boy matching Brian Anderson's description. The girl ran away as if her mother were a demon. Actually, it was your mother, Buffy, who suggested she call him, as I'd mentioned him to her at the benefit, and . . ." He trailed off, no doubt realizing he was treading on very thin ice.

There was a long pause before Angel said, "You were talking about cattle mutilations."

"With Jamie," Xander supplied.

"And UFOs," Angel pushed on.

Buffy cleared her throat. Fun and games and awkward moments aside, there were matters to discuss. "Okay, so Angel and I will—"

Just then a hunched old man staggered up to them and Angel put a warning hand on Buffy's shoulder.

"Tuppence for a poor old man?" he said. His hair was filthy and matted, and he was missing most of his teeth. And two of the fingers on his left hand. "A penny, a pound, for no friend of the Crown?"

"They sang this in *Mary Poppins*," Xander observed. "There's a possibility you're violating copyright, my good man."

The beggar tugged on Buffy's arm with his truncated left hand. "Can you spare something for an outcast then?" He leaned toward her and dropped his voice to a whisper. "My young miss," he hissed at Buffy. "The boy. He is a—"

"Well, old fellow, what tricks are you up to?" Robin Hood boomed as he strode up to the group. Some of his currently less than merry men accompanied him. A Friar Tuck type, only with a strange, artificial cast to his features, and a woman in a green flowing dress and deep, emerald-green eyes. Each took one of the arms of the beggar and began herding him away.

"I said nothing," the beggar said anxiously over his shoulder. "Tell them I told you nothing!"

Buffy raised her chin as she regarded Robin Hood. "What's the deal?"

He raised his chin and matched her steely gaze. "I apologize for the scoundrel," he said. "The man's a thief and a rapscallion."

There was something about his look that put Buffy so very off. Oh, not the defiance or the rudeness, but

93

something very deeply sinister. If she hadn't been the Slayer, she might have taken a step or two backward, putting more space between herself and that look.

But she was the Slayer, so she stood her ground.

"Yes, let's be off, then," Giles said, motioning for Buffy to go with him.

"The night is young," Robin Hood protested. "Surely you can stay a while."

Buffy started walking in the direction of the parking lot. Angel caught up with her.

Then Cordelia let out a bloodcurdling shriek that sent them rushing back in the opposite direction.

"Look!" Cordelia howled, her hazel eyes wide with horror.

Above her head she held her Renaissance costume. The gauzy ruffled blouse and crimson waistcoat were shredded. The brilliant red skirt was nothing but a collection of tatters.

"Good Lord," Giles said. He took the outfit from Cordelia and examined the damage. As Buffy approached, he held it out to her. Robin Hood and the rest of his posse had moved on. It was just the gang, staring at Cordelia's ruined costume.

"I'm getting my money back," Cordelia said. "No way am I paying for that. Plus I should get damages for emotional distress. I really liked this dress!"

"Me, too," Xander said sadly.

Cordelia stomped away.

"Cordelia, perhaps that's not a good idea," Giles called after her. He regarded the kids. "I've not been here much today," he said, "but what little I've seen, I've found off-putting, to say the very least."

"Tell me about it," Buffy said, adding, "I'll cover Cordelia." She looked at Angel. "I'll be right back."

Cordelia was already halfway down the row of stalls by the time Buffy caught up with her. She was a woman on a mission, and when Buffy suggested she forget about the dress, Cordelia would have none of it

"You saw how expensive this thing was," she said hotly. "You couldn't even afford yours. If you went into Neiman's and bought a pair of shoes—not that you would, obviously you do not know your way around a decent shoe department—and then you went over to lingerie for something in a bustier and maybe some matching tap pants, except those are so out, and you discovered that some demented psycho-loony had cut up your shoes when you accidentally left your shopping bag in the bathroom, would you just sigh and go, 'Oh, well'? I think not."

"Cordelia, this place is weird," Buffy said. "Talk about psycho, just look around you."

"May I remind you, I didn't want to come here." Cordelia gave her raven hair a toss. "But I showed, and I entered into the spirit of things, and I am not going to be penalized for being a good sport. Here we are."

She sailed into the tent where she and Buffy had tried on their costumes and marched up to the makeshift sales counter. "Service!" she snapped, tossing her hair again. It amazed Buffy how many different emotional punctuations the girl could manage with her hair. It must have taken years of practice.

"Aye, mistress. Anon, I come," croaked a voice from deeper inside the tent.

An elderly woman Buffy had not seen before slowly limped to the counter. One of her eyes was milky and her lower lip was turned down in a frozen grimace. The lines on her face seemed carved there, deep and painful. Buffy watched her as Cordelia wound up for the pitch, the perfect picture of righteous indignation.

"I mean, look at it!" Cordelia held the dress above the counter.

"Mistress, we cannot be responsible for your goods after you leave our company," the woman said.

"What?"

Cordelia looked as if she might leap across the counter and strangle the woman. Despite the strangeness, Buffy couldn't help but grin. Cordelia had once told Buffy she, Cordelia, was the Slayer of dating. But she was also the Slayer of consumer abuse.

As Cordelia informed the woman that under no circumstances would she keep this piece of garbage, etc. and so on, it occurred to Buffy to tell Cordelia to keep it and then cancel the charge on her AmEx. Situation solved. She was just about to turn around and tell her that when she caught sight of a blue-and-red jester's cap disappearing behind one of the dressing room curtains.

Buffy crossed and pushed back the curtain, but there was no one there. However, the back partition of the dressing room hung askew. Buffy stepped around it and found herself in a storage area. Rows of Renaissance costumes hung bagged in plastic from overhanging dowels.

And the door—a real door—to this area was ajar.

Hesitating, Buffy listened to Cordelia's rant and figured she could hold her own for another minute or two.

Buffy went through the door.

Whoa, backstage.

She stood in a sort of alley created by the backs of

the stalls, which faced outward toward the lanes in two rows. Here were the plastic trash bags brimming with garbage and packing material. Someone's rubber sandals were plopped onto a beach chair with a beer and a *Sunnydale Press* beside it. Suddenly, a bit of the menacing air that seemed to permeate the Faire dissipated.

There was an old outdoor grill up on cement blocks, and a row of hot dogs cooking on top, already fat and charred. Nobody was cooking, but from the looks of it, they'd be back any moment. It made the people of the Faire a bit more real to her, and Buffy took a breath. Real. Solid. Which meant if they were causing some kind of trouble she needed to know about, she'd have no problem kicking some butt if necessary.

"If it bleeds," she whispered to herself, "we can kill it."

The distant jingle of bells drew her to the left. She followed, growing more cautious, wondering if this was a trap or a diversion, unsure if she should continue on or go back to Cordelia.

"Excuse me?" she heard Cordelia shout.

Buffy almost turned around. Cordy wasn't getting anywhere and it'd be better all around if they just left without causing any trouble. But that poor guy in the jester costume had seemed so . . . sad. Buffy went on, following the sound of tinkling bells.

Roland, the jester, stepped into the alley with an armload of purple fabric. It was King Richard's robe.

He saw Buffy and for a moment he stood frozen, staring at her. He looked sadly comical in his jester's costume minus the hat. Then he unfurled the robe and hung it over a clothesline. He picked up a thick wooden stick and started whacking it against the robe, beating the dust from the garment. His movements were awkward and slow, as if he were exhausted.

Buffy came up beside him. For a moment she silently watched. Nice curly brown hair, big brown eyes. The pieces were there for good-looking, but there was something really wrong with this guy. She couldn't put her finger on it, but it was as if his skin didn't fit right, or something. He almost looked old, except that he didn't. Maybe it was the way he squinted, or his clumsiness as he slammed the stick against the robe. Dust rose in a little cloud, and Buffy coughed into her hand. He looked at her questioningly and set down the stick.

"We used to think I was allergic to house dust," she told him. "Then my parents went out of town for two weeks. So, just as an experiment, I let that darn dust pile right up. All in the name of science, you understand. I still had a runny nose. Turned out it was our cat."

She expected at least a polite smile. She was disappointed. He looked at her as if she were a creature from another planet. She almost said, "Hey, how about them cattle mutilations?"

Instead she said, "When they throw you around like that, does it hurt?"

To her unpleasant surprise and acute discomfort, he flinched, his brown eyes growing distant, and he lowered his head and said, "Yes."

"Then, um, why?"

"There's not much else to be done."

Hmm. Interesting answer. She put her hand on her

98

hip and said, "Well, food service is always a field loaded with advancement. And you get all the free hairnets you want."

He still didn't crack a smile. He only stared at her with kind, sad eyes. Hurt eyes.

"I'm Buffy." She held out her hand.

He didn't shake with her. "Roland."

"Summers," she added.

Silence.

O-kay. She gestured to the cloak. "So, is he your dad?"

Roland's eyes jittered nervously left, right. He gave his head a tiny shake and said, "I need to finish."

"Can I help?"

He looked at her very oddly. And then suddenly it occurred to her: what if he was a runaway?

"Hey, listen," she said.

"Roland!"

Roland jumped a mile. It was King Richard, and he sounded pissed.

"Lad, answer if you know what's best for you!"

Roland stiffened. Buffy reached out a comforting hand but he actually stepped away from her. She figured he was embarrassed—more than once, she had humiliated a guy by helping him out, keeping him from getting pummeled or worse. It was this guy code thing that it was better to get the crap knocked out of you than have someone, anyone, most especially a *girl,* save you from that fate. That was something she did not get, except that it had happened enough times for her to turn her back when requested.

And from what she could tell, Roland was making the request.

"Yeah." She cleared her throat and lifted her hand in farewell. "It's been . . . what it's been." She turned to go.

"Goodbye," he said, so faintly that for a moment she wasn't sure he'd spoken. "Godspeed."

She turned back. His eyes were wide and frightened.

"You don't have to stay," she said in a rush, but then the clomp of boots told her that His Royal Painness was about to make his entrance.

She hurried back down to the costume shop, where the milky-eyed crone of a shopkeeper was bitterly muttering, "And here is your copy."

"Thank you," Cordelia said crisply. In triumph, she displayed her charge card credit slip for Buffy to see and admire. "Let's go."

"Trashed," Oz confirmed, as he slid back out from under Giles's car. He wiped his hands on the newspaper Willow offered him, wadded it up, and kept it. Some guys were thoughtful that way. Other guys would just hand you back the yucky newspaper like they figured you wanted to keep it as a memento.

Oz added, "I don't know how you drove it back over here."

"He's used to driving it thrashed," Xander said. He frowned slightly. "Where are our other lovely wenches?"

The parking lot wasn't as crowded as when they'd arrived. Now it looked more like what it actually was: a stretch of hard-packed dirt that had once been a field. Giles's car was tucked in between a Jeep Cherokee and a pair of ancient Harleys with big-breasted barbarian women painted on the side. Xander had become an instant art critic when they'd passed the motorcycles.

Willow looked back at the Faire. Seen at a distance like this, it looked kind of puny and tacky. Of course, they hadn't seen the Shakespeare scenes, or gone to the lute concert. Those might have been really cool. But all in all, she was glad they were leaving.

"Do you have triple A?" Angel asked. "You can call for a tow."

Not for the first time, Willow found it hard to really accept all that had happened since she had met Buffy. Evil curses, monsters, trips to hell and back, and all that Romanian! But weirdest of all maybe was that Angel, who had lived in the 1750s, could stand there so calmly and talk about the auto club. It was moments like this she had to pinch herself.

Then Oz squeezed her hand. Maybe that was weirder, a cool guy like the lead guitarist of the Dingoes thinking *she* was cool.

Oz grinned as if he knew exactly what she was thinking. Willow wouldn't have been surprised. He could turn into a werewolf, so maybe he could read minds, too.

Then Buffy and Cordelia appeared, walking along as if they were the best of friends, and Willow knew that *that* took the weirdness prize, hands down.

Yes. Definitely.

The two approached, and Giles said, "Good. Let's be off, then. Buffy, you should patrol."

"Giles—" Buffy began.

"I'd like you to check out the mutilations first, if you don't mind."

"Morbid much?" Cordelia asked.

"Cordelia, Buffy is the Slayer. Unsavory as these

attacks may be, it's her responsibility to investigate them."

"I'll go with you," Angel said.

"Ah," Giles said, then clamped his mouth shut. There was an awkward moment. Willow caught Buffy's irritation, and wondered at it. She might be the Slayer, but Willow thought she ought to cut the Watcher some slack. They were all a little gun-shy around Angel.

Angel looked to Buffy, clearly oblivious to Giles's anxiety and very eager to be off. Willow felt so sorry for them. Things certainly weren't working out as they had planned. They tried to make the best of it, but there wasn't much left to work with. Oz, well, that was happening pretty well. Three nights of werewolf, twenty-seven of pure guy. It was a good percentage.

"Yeah, about that going thing," Xander drawled. "Be sure to take a cross or two, Buff. Maybe spray on some *eau de garlique.*"

"We don't think it's vampires, Xander," Giles said.

"I know that," Xander replied, gazing straight at Angel.

Buffy shot him a look. Xander didn't flinch. He, of all of them, was the most blatantly not okay with the A-man, and on occasion he didn't mind letting other people—including Buffy—know it.

However, it was obvious that everyone including Xander wanted to get away from the Faire. Willow was sorry. It seemed like every fun thing in town eventually became the negative fun thing.

It was Cordelia who seconded the motion. "Yeah, okay, let's get out of here. This bunch is not exactly high on the normal chart. How new, how different, for an excursion with Buffy. I just know someone will try to kill at least one of us—probably me—before the weekend's over."

"We can hope," Xander zinged, ducking. But Cordelia just rolled her eyes and sighed.

"What time is it, babe?" Oz asked Willow gently.

"Time?" she asked, then jumped. "Oh!" She grabbed Xander's wrist. "When did you get this watch? What happened to Tweety? Oh, my gosh! Oz, I've got fifteen minutes."

Oz nodded. "We can make it, if you promise not to tell your parents how fast I drove." He put his arm around her and said to the others, "We have to book."

Giles said, "Ah, speaking of which. Cordelia, would you mind very much giving me a lift to the library? I'll call there for my tow."

Looking a bit confused, she reached into her purse. "You can use my cell phone. They'll take you right home."

"Yes, well, there are a few books I need," he said.

"Oh. Books. Of course. I get it now." She looked at Xander, who shrugged.

"I don't care where we go, Cor, as long as it's away from here."

"Well, then," Giles said, punctuating their decision and their unease. He glanced at Buffy. "I should think a bit of alacrity's required regarding the cattle."

It was a capitulation about Angel's going with her, but Willow wasn't certain that Buffy realized it. Or cared.

Instead Buffy simply stared at him.

The Watcher translated, "Hurry. They're certain to move the carcasses tonight."

"Now that you guys are done with your planning, maybe I can make the point I've been saving for the last ten minutes. There's this boy," Buffy said. "I think they're abusing him and . . ."

"We can always come back. The Faire will be here for quite a while." Giles took off his glasses. "Unfortunately."

"Maybe it'll disappear," Willow murmured, though no one but Oz heard her. He gave her hand a tug.

"Something wicked," Oz said, "this way has come."

Giles nodded at him. "Indeed, Oz, I'm afraid you're right. And nicely put, I must say. It's a pleasure to know that one of you reads."

"Hey," Willow protested. "I know my Bradbury, too." She lifted her chin. *"Something Wicked This Way Comes.* About a spooky . . ." She looked back over her shoulder. "Carnival," she finished weakly.

"But this isn't that," Oz said profoundly, comforting her. "Spooky, well, yeah. But carnival, no. See?"

Willow smiled. *"Si,"* she agreed.

Staring into the darkness in Weatherly Park, Shock searched for Treasure. He heard a noise, footsteps maybe. Or the pitter-patter of little animal feet. He whispered, "Treasure?"

In a clearing in the forest:
The first shimmering of the dark.
The soft laughter of the damned.
Dogs stopped their barking, lay down, whimpered. Cats arched in fear and hissed at shadows. Babies awoke, inconsolable.

And the little town that sat upon the mouth of hell gasped in fear.

Chapter 5

In the rural outskirts of Sunnydale, higher in elevation than the town itself, along the northeastern side of Route 17, lay some pasture land abutting the entrance to the Los Viejos National Forest. The forest was composed primarily of evergreens, and there were huge granite boulders that rose in the sky like cliff dwellings. As it was out of the way, it wasn't on Buffy's normal patrol route. So she didn't know the terrain, and that did nothing to relieve the tension that had grown during the Renaissance Faire.

Level with the pasture land, she and Angel crouched behind some manzanita bushes as the moon shone down on a gulley about twenty feet away. In the dry wash lay three dark shapes—the dead cows. Yellow police tape had been stretched between some trees, but otherwise, it appeared the authorities had quit the scene. Buffy was surprised, and she wasn't quite ready to believe it.

So they stayed hidden, hunkered down so closely together that Angel's thigh rubbed against hers. Buffy's muscles tightened and she began to lose her balance. She had to steady herself against him.

He put his hand over hers and pointed.

Sure enough, someone with a flashlight fanned the beam over the three stiff, dead forms, then in the immediate area surrounding them, then moved toward the street.

They heard the sound of a motor starting. On the two-lane road to their right, red and blue lights strobed and a police car pulled away.

"They'll probably be back soon. With a tractor to haul the carcasses away, something like that," Buffy guessed.

Angel nodded. "So we go for it?"

"We go for it."

She moved with purpose. One thing she had learned about being the Slayer: when you were walking among the wicked, you had to keep your mind on two things: destruction, and survival.

As they covered ground, Buffy said softly, "Be careful. There might be small animal bodies around here." Then she caught herself, half-smiled, and said, "But I guess you would be able to smell them."

"Yes," he said frankly, "I would."

They crab-walked closer to the cattle. Then Angel frowned and whispered, "Did you hear that?" When she shook her head, he persisted, "That crying? No. It's dogs. They're howling."

She listened for a few seconds. "I don't hear anything."

"Really? I swear, Buffy, they're so loud they could wake . . ." He trailed off and dropped his gaze.

"The dead," she finished for him.

They looked at each other. He smiled his sad smile, the one that reminded her of everything she had once hoped they could have, but now never would.

"You have such a way with words," he said.

"So my English teacher tells me," she replied. "Only, it's the wrong way."

"I haven't been to school in over two hundred years. Sat in classes, I mean. Before I was changed, I wasn't much in the book-learning department either."

"We have so much in common," she flirted. Uselessly.

Somewhere nearby, a twig snapped. Buffy tensed, glanced at Angel. He had heard it, too.

She gestured to stay still. They had patrolled together so much that such a precaution was unnecessary, but she was used to being in charge, telling anyone with her—the Slayerettes, especially—what to do.

Another snap. Buffy watched Angel, whose head was turned slightly in the direction of the sound. As if he knew she was looking at him, he reached out his hand. Without hesitation, she took one of her stakes from her belt and placed it firmly in his grasp. Swiftly, she got one out for herself.

Angel jerked again and looked at her. She stared back at him. Evidently he had heard something else that she couldn't.

Then something small leaped onto Buffy's back and bit her, hard. She shrieked in surprise and instinctively rolled over to crush the thing just as another one landed on her shoulder. Sharp claws or teeth broke the skin as she grabbed at her attacker, catching at it and pulling it away from her body. Her blouse sleeve tore away with it, and it waved the bloody fabric in a tiny, mottled fist, its hands ending in miniature, curved talons.

It was some kind of weird, misshapen creature that vaguely resembled a human, with a head, arms, and legs, only its skin was a mottled, graveyard green and gray, its eyes glowed red and blank, like a mole's, and its ears were batlike, long and pointed. Her mind flashed to a character she'd seen in old Spider-Man cartoons: Goblin-man or something.

Then teeth bit into her flesh, and Buffy cursed loudly and batted another of the things from her calf. The one she held in her hand wore some kind of crudely woven clothing, and as she stared at it, it shrieked and struggled to attack her, its teeth clacking wildly.

"Yeow," Buffy said, amazed.

"Buffy!"

Angel was beside her in an instant. She showed him the creature, keeping it a good arm's length from both of them as it flailed and slashed at her hands with its talons. Then it threw back its head and shrieked and cackled at the same time like a complete lunatic.

"Is that what you heard?" she asked.

He shook his head. "Not at all." He gestured for her to give him the creature, but she kept hold of it.

"He's happiest here," she said.

Then suddenly, another of the creatures flew through the air. And another. They were dropping from the trees and flinging themselves through the air from the undergrowth. Buffy kicked one away at the same time she ripped another one off her back. Then her chest.

Angel was faring no better, waving his arms as at

least a dozen of them clung to him, biting and tearing at his duster with their knifelike talons. Despite his obvious pain, he managed to yank one of the creatures off. Two, three more of the creatures took its place.

More than a dozen of them bit and clawed at Buffy, all over her body, as she struggled, overpowered, trying to keep her mind clear. Destruction. Survival.

She kicked at them, pulled at them, fell into a forward roll and then flipped back up to a standing position. Maybe one dropped off, while six took advantage of her contact with the ground and leaped aboard.

They were drawing blood, and they were causing damage both to her body and her hot velvet tank top and leather pants.

She staggered toward Angel, flailing as if she were on fire, until she reached him. With both hands, she tore one of the creatures off him, stomped it, made a fist and smashed another one in the head as she snap-kicked one more off Angel's calf.

Angel began to attack the creatures on Buffy. Soundlessly they worked at freeing each other. Incredibly, the creatures never stopped their maniacal laughter and screaming even as Buffy and Angel worked their way through them.

More of the creatures descended on the pair, and still more, until they were completely surrounded. There might have been a hundred.

Buffy was slashed and torn, and as she assessed the damage, she realized that if she couldn't figure out some way to stop them, they just might kill her.

As one of them sank its teeth into Buffy's hand, Angel whipped his head up. As if they shared one mind, the creatures immediately leaped away, then skittered into the copse of trees. Shrieking and laughing, they darted like animals under bushes, reappearing on the other side, massing in groups, then breaking away, racing headlong for the trees.

"Let's finish them off," Buffy said, panting as she half-limped, half-ran after them. She was bleeding. She hurt all over.

"No, Buffy," Angel said. "They aren't alone."

She pressed against the stitch in her side and tried to catch her breath. "What?"

"Someone called them off," Angel told her, pointing toward the trees. "With a hunting horn."

Buffy frowned. "Yeah, well, we'll kick Horn Guy's butt, too," she said.

She started forward again. Then she felt a sudden rush of dizziness, tripped over an outcropping of rock, and fell to her knees. Something on the ground shone brightly in the moonlight.

"Buffy," Angel said, dropping down beside her. "You okay?"

"Hey, look at this." She stared at the locket in the grass. The moonlight glinted off a shiny, heart-shaped locket . . . engraved with the name CONNY.

"Oh, God," Buffy said.

Xander had gone to the lounge for snack food. Cordelia was just saying goodbye to Giles when Buffy limped in to the library, holding the locket. Angel trailed behind, staring back over his shoulder as if he expected the devilish creatures to attack once again.

"Good Lord, what happened to you?" Giles demanded, rushing toward Buffy. "Cordelia, go to the girls' bathroom and get some paper towels and water."

Cordelia, looking freaked, ran past Buffy and stopped at Angel. "Wow, you guys look awful," she said, "except, of course, that you look better in general," and ran on.

"What happened?" Giles asked, as Buffy slowly sank into a chair at the study table. She groaned.

"It's a good thing I'm the Slayer and he's a vampire," Buffy said, "or we'd probably be dead."

Giles began examining her wounds. "You were attacked?"

"No," she said. "We went bowling."

"Fair enough, it was a stupid question." He went into his office and came back with a first aid kit. "Angel, you should sit down as well."

Gingerly Giles applied some antiseptic to the cuts on Buffy's arm. It stung a little, but she barely noticed as she stared at the locket.

Angel crossed the room slowly. His silk shirt and leather pants were ripped, revealing parts of his thighs and a peek of his right hip. There was a long scratch on his chest that crossed from one side of his rib cage and plummeted toward his other hip. And as for his face . . .

She caught her breath. He was gazing at her. He smiled painfully, and she knew he missed her, too. Missed her touch. Missed touching her.

Resolutely, she made herself look away.

"These things . . . I saw them once, a long time ago. As a boy," Angel said, his voice tinged with irony and sadness. "I thought I had had a nightmare. I cried out for my mother."

"Indeed?" Giles listened intently as he put gauze over the biggest cut on Buffy's arm. Then he stopped and examined her skin more closely. "These bite marks are identical . . ."

"We've found our interdimensional raccoons," Buffy said.

Angel shrugged. "Until now, I always thought I'd really dreamed them. We used to call them the wee folk."

"Leprechauns?" Buffy asked, astounded, wincing as Giles applied more antiseptic to her arm. "Like in those movies?"

"No." Angel described them to Giles, searching for the right words. "I don't have any idea if those legends are true, but these are completely different creatures. They're elfin, but very tiny, almost gnome-like."

"Dark faerie?" Giles mused.

Angel shrugged. "We called them the wee folk. Not nice creatures. If anything went wrong, we believed they did it. If your milk soured, or your child got sick—"

"Or you failed math," Buffy added. "Useful." She remembered the locket. "We found this."

Giles put down the kit and looked at the locket. "Conny." He was quiet for a moment. "Buffy, do you recall my mentioning the woman who runs the run-away shelter? I believe her missing daughter's name is Connie."

"Connie DeMarco," Buffy said. "Yeah, I know." Her voice was ragged. "Only, I'm thinking—well, okay, hoping—that it's a different girl. Conny some-body else."

"I've seen the name written down. Your mother

had a big list in the gallery, along with their faces." He examined the necklace. "I'm fairly certain it was spelled the other way. I wonder if I should phone Jamie."

"What would her locket be doing around the site of a cattle mutilation?" Buffy asked.

"There's more," Angel said. He looked hard at Giles. "I heard a hunting horn. And the baying of hounds."

"Hunters," Giles said. "There's nothing to hunt here, in the sense of normal hunting, anyway. No deer or elk, not even ducks. Were they your usual hunters? Camouflage jackets, that sort of thing?"

"I said I heard them," Angel replied. "I didn't see anything."

"Because they were up in the forest," Buffy filled in. "And it was dark."

"They called the wee folk off." Angel daubed at a cut on Buffy's face. "Buffy's right in saying the faerie could have killed us, but when the horn blew, they took off." He glanced at Buffy. "Buffy couldn't hear the horn. Or the dogs."

"It's all those evil rock concerts I've been attending," Buffy said. "Ruined my hearing."

Just then Cordelia burst back in with Xander in tow. "Hey, Buffy, what are you going to tell your mom? I'm thinking car accident, at least." Then she caught herself. "Oh, that's right. She *knows.*"

"Oh, my God, Buffy, what did he do to you?" Xander cried, then stopped when he saw Angel, nostrils flaring in distaste. "Dead Boy," he said, by way of greeting.

"We were attacked by the anti-pixies," Buffy said. "These weird little thingies."

Xander stared down at Buffy with real concern on his face. It was not the smoldering look Angel had given her. Xander was freaked. Angel had known that the Slayer would heal. Xander had forgotten that, or still didn't quite get it. He was seeing a badly injured friend. Buffy didn't want to remind him that he had seen it before, and he would see it again.

"Cordy, no mom could see her kid messed up like this and not have a total meltdown," Xander said, then added, "I think."

Buffy said nothing. It would be another night of climbing in through the window. With any luck, her mom would not be sitting on her bed with tears in her eyes.

Lately, her luck had not been so good. But it was better than Conny's.

Giles said, "Buffy, if you need to go home, Cordelia and Xander can take you. Angel and I will look into this a bit further."

Not a temptation. "No," Buffy told him, "I'll stay, too."

"If you're sure you're up to it," Giles said. She nodded again.

He looked at Cordelia. "I believe I heard a rumor that some of you have been getting into trouble for staying out late. If that's the case, I suggest you put in an appearance at home as soon as possible."

"Great!" Cordelia enthused. Then she frowned and said, "Oh, but I was so hoping to help you look through all those moldy books for pictures of monsters." She shrugged. "Too bad. My terrible loss."

"Good night, Cordelia," Buffy said dryly.

She reached for Xander's hand. "I'll take you home."

Xander began to protest, but Buffy cut him off. "Xand, we've got a lot of eyeballs here," she said. "Your parents are probably wondering if they should call nine-one-one."

He smiled unhappily. "No, Buffy, really, they're not."

"Xander, I'd feel better if you made sure Cordelia's car checks out. Who knows where these creatures are hiding?" Giles said. "Obviously, they were in my car. They could be in hers as well."

"Ew." Cordelia made a face.

"Okay," Xander said. He took another look at Buffy. "When we find those little monsters, I'm going to take each and every one of them out."

Buffy smiled at him. "I know."

Cordelia leaned around Xander and said to Buffy, "To hide all those scratches and stuff? Lots of foundation. But apply each coat thinly, let it dry, and then apply the next. You can't just glob it on. That's why you look so cakey half the time."

Then she smiled kindly and left the library with Xander in her wake.

Buffy sighed. "The other half of the time, I look so bloody."

"So, it seems as though we've had an encounter with dark faerie," Giles said, crossing into his office. "Hmm. I believe I've got some reference books." He began making a lot of book-moving noises. "Quite a number of them, actually."

Buffy sighed. "There's a surprise." *Maybe I should have gone home.*

"Buffy, Angel, would you like some tea?"

"Sure," Buffy said. "If you're buying."

"I'm brewing. " He peered out of the office, seemed

to consider his hospitality a moment, and then said, "Angel?"

"Thanks," Angel replied, sliding into a chair next to Buffy.

Buffy's mind was racing as she tried to make sense of what had happened, to find connections. It seemed somehow that everything that had been happening in Sunnydale of late was connected. Little Timmy Stagnatowski—his parents had only thought he'd run away. But this girl Conny, and Jamie Anderson's son, they were the real thing. And that boy at the Renaissance Faire. Roland.

Buffy said, "You know that boy Roland? At the Faire? No, you don't know that boy Roland. He's a runaway, Giles. I'm sure of it." She thought for a moment and picked the locket back up. "Like Conny."

A clearing in the forest:
The Gathering, as the Hunters converged. Shapes shimmered in the moonlight, searching for form as the dark faerie swarmed, cackling and frolicking. The breath of the Hunters blew like fog, the panting of the hellhounds and stallions roiled like smoke.
A phantom horn blew.
Dogs bayed.

Half-crazed, exhausted, and alone, Shock sat crouched behind a boulder as the ugly little creatures pranced. He had followed Treasure's screams to this place, hitching a ride with a trucker on his way to L.A.

That he could still hear her screaming baffled and terrified him. He hadn't been able to find her anywhere.

Beyond the rock, the little monsters cackled.

Shock crawled away as silently as he could. He couldn't handle this alone.

After all these years, it was time to go home.

Hours later, heads crammed with stuff about wee folk and dark faerie that still didn't make sense with what was going on, Angel and Buffy made their good nights to Giles. The librarian, on the phone with various Watchers all over the globe, had stared at them for a beat too long, then given his head a shake and said, "Good night."

It didn't take much to remind Buffy that Angel had snapped Jenny Calendar's neck, but so often it had been Giles who had come to Angel's defense when Xander trashed him, reminding him that Angel was Angel now, not Angelus. So it hurt when it was clear Giles was uneasy to see Angel and her alone. They knew they couldn't . . . be together ever again. They were trying to accept it. Surely Giles didn't think they would risk Angel's soul again, in a moment of reckless passion?

At Buffy's door, Angel paused and Buffy said, "My mom's not home. Would you like to come in?"

Slowly he shook his head. "Not a good idea." He gestured to her wounds. "You should soak in a hot bath and take some aspirin. You're going to be sore tomorrow."

"You won't be," she chided.

"Maybe a little."

Then he kissed her, just a bit. Not a boyfriend kiss. But not just a friend kiss either. Which was fine, because Buffy figured it was time for them to invent a new kind of relationship. Neither of the others had really worked out for them.

Yet as they stood beneath the stars, torn and cut from fighting side by side, she couldn't help but tighten her arms around his neck and kiss him the way she used to. And even as she did it, she thought, *Oh, God, I'm being so stupid.*

It was Angel who caught his breath and moved gently away.

Then he turned and walked into the night.

Chapter 6

THE NEXT MORNING, AS SOON AS IT WAS A DECENT HOUR, Giles accompanied Jamie Anderson to the home of Liz DeMarco. The streets of her neighborhood were lined with broken-down cars and overflowing trash cans. A family in a tinderbox of a house was holding a yard sale. A box near the curb read USED SHOES 25 CENTS. Two large women in flowered housecoats were pawing eagerly through it.

They turned left at a combination mini-mart and gas station, then drove two more blocks.

Jamie pulled over and said to Giles, "Be sure to lock."

It was a sad little apartment redolent of gas fumes and motor oil. On the wall above the television set was a statue of the Virgin Mary with outstretched hands. A crucifix hung above a short, dark hallway.

Giles wondered if he told Mrs. DeMarco of the

things he had seen and done, if she would retain her faith. It was even possible that his revelations would serve to strengthen it. However, today was not the day to test her.

"Artie?" she called uncertainly, when Giles smiled kindly through the frayed screen door and asked to come in. He had called ahead, and she had murmured, "Oh, my God," and asked him to come over right away. Distractedly, she explained that she'd been on her way to Mass, but she would stay home and wait for him and the thoughtful police officer who had returned her call. He had promised to move heaven and earth to find her Connie.

The small front room was littered with flyers about the shelter, boxes, and piles of what appeared to be used clothing. The couch was covered with grocery sacks. Flushing, she picked one up and looked around for a place to put it back down in the crowded room.

"Please, sit down," she said, glancing over her shoulder down the hall. "My husband . . ." She ran her hands through her hair. "He, well, he's so angry. At her." She took a breath. "Please, show me the locket."

Wordlessly, Jamie Anderson pulled a plastic bag from a manila envelope he carried. The envelope was marked EVIDENCE, POSS. HOMICIDE. Giles hoped Mrs. DeMarco had not noticed that.

As soon as she saw the bag, she gave a little cry and sat in the space on the couch. She leaned forward and buried her face in her hands. She nodded.

"It's hers." Her voice trembled. She burst into tears. "You found nothing else?"

"No, ma'am," Jamie said in a low, soft voice. "It's

very possible it was dropped by accident. That sort of thing."

Giles wasn't sure that she had heard him. She continued, "She had this boyfriend. This . . . Bobby. His family's illegal. His mother used to clean house for the people who own the garage where my husband works. The father, I don't know where he is."

She wiped her face. "He gave Connie that locket for her birthday. He didn't know how to spell her name. He barely speaks English. I—I saw them . . . together. I was worried. You can't be too careful these days. Kids grow up so fast."

She took the plastic bag. Jamie said, "Please don't open it, Mrs. DeMarco."

She turned the bag over, staring at the locket through the plastic. Running her fingers over the name. She looked on the verge of losing her composure again, but she held steady. Giles admired her enormously.

"I'm afraid I lost my temper with her. She made some remarks. I—I insulted the boy. I didn't mean to. I was ashamed of what I was saying even while I was saying it."

"Remarks, ma'am?"

Mrs. DeMarco looked down at the locket.

"What Liz don't want to say is, she told her he was a moron," boomed a voice from the hallway. Then a man in a stained blue work shirt with wet, dark hair strode into the room. It was clear he had just stepped from the shower. In his day, he might have been what one considered a burly man. Now, he had run to fat.

"I'm Connie's father. What's she up to? Did you find the little tramp?"

"Artie," Mrs. DeMarco said, raising a face filled with pain toward her husband.

"She is a tramp, going with all them boys. We've warned her. Look at us: got married way too young." He seemed to catch himself. "Not that we ain't happy. But Liz here, at least, she could've gone to college. That brat wrecked her figure, screwed our futures." He shrugged. "Then she does this to us."

Jamie nodded. "I see."

"Oh, you don't see nothing," the man said in hostile tones. "You see a cheap apartment with a fat, mean husband. You don't see the years we tried to make her happy, give her everything. I'm bitter, I'll give you that. But I wasn't always. Lot of other guys woulda run, but I stood up. I did the right thing." He sighed. "I was just a punk kid. Seventeen years old. But I did the right thing."

Mrs. DeMarco sobbed on the couch. "What aren't you telling us, Detective?" she asked. "She's dead, isn't she?"

"Ma'am, I sincerely hope not." Jamie put the plastic bag back into the envelope. Giles noted that Mr. DeMarco had not asked to see it. "I truly have no other information at this time."

She nodded. "I'm going to the shelter after I go to see my priest," she told him. "If you hear anything . . . ?"

"I'll call you there." Jamie patted his pocket. "I have the number."

"Okay."

"Good day, Mrs. DeMarco," Giles said.

"You're the librarian," she said to him. "The kids at the shelter, some of them talk about you."

"Indeed?" He was a trifle alarmed. "And what do they say?"

"They think your accent is cool." She smiled weakly. "Some of the girls want to know if you know Prince William."

His smile was sad. "Lie to them."

"I do," she said painfully. "Every single day."

Jamie inclined his head. "Mrs. DeMarco. Mr. De-Marco."

The two men left together, Jamie leading the way. The screen door banged behind them.

"What is it with you?" Mr. DeMarco yelled at his wife. "Always with the priest, always with that damn shelter. What about me? I'm falling apart."

"Artie, I'm sorry," Mrs. DeMarco said. "It's just that I have a chance to do some good—"

"Yeah, you done real good with that little piece of work. When she comes home, I'm going to beat her—"

"You are not going to touch her!" she shouted.

Jamie ticked his glance toward Giles as they got into Jamie's police car.

"That's the way people think all of us are," he told Giles. "They think if your kid has run away, there's a reason. You're molesting them, or you're beating them. It's never . . ." His voice trailed off. "It's never that they just left, and you have no idea why." He wiped his forehead. "Man, I could use a drink."

"Steady, old man," Giles said.

Jamie sighed, nodded. "I know. I'll find out tomorrow if I still have a job. Need any help at the library?"

"It's a dismal job, really," Giles said. "Being a high school librarian, I mean."

"So's being a cop in this day and age."

They traded looks of commiseration.

"Could you drop me at the library?" Giles's car was in the shop. Not the one where Artie DeMarco worked. One where they told him it would probably be cheaper for him to buy a new car than to fix his ancient Citroën.

He had told them to salvage his car at any costs. Newer was not better. Not even in America.

Joyce parked her car and glanced uncertainly around. The shelter was in the worst part of town and in a very run-down building, so bad that on the second story, all of the windows were broken. It was brick, and with a lot of work—a tremendous amount of work—it could be charming. It must be a very old building. Brick was unusual in southern California because of the earthquakes.

She couldn't help but admit to some disappointment. When she'd offered to hold the benefit, she'd pictured a sunny little place somewhere, kids playing Ping-Pong, that sort of thing. Naive, she knew, especially when compared to the reality: raucous music, so loud she could barely hear herself think. Posters about AIDS, teen pregnancy, and suicide had been pasted on either side of the peeling brown door. It hadn't been like this when she was a girl. Why, in her high school, there hadn't been a single—

Oh, yes, there had.

Her hand on the door, she froze.

There had been a girl named Elise Alexander, and she had killed herself. Handfuls of pills. No one knew exactly why. Some said it was a boy. Some said something awful had happened to her. It was the talk of the school, and yet no one really knew anything.

Now Joyce vividly recalled her own mother saying, "That poor girl. She had nowhere to turn."

So maybe it didn't matter that as she opened the door she was greeted by the din of what passed these days for music, a choking cloud of cigarette smoke, and a handful of very hostile young faces staring back at her. Boys with enormous, elaborate tattoos and girls in makeup that hardened and aged them. The kids all tensed as she stood in the doorway. Pasty white faces and closed, angry dark ones.

Frightened ones.

She paused on the threshold, scanning for Liz DeMarco.

A boy about Buffy's age strutted over to her. He wore jeans belled so big around the legs you could fit a mop bucket in them. His faded T-shirt said THE MERMEN A GLORIOUS LETHAL EUPHORIA.

"You a social worker?" he asked with disdain. "Or a cop?"

"Neither," she said. "I came to see Mrs. DeMarco. She's a friend of mine."

"Liz?" He gestured with his head. "She's in the back."

"Thank you." She smiled at him. He didn't smile back. Instead, he slouched away and noisily straddled a metal folding chair. Glowering beneath a sign that said, NO SMOKING. CALIFORNIA STATE LAW, he lit up a fresh cigarette, stared at Joyce, and exhaled the smoke in a long, slow breath.

She pitied him. It took so much effort to be that angry. He must figure he had just cause.

Maybe he did.

She hurried to the back and found Liz hunched over a battered desk with a pile of what looked to be bills at her elbow and a checkbook held open with a coffee cup.

But Liz was not writing checks. She was crying as if her heart had broken.

Joyce hurried to her, squatted beside the desk, and touched Liz's arm.

Liz started, then melted into Joyce's embrace. She said, "They found her locket."

Joyce knew that. Liz had told her that on the phone. But now she said, "Oh, Liz," and let the woman cry.

"She's dead. I know she's dead," Liz sobbed. "My baby's dead."

"We don't know that." *And for sure in Sunnydale we don't know that,* Joyce thought.

"She loved that locket. She loved that boy. I should have let her see him." She fought to compose herself. "You know, you worry about if they go with the wrong one. My mother worried about that."

She was right to. Joyce had to bite back the words. She thought Artie DeMarco was one of the most obnoxious men she'd ever met. According to Giles, Liz worshiped him, which made no sense to Joyce at all.

Liz sat up and opened a drawer. "I have a box of Kleenex somewhere," she said.

Joyce rummaged in her own purse. "Here." She handed the other woman a tissue.

"Thanks." She blew her nose. "The thing I don't understand is why she hates me so much." Liz's face clouded. "I think she thinks I'm sorry she was born. That she ruined my life. You see we, um, we had to get married. But I've always loved her. She's the joy of my life."

Joyce patted her arm. "Kids get mixed up sometimes, Liz." *And so do their parents.*

But Liz would not be comforted with empty platitudes. "Every night I lie awake, going over and over the things I've said to her. We've had our fights, sure. What mother and teenage daughter haven't? But for her to believe that I hate her. I've never given her any cause to believe that."

Joyce didn't know what to say. She really didn't. So she did what she had wanted to do so many times with Buffy.

Hold her, saying nothing.

Just hold her.

Buffy lay across her bed, sore and bruised, as Angel had predicted, and heard the front door close. She held the phone to her ear, half-listening as Willow continued, "So I just think you should be careful, Buffy. I'm only telling you this because I care about you."

Buffy opened her mouth to protest, but the memory of Angel's kiss weighed heavily on her mind. "I know we can't . . . seize the moment again, Will," she said. "But we, we'll, we're trying to find some way to at least stay in each other's lives." She sighed.

"I don't mean to make you feel bad," Willow said sincerely.

"I know." Buffy sighed again. "You're a friend to me, Will. I'm glad you're saying these things because I need to hear them."

"It's not because he tried to kill me," Willow persisted. "Well, kill me, yes, maybe that has something to do with it. A little. But I don't want him to hurt you. In any way."

Tears welled in Buffy's eyes. "I know."

"Buffy?" Joyce called.

Buffy huffed. "I should go. My mom's home and I'm sure there're groceries to bring in or artworks to uncrate or something."

"It's probably 'or something,'" Willow offered. "Like she wants to take you to the mall for new shoes."

"That's definitely it," Buffy drawled.

"What did she say when she saw you?"

Buffy bit her lower lip. "Now that you mention it, she hasn't seen me yet."

A beat. "You're pretty messed up."

"Well, at least I don't have to pretend I'm in a gang. Or a rock band."

They both chuckled grimly.

"How is it over there?" Buffy added. They hadn't really caught up on Willow's deal with her parents and Oz, and Buffy was sorry.

"The same, I think. They want me to go out with a nuclear physicist."

"Who would be way too old for you," Buffy pointed out reasonably.

"Buffy?" Her mother sounded a little exasperated.

"I do have to go," Buffy said. "I'm sorry, Will."

"Later."

Buffy hung up and swung off her bed just as her mother started up the stairs. Crossing the room to her mirror, Buffy glanced at herself. Grimaced. She looked terrible. Keywords: Foundation. Cakey. Car accident. Bloody.

Sheesh.

She took a deep breath and faced the doorway.

"Oh, my God," her mother said when she saw her.

"Um, hi," Buffy said perkily. "Did you have a nice time at the shelter?" Then she remembered why her mother had gone there and dropped her act. "How is Mrs. DeMarco?"

"My God." Joyce came to her and gently cradled her face. She stared at the bruises. "Buffy, do you . . . can't you . . . ?"

Buffy swallowed hard. "Mom," she warned, "we've been over this a million times. I'm the Slayer. It's what I do. What I *have* to do."

"You're my baby," Joyce said softly. "Buffy, let's talk. Really talk." She hesitated. "I have to go to the gallery now. And I have a meeting tomorrow night with the police. We're trying to get the department to organize a runaway task force. But Tuesday evening I want to talk as soon as I get home from work."

Buffy said steadily, "Okay, Mom."

Her mother let her go. "I think you should stay home from school tomorrow."

"Your wish is my command," Buffy said lightly.

Joyce left the room.

Buffy picked up the phone and speed-dialed.

Willow's line beeped.

"Um, hello?" Willow said.

Buffy smiled. "Let me guess. Oz is on the other line."

"Oh, gee, Buffy. I can tell him to call back later."

"Never mind. I just wanted to tell you this dumb joke," Buffy assured her. "It'll keep."

"Oh, no, go ahead. What is it?"

"It's okay, Will. Go talk to Oz."

They disconnected.

Buffy whispered, "Me. I'm the joke."

On Tuesday afternoon, Oz's van was parked in front of Willow's house. Buffy sat in the back with Willow, Xander, and Oz, idly picking at her bandages. Her mother had decreed that she looked passable enough to go to school, and so she'd shown up in biology class just in time to fail a pop quiz.

Now, glancing up, she caught the movement of the curtains in the Rosenbergs' living room. Poor Willow. Her parents were spying on her. Buffy's buddy seemed oblivious, her attention split between the matter at hand and admiring Oz in his bowling shirt.

Xander clapped his hands and said, "Okay. As former treasurer of the We Hate Cordelia club, and current Semi-Grand Poohbah of World Slayage Incorporated, I open this meeting of We Jolly Four. Or is that 'Us'?"

Buffy held out her hands. "Roland's in trouble. And we all had a wiggins at that Faire. Meanwhile, these evil pixie-things had a locket that belonged to a missing girl. Whose mother runs the runaway shelter, by the way, and is now my mother's new best friend. And Cordelia's dress was slashed—at the Faire—like I'm slashed. So I'm starting to wonder if maybe it's all connected."

"Isn't it always?" Oz said, as if the plain fact should be obvious to them all.

"I'm wondering, too," Xander said. "So, shall we take us to the Faire?"

Oz nodded. "I'm in."

Willow nodded. "Me, too."

Xander said, "That makes it a foursome. But not a double date," he added, his tone a little wistful. "Gee, too bad Cordy has a hair appointment. You just know she'd love to come with us."

Willow smiled. "She has nice hair."

Oz's adoring look was not lost on Buffy. Or Willow. Or Xander.

"Okay," Buffy said. "But you understand, we'll be crashing. We're known there now, and if something's going on . . . well, we already know something's going on. We just don't know what it is." Buffy checked Xander's watch. He had given up the Tweety Bird for something that wouldn't humiliate Cordelia. That made Buffy sad. Xander was Xander, not some guy from GQ. If that's what Cordelia wanted, she should find it, not force-fit him into some fantasy she had.

"Look," she said, not wanting to say what she had to say. Because she had no right to force-fit these guys into something they might not be—or might not want to be—either. "Maybe you guys should just sit this one out. Maybe Giles is right." She looked at Willow. "Your parents are already angry enough with you."

"They aren't angry, exactly," Willow offered, and jerked as if she had just remembered Oz was sitting next to her. "They just want me to um, study hard so I can go to college."

Oz shrugged. "You're a studying machine, Willow. It'll be cool."

"It'll be cool," Willow said meaningfully to Buffy.

"Buffy, look at you," Xander said. "No offense, but after the other night, you aren't exactly prime real estate. If you never needed us before—which you did—you most definitely need us now. We're in. The Slayerettes reign supreme. Period. End of story."

"Thanks, guys." Buffy took a deep breath. "We'll meet up later, then. I have to go home now. My mom took one look at me Sunday morning and asked me to pencil in plenty of 'quality time.'"

She looked at the pitying faces. "Which could mean a long talk about my bizarre direction in life, doubtless disguised as a lecture on my most recent rash of bad grades and unexcused absences, or it could mean a pigout on freshly baked cookies which we, in a moment of bonding, freshly bake ourselves."

Xander raised a finger. "If Cordelia were here, she would remind you that lectures aren't fattening."

"And I would be so grateful." Buffy smiled tightly.

"Hey, just trying to brighten up your day."

Willow bailed while everyone else climbed into seats in the van. Oz started the engine and Xander said, "On your mark, get set, stall."

And they were off.

In the library, Giles shook his head and put aside *Phantom Hunts: Myths and Legends.* Perhaps these hunters of Angel's were masquerading as Renaissance Faire personnel. To capture runaway children?

The library phone rang. Absently he picked up. "Giles," he said.

"Rupert? It's Jamie Anderson."

"Yes."

He braced himself for bad news about Connie DeMarco. On the Hellmouth, one expected nothing less. Except that Jamie Anderson had not been so much as reprimanded at work for public drunkenness. His superior had taken him into his office and asked him how he was, then meaningfully told him to be careful. That was it.

And that was good news, after all.

"Rupert, my boy has come home! My son's with me here, right now."

"Oh?" Giles smiled broadly, quite astonished. "That's wonderful. Brilliant. I'm absolutely delighted for you."

"All these years. I was going crazy . . . well, you know that. You know what it's like to lose someone . . ." The man broke down into sobs.

Suddenly a new voice was on the phone. "Um, you the dude found Treasure's locket?"

"Treasure . . ." This must be the son. Giles said, "You mean Connie?"

"Yeah, that's her. Listen, I gotta talk to you about what's goin' down." He hesitated. "My old man don't believe me, but I know what I saw. He said I should talk to you, that you do all these occult studies or something. He saw some books in your condo."

Oh, dear. *I have to be more careful.* "Go ahead."

"Not on the phone. Can you come to my dad's?"

Giles hesitated. He had placed several calls to other Watchers about the dark faerie, and he was waiting for answers.

"We'll come on over to the library," said Anderson, senior, who had apparently taken back the phone.

"Very good. I'll see you when you get here. And Jamie, I'm very pleased for you."

"Thanks, Rupert. I couldn't have made it without you, really."

Giles smiled.

They hung up.

As if on cue, the fax machine went off, and he nodded to himself as he checked his watch. Good show. It had taken someone a mere thirty minutes to reply to his request for assistance. Not at all bad, considering the lack of organization among his peers *and* his superiors.

He bent over the machine, reading. It was from Frau von Forsch. She was an excellent researcher, and Frankfurt University, where she was based, possessed an extensive mythology library. On her cover sheet, with some scrawled English: *Here you go, freund Giles. The Dark Faerie ride with the Wild Hunt. This I found cited many times. More follows.*

His lips parted in surprise. A poem?

Erlkönig
(The Erl King)

Who rides by night in the wind so wild?
It is the father, with his child.
The boy is safe in his father's arm,
He holds him tight, he keeps him warm.

My son, what is it, why cover your face?
Father, you see him, there in that place,
The elfin king with his cloak and crown?
It is only the mist rising up, my son.

"Dear little child, will you come with me?
Beautiful games I'll play with thee:
Bright are the flowers we'll find on shore,
My mother has golden robes full score."

Father, O father, and did you not hear
What the elfin king breathed into my ear?
Lie quiet, my child, now never you mind:
Dry leaves it was that click in the wind.

"Come along now, you're a fine little lad,
My daughters will serve you, see you are glad;
My daughters dance all night in a ring.
They'll cradle and dance you and lullabye sing."

Father, now look, in the gloom, do you see
The elfin daughters beckon to me?
My son, my son, I see it and say:
Those old willows, they look so gray.

"I love you, beguiled by your beauty I am,
If you are unwilling, I'll force you to come!"
Father, his fingers grip me, O
The elfin king has hurt me so!

Now struck with horror the father rides fast,
His gasping child in his arm to the last,
Home through thick and thin he sped;
Locked in his arm, the child was dead.

—*Johann Wolfgang von Goethe*

Giles pursed his lips. "Frau von Forsch, you're being a little too oblique, I'm afraid."

He crossed to his office and picked up his phone, remembering just in time to use his phone card. There had been a number of queries about why a high school librarian had to make so many international calls. Of course, Giles made certain that he paid for them, but nevertheless, the mere fact that he appeared to spend hours chatting with people in places such as Kingston, Macao, and Sydney raised a few school board eyebrows.

So, discretion and all that.

He dialed Germany.

Frau von Forsch answered on the first ring.

"You got something pretty crazy going on over there, *ja?*" she said.

It was almost 10 P.M. The Faire was due to close in a few minutes. Buffy—wrung out not from cookies, but an awkward and painful conversation on the beach, as if their house were just too small for the issues between mother and daughter—stood with the others. They studied the chain-link fence, which was covered with pieces of wood painted to look like castle blocks.

"Piece of cake," Buffy said.

With a glance left and right, she tried to vault over the fence, then caught herself as her bones felt like they were being crunched together. She was still thrashed from her battle with the dark faerie. She fell back down, sucked in her breath, and started to try again.

"Hold it," Oz said. He pushed on the gate. It swung open. He glanced at Buffy, who shrugged.

Buffy led the troops.

As per their plan, they fanned out, Buffy taking the route that most likely led her to the alley where she had last seen Roland. Her best guess was that if the King Richard show was over for the night, the poor guy might have to clean the robe again. Otherwise, she had no idea where to look.

She tiptoed down the row of shops and food stalls, searching for an entrance through to the interior without actually going through a shop.

Then she heard a voice raised in anger, and she

crept closer, keeping to the shadows cast by a purple tent decorated with black moons and stars.

"You thick-headed sod! You ungrateful wretch!"

It was King Richard. And that was the noise of a fist hitting flesh.

And that was a groan.

Buffy was about to run through the tent when a hand clasped her elbow. It was Xander.

"You bloody idiot!" Richard shouted.

Willow crept into the tent as Buffy mouthed a protest, then followed her. It was empty. Oz and Xander trailed behind.

At the opposite end, Buffy carefully pulled back the tent flap. Willow audibly gasped.

Roland was on his knees, doubled over and groaning. King Richard stood over him, wielding the same heavy stick Roland had used to beat the dust from his cloak. He struck Roland over the head with it, then across the back.

Again. Again.

Roland cried out and fell forward, bracing himself with his palms.

"Buffy," Willow whispered, agonized.

Buffy took a step forward.

"Down, girl," Xander whispered.

Buffy nodded. He was right. She had to choose her moment. But this was terrible to watch.

"When I come back, you'd better have my boots shining," the king said to Roland. "And if they aren't, you'll clean the stables with your tongue."

He kicked Roland, hard, and the boy rolled over on his side. He didn't move. Buffy closed her eyes, wondering if he was dead.

As soon as the king left the area, the group threw back the tent flap and raced over to Roland. Buffy clamped her hand around his wrist.

"Oh, my God, he doesn't have a pulse," she whispered.

"That's an unreliable measuring technique," Willow ventured.

Xander ran and got a blanket and threw it over Roland, who coughed and moaned. Buffy gently patted his cheeks, staring at his mottled skin.

"Roland, come on," she whispered. "We're getting you out of here."

"Yeah, and calling the cops," Xander added angrily.

"No!" Roland rasped, bolting upright. He could barely speak. "No authorities, I beg you."

Buffy frowned. "But that creep ought to pay—"

"No." Roland shook his head. "I won't speak to them."

Xander looked at Buffy. "This is a conversation that can wait," he said earnestly. "We've got to get him out of here now."

Buffy nodded her head. She hoisted Roland to his feet and slung his arm around hers. His clothes were little better than rags, but his brown eyes shone with a moist glow that was almost . . . saintly was the word that came to mind, but Buffy decided it was too much, and pushed it away.

"Can you walk?" she asked him.

He nodded.

"Good. Walk fast."

Draping the blanket around his shoulders, Buffy and her friends hurried him to the exit.

* * *

Oz drove the van in silence, trying with a look to reassure Willow that everything was going to work out all right. But if there was one thing he had learned in the time since he had met this very interesting group, one did much better if one just went with the flow. Another thing he'd learned was that things didn't always work out all right.

So while Xander and Buffy pelted the poor guy in the backseat with questions, Oz said to Willow, "Devon got a sub for me for the gig."

"How'd he take your excuse?" she asked.

He shrugged. "Hey, we all have to go to weddings. And I gave him more than a week's notice." He slid her a lazy grin, which grew as she blushed.

She was such an amazing girl.

Buffy looked out the window and said, "My mom's probably asleep. I'll go on in and explain—"

"No," Roland said, his eyes wide and terrified. "No one must know where I am. No one."

"But, Roland," Buffy began, "there are people who can help you. My mom just had an art exhibit for a group that helps runaways, they have a shelter—"

"No." He held on to the seat. "If you tell anyone, I'll run away again."

Xander said to Buffy, "Your basement." She wrinkled her nose. "It's late, and he's all messed up, and let's just leave the grown-ups out of this one, okay?"

Still Buffy hesitated.

"Okay," she said finally. "We've got one of those inflatable mattresses for camping. And I'll get some blankets."

"Shelter is all I ask," Roland pleaded.

* * *

Buffy's mother had left a note that she had gone to Elmwood to supervise the packing of the Cassatt paintings that had been on loan, and would probably spend the night there. Buffy was relieved; that made things simpler. The beach talk rang in her ears. Her mother didn't want to be excluded anymore. Didn't she realize that what she was asking for was just going to complicate Buffy's life?

On the other hand, Buffy thought, her being the Slayer had certainly complicated her mom's life quite a bit.

When she had made sure Roland was settled in, Buffy went to bed, her mother's justifiable anxiety competing for attention in her mind with the whole mystery surrounding Roland and these little dark faerie creatures. She tossed and turned and stared at the clock, promising herself that at midnight, she'd go and check on Roland. Now she glanced at the clock one more time. Eleven twenty-one.

Close enough.

She threw back the covers and got up, glancing down at her T-shirt and boxers. This assignment called for a robe.

She was just about to cross to her closet when Angel clambered through her window with incredible speed, lunged at her in full vamp-face and threw her across the bed.

"Uh," she said, astonished.

"Buffy, close your eyes," he whispered, yellow eyes burning and intense. "Don't move."

"Angel," she said, starting to sit up. "What?"

He threw himself on top of her, pinning her to the mattress. "Close your eyes," he growled. "Don't make a sound. Don't even breathe."

A freezing wind whipped through her room. It shrieked as it blew, making her start violently. Reflexively, she tried to bolt out of her bed.

Angel gripped her tightly, his body holding hers in place. One hand was around her wrist. Her other arm was wedged beneath his side.

"It's the Wild Hunt," he whispered. "They're riding through Sunnydale, Buffy. They're hunting for souls. If you look, they'll take you."

Chapter 7

Outside Buffy's house, the shrieking was joined by the sharp howling and panting of dogs, fierce and predatory. Her window was second story, but the sounds, the very presence of the dogs, seemed to be coming right at her. She stiffened and started to open her eyes, but Angel covered them with his hand.

"The hellhounds," he said. "They run ahead of the Hunt. Their paws never touch the earth."

"But . . ."

"Hush. They'll hear you. They'll find you."

She swallowed in the blackness as he kept hold of her, his left hand capturing and holding both her wrists. His other hand was pressed tightly over her eyes. His mouth was pressed against her neck. She knew he could feel the vein throbbing as her heart thundered. She had once said to him, *When you kiss me, I want to die.* But sometimes, truly, she thought she would die from not being kissed by him.

She shifted beneath him, and Angel shushed her. His chest pressed against hers. She felt the long muscles of his thighs as he forced her to lie still.

She heard horrible laughter, and gibbering, and the mournful dirge of some kind of horn. Angel released his grip on her wrists, taking one hand and holding tightly, as if willing her to stay silent.

There came the scurrying and scratching of dozens of tiny feet, perhaps a hundred. A ripple of disgust ran through her, and Buffy shivered. She was . . . Buffy wasn't just afraid. She found, to her horror, that she was frozen in terror, wallowing in a kind of helpless panic she had never felt before. It was senseless fear, beyond her own conscious mind.

As if her soul itself were terrified.

The Slayer whimpered.

"Sssh," Angel urged. "Those were the dark faerie. They must be scouts for the Hunt. Now the Huntsmen are coming."

Then the room thundered with hoofbeats; the windows and walls and the doors rattled with a gale force. Buffy bit her lower lip to keep from shouting out; it wasn't her way to cower, and everything in her longed to jump up and face this Wild Hunt.

The hoofbeats came louder, louder still. Buffy braced herself to be trampled. She was shaking with cold; it was as if she had been plunged into a sea of ice.

"Their leader wears the horns of a buck. He's shaggy and no man can see his face and live," Angel whispered. "All heads must turn away when the Hunt goes by."

"Angel . . ."

"Hush, Buffy. My soul is my curse, they can't take it away," he said. "But they can take yours."

143

The room resounded with howls and thunder and Buffy's own heartbeat roaring in her ears. Her body ached with cold. Pinned beneath Angel, she could barely breathe.

Then there was another weight on the bed, pressing down, coming close to her foot. She heard Angel gasp.

And then it was gone.

Still, the riders came, maybe passing over her, or through her. She couldn't see. It was driving her crazy that she couldn't see.

She heard the whinny of their horses.

The crack of a whip.

Laughter, evil and deep.

She smelled the odor of damp earth, and sweaty animals, and something else she could barely place, as if someone had lit a hundred matchbooks and blown them all out at the same time.

From outside, on the street, she heard an agonized scream.

"Dad! Daddy!" Brian Anderson shouted, as the darkness flared and huge, howling black dogs circled around him. Shock had heard the chaos in the street and run out to see what was happening.

Now he was caught in a whirlwind. Shock turned away from the dogs, shouting again for his father. But what he saw made him scream and throw his hands to his face.

Dark, cloaked shapes on black stallions galloped across the sky. At their head, a looming shadow with an enormous cape made of screaming faces stared at Shock, and his eyes glowed red and evil. His head was helmeted, but hair whipped wildly behind him. Antler horns crowned his head, but Shock couldn't tell if they were part of the helmet, or poked *through* it, actually growing from the horseman's head!

Huge black dogs raced ahead, making no sound, until all at once they threw back their heads and howled. Flames shot from their mouths and nostrils.

The horned man pointed straight at Shock.

In a huge, faceless rush, everything flew at Shock. Dogs leaped on him, jaws snapping, worrying at his hands and face as if his flesh were pieces of leather. Then the little creatures he had seen in the forest leaped from the backs of the dogs and the saddles of the hunters and flew at him, tearing at him, savaging him as he sank to his knees.

Around him, the wind screamed, the dogs' burning breaths flared like comets. Then the riders came for him, lances raised in huge hands wrapped in black leather gloves. One whipped a net over his head, threw it—

"No!" Shock screamed, covering his head. He was thrown back against the pavement, then lifted into the air like a doll, caught inside the net, thrown roughly across a saddle. He tried to raise his head. A hard blow slammed against the back of his neck.

"Brian!" his father called from far away.

"Daddy," Shock—not Shock, Brian, Brian Evan Anderson was his real name. He was Brian and his father was Jamie Anderson, a policeman, and while Brian had been gone, his mom had died—Brian, who had wanted to be someone else so very badly, because he had had no idea how much his parents loved him. Because he had had no idea how to love himself.

Brian, who had seen a dead man crawl out of the

ground. Brian, whose hair now turned completely white, raised one hand feebly, thinking, *If my father can touch me, he can save me.*

"Daddy," he whispered, and then he went limp.

Jamie Anderson heard the receding hoofbeats, heard his son cry his name, saw just the shapes of the horses in the darkness and then the riders were gone. He fell to his knees and threw his arms wide as the sounds of the horses and the baying of the hounds disappeared in the darkness.

"No! Please no!" he shouted. "Not now!"

Buffy's head ached. Her body was straining to move, to act.

The screaming outside stopped abruptly.

The howling of the wind subsided. The scurrying and scrabbling sounds grew faint. The hoofbeats, fainter still.

Then there was nothing.

It was over.

Angel exhaled against Buffy's neck. He said, "I have to go. It's almost dawn. But don't leave your room until first light. Until then, they can come back."

He released her and moved away, and Buffy was sorry.

Angel crossed quietly to her window and peered out.

"I heard someone screaming," she said, sitting up. "I mean, besides all the supernatural-type screaming."

"I did, too. I don't know who it was, but it probably means they were taken," Angel told her, still scanning the street. "By the way, that friend of Giles's, the cop? His son showed up."

"Oh, that's good!" she cried.

"Hush!" He whirled on her. "He and his son went to see Giles at the library. Giles tried to call you, to tell you what they pieced together. He left me a message, and I tried to call him back. I'd remembered one of the legends about the wee folk: some of the myths say that they ride with the Hunt. Since I'd heard the horn the other night . . . I was afraid you'd look and the Hunt would take you."

"Roland," Buffy said suddenly, and started for her door. "There's this runaway kid in my basement. I've got to check on him."

"No, Buffy!" Angel whirled around. "You've got to lie low until first light. Their nets are open. They're still out there hunting."

"But he's down there. He won't know all this stuff."

"No!" Angel threw her back down and held her there. "You can't help him now. There's a good chance they've taken him already."

"Oh, no." Her eyes widened. "Maybe he would have been safer where he was. Angel, what if I've let them take him?"

"You didn't know. Nobody did." He regarded her seriously. "Giles sent me to warn you. I was all over Sunnydale looking for you."

"I went back to the Faire," she said, and flared at his look of disapproval. "Hey. I'm the Slayer. I don't exactly leave a trail of breadcrumbs wherever I go."

"I know." He touched her cheek. "Once it gets light, go to Giles. He'll explain everything to you. Everything we've figured out, anyway."

"Seeing as it's a school day, I'll be at school," she said dryly.

He managed a smile. "I have to go, Buffy. It'll be dawn soon."

She nodded. "Go."

"Don't check on your friend until first light," he said again.

"I won't."

Lying on the bed, she watched him sling one leg over the sill, and then the other. Then he looked at her one last time, and slid out of sight.

With wide eyes, Buffy waited anxiously for the dawn.

It wasn't supposed to be like this. She wasn't supposed to be afraid of the dark.

The dark was supposed to be afraid of her.

Bernie Sayre was almost asleep when he heard something rummaging in the trash can outside.

He bolted upright, frightening Simon off his bed, and winced at the pain in his hip at the sudden movement.

More gingerly, he swung his legs over the side of the bed, stepped into his slippers, and grabbed his robe.

"Okay, now I'm going to get you," he muttered as he shuffled along, pulling on the robe and belting it. "You just stay there. I'm coming for you now."

As quickly as he could, he grabbed his flashlight and headed for the kitchen door, muttering to himself. For two weeks, something had been tormenting him. Going in his trash. Ripping up his letters in the mailbox. Even chewing on the wiring of his house.

Raccoons, the police said. Varmints. Maybe big rats.

Vandals, Bernie said. Teenagers. Hoodlums. No raccoon ever ripped up letters.

No teenager ever chewed on wiring.

"I'll show 'em," Bernie grunted, as he took the three steps from the kitchen door to his backyard.

Then Bernie Sayre froze.

On the other side of his yard, a hideous figure dropped over his wooden fence and squatted to catch its balance. It stared straight at him. Its face was like a nightmare, all scarred or burned or maybe it was a mask. Its eyes glowed yellow. Its teeth were large and pointed.

"You punk kid! You don't scare me!" Bernie shouted, raising his fist. "I've already called the cops, so you can take off your stupid disguise and face me like a man."

The figure leaped on him and knocked him flat.

"Hey, hey wait!" Bernie shouted, flailing. The pain in his hip was unbearable. "Hey!"

It straddled him and sank its teeth into his neck. The thing was wounded, too, and its blood dripped down onto Bernie's face. Bernie shrieked in terror and in agony.

Then he was silent.

His eyes were wide open.

But Bernie Sayre saw nothing.

He did not see the vampire slake its thirst and pull away with satisfaction from the drained corpse.

He did not see its confused frown as a horde of misshapen green creatures burrowed in the trash can, then dropped to the ground and skittered toward it. They gabbled and pranced, advancing on it hungrily, as it had advanced on the human.

He did not hear the booming thunder of hooves as a

night-black figure on a jet-black stallion swooped down from the midnight sky.

The shadow put a bolt to a crossbow, as its mount threw back its head and whinnied. Fire erupted from the horse's nostrils like gas jets.

The figure let the bolt fly. The projectile slammed directly into the vampire's chest.

With a shriek, the vampire exploded into dust.

The dust settled on Bernie's open eyes.

His blank, unseeing eyes.

Finally. The sky was red with sunrise as Buffy dashed downstairs.

She threw open the basement door.

"Roland?" she called, peering into the darkness. She had left the light on. He must have turned it off. She flicked the switch back on and raced down the stairs.

To her intense relief, he was seated on the air mattress. His back was to her, but he looked fine.

"Oh, thank God. Did you hear all that stuff last night?" she asked, and thought about trying to explain. But no, Roland was just a runaway. After Giles's admonishment, the last thing she should be doing was trying to tell someone else about the Hellmouth and its nastier residents . . . and visitors.

Roland didn't move a muscle. Now that she thought of it, he hadn't so much as turned when she'd come thundering down the stairs.

"Roland?"

Suddenly worried, Buffy darted around in front of him and crouched down. His eyes were closed, but he seemed almost too still, too silent, to be sleeping. His lips were parted, but he didn't appear to be breathing.

He didn't move a muscle. He sat completely still, like a statue.

"Roland?"

She felt for his pulse and jerked her hand away. There was no pulse, but there was something else: his body was like ice. It was as if he were frozen solid. She thought of the fierce wind, and wondered if this was what you looked like after the Hunt took your soul. If all that was left was skin and—

"Dirt?" she said, astonished.

She raised her hand and studied the brown smudges on her fingertips, rubbing them together, judging the texture, staring at it again.

On Roland's neck, her fingerprint stood out as if she had dipped her hand in paint.

Or dirt.

She peered at him, almost nose to nose.

He was made of dirt.

In a clearing in the forest:

Evil, shimmering into being.

The soft laughter of the damned, the shrieks of their freshly captured prey.

The hellhounds battling over the scraps.

Dogs stopped their barking, lay down, whimpered. Cats arched in fear and hissed at shadows. Babies awoke, inconsolable.

And the little town that sat upon the mouth of hell started screaming.

Chapter 8

Buffy THREW ON JEANS AND A BLACK BOATNECK BLOUSE
while she called each of her friends in turn. So far, so
good, and she relaxed enough to pin her hair up with a
butterfly clasp. But the hand that held her portable
phone began to shake as she said carefully to Mrs.
Harris, "So you don't know if Xander came home last
night?"

"Well, I'm pretty sure he did," Mrs. Harris said in a
flat voice. In the background, *Good Morning America*
blared so loudly Buffy could barely hear her.

"So he might have already left for school?"

"Yes, he's probably at school," Mrs. Harris replied,
obviously distracted by the television. "Try him
there, Buffy."

"Thanks. Uh, some storm last night, huh?"

"What?"

"Nothing, Mrs. Harris. Thanks."

Buffy hung up. All accounted for except Xander.

And Giles, but he was probably already at the library. She'd catch up with him there.

Buffy didn't get to school until the middle of fourth period. It wasn't until she walked through the door that she realized she had left her books behind. Not that it mattered. After the past twenty-four hours, she knew there was no way she'd be able to pay attention in class, with or without a book.

Outside, it was a beautiful fall day—sunny and unseasonably warm, even for southern California. Buffy barely noticed. She felt cold. Almost numb. With the students in class, the halls of Sunnydale High were eerily deserted, and it bothered her. Buffy didn't want to be alone.

Behind her, there came a sudden clatter, and she turned with a start. Down the corridor, a sophomore she thought she recognized scrambled to pick up the books that had tumbled from his locker. He looked frantically up and down the hall, and Buffy knew from his eyes that he wasn't supposed to be out of class any more than she was.

She felt a little less alone, but even colder than before. The noise had been nothing but the rattle of a locker door, the slap of books hitting the linoleum, but her heart was still pounding.

The Slayer was spooked. No denying that.

She hated it.

Buffy picked up her pace, kept her eyes straight ahead, and tried not to recall how pale and gaunt she had looked in the mirror before she'd finally calmed down enough to leave for school. She'd covered Roland with a heavy blanket, but couldn't think of anything else to do.

Uh-uh, this was definitely one for the Watcher.

Giles would have some idea of what to do. Some kind of answers. Anything would do, at this point. For the last few days, nothing had turned out to be exactly what it seemed, and it had Buffy considerably off balance. Off balance was not at all healthy.

With a sigh of relief, Buffy reached the swinging double doors of the library and pushed them open with both hands, like a gunslinger entering a saloon. Her boot heels clattered on the tile. She heard him fumbling around inside his small office—probably making tea, she thought.

"All right, Giles," she called. "Fill me in. What do I need to know about something called the Wild Hunt? And have you touched base with Xan—"

Buffy stared expectantly at the door to the office, then blinked in surprise as a gray-haired woman wearing glasses emerged with three hardcover books under one arm.

"I don't know how Mr. Giles puts up with that kind of disrespect, young lady," said the old woman, "but in my day, a student would never have spoken to a teacher like that. Not to mention that you really ought to be doing your own research rather than relying on the kindness of your school librarian."

She stared disapprovingly at Buffy.

"Who are you?" Buffy asked. "Where's Gi . . . I mean, Mr. Giles?"

"Mr. Giles has called in sick for the day," the woman replied. "I'm Mrs. Winston, and once upon a time, *I* was the librarian here. I've been retired seven years now, and I thank the Lord for it. Mr. Giles isn't exactly the soul of organization, is he?"

The woman had seemed to relax a moment, but now that stern gaze was back on Buffy.

"And you, young lady," she said. "Aren't you supposed to be in class?"

Buffy blinked. Couldn't think of a thing to say. This was the last thing she had expected. Giles never called in sick, with the exception of a few days not long after Jenny Calendar had . . . had died. There were so many things happening in Sunnydale, so many questions running around in her mind, and Buffy didn't think she could find the answers on her own. She needed Giles.

Then again, he had gone on patrol in her place several times. Maybe she could switch roles with him again, only this time, in a different way.

"Uh, actually, I'm working on a research project," Buffy said, and then flushed a bit. "Like you said, I really should do the work myself, but I really need some of the obscure books Mr. Giles has in his collection. I was hoping he could help me, but maybe you could . . ."

Mrs. Winston looked scandalized. "Oh, I'm afraid not, my dear," the woman said in a hushed voice. "Mr. Giles's things are Mr. Giles's things, and no one must touch them but him. I'm certain if you come back tomorrow, he'll be more than happy to assist you. Neat he is not, but Mr. Giles is a very kind man, and he does love books."

Buffy sighed, mumbled a thank-you, then turned and pushed out into the hallway. Behind her, she could hear Mrs. Winston saying, ". . . still the library could certainly benefit with a bit more light. It's so depressing in here."

Buffy stood in the whitewashed hallway for several seconds, completely oblivious to the walls festooned with bulletin boards bearing multi-colored messages about everything from anti-smoking campaigns to henna body painting. Most of the lockers had their own color, multiple stickers and temporary tattoos that the custodians had only half-heartedly attempted to remove.

As she stood there, trying to figure out what to do next, her eyes focused on a poster for the big game on Saturday. Only a few more weeks until homecoming, she thought.

She wished that she had the luxury of caring.

But next to the poster for the football game was a flyer for the runaway shelter with a picture of little Timmy on it. She wanted varsity sports to be important in her life, but Buffy's life was just . . . too real, too soon.

So, what next, she thought. She could go to Angel's, though he didn't seem to have much more to offer than warnings and horrific legends the night before— back to his old tricks, her Angel. Well, not *her* Angel, exactly.

So, no help there. No help from the mysteriously disappearing Giles. No help from . . .

It struck Buffy, just for a moment, that Giles might not have called in sick at all. That the principal might simply have assumed he was sick and asked Mrs. Winston to cover for him. Okay, all right, Angel had told her not to look as the Hunt had ridden, but what if Giles had decided to take on the Hunt himself? What if Xander had joined him?

What if it had taken him and Xander both?

The chill that had been surrounding her all morning seeped down into Buffy's bones, even as a fire of anxiety began to burn inside her. Anxiety and a bit of nausea as well.

Buffy pushed it all away. She was afraid, and not just worried for her friends, without really understanding why. But fear was part of the job. If she was too stupid to be afraid when there was reason to be, she'd have been dead a long time ago. No, she was the Slayer, the Chosen One. Buffy didn't know exactly what was going on, how it all fit together, but she could feel the malevolence crackling in the air, even with the sun shining outside. Something evil was coming . . . was probably already here.

Somehow, she would find a way to stop it.

Just as she had that thought, the school bell began to ring and Buffy winced at the volume, the noise spiking into her head. She prayed for it to rain Advil, but no such miracle. Instead, she was surrounded by hundreds of other students, all on the perilous journey to the cafeteria for lunch.

Buffy let herself be pulled along by the tide of hungry teens.

"Please, for my sake, can we not talk about this here?" Cordelia begged, her expression pitiful. Framed by her black hair, her large hazel eyes reminded Buffy of one of those velvet paintings of sad-eyed children. "Aren't I being courageous enough just being seen with you all in public?"

Buffy paused. Cordelia maintained her pleading expression. But she definitely did not look like a child, dressed in a flame-red, short-sleeved Angora sweater, black pants, and talk about stacked . . . heels. Buffy glanced around the cafeteria. Despite Cordelia's efforts toward *hot* couture, nobody was paying attention to them. Nobody ever did. But just this once, she didn't see any harm in being circumspect.

"I'll try to behave," she told Cordy, who nodded in satisfaction, took a quick look around, and then gave her attention back to Buffy.

Xander—wonderful Xander, wonderfully safe and here with them—was using his fork to pry all of the cheese and bread off the burned crust of his Sicilian pizza. Typical Xander behavior, but Buffy knew him. He was too quiet. Then there were those Giles-like bags under his eyes.

Willow, too, seemed slightly askew today. They all did. Nobody looked his best, nobody was really laughing.

"All right, then," Buffy went on. "As vaguely as we can, what do we know?"

Willow offered her usual earnest face, though her eyes were not as wide, nor her manner as pleasant as it almost always was. Buffy couldn't blame her. She herself had been too distracted by other things to pay any attention to the local news this morning, but the entire town was reeling.

"At least twenty-three people missing overnight," Willow said somberly. "And . . . and seven confirmed cases of crib death."

She looked stricken. Xander put down his fork and blew air out his cheeks.

"Oh, my God," Buffy whispered. "The Hunt must have ridden all through Sunnydale."

"Mrs. Blake's little girl . . . she was one of them." Cordelia had a quaver in her voice Buffy had never heard before, not even when the other girl had been faced with the horror of seeing the corpse of a boy she'd been dating.

"She had asked me if I could baby-sit sometime," Cordy added, then looked away, as if searching for anything else to focus on.

"Mr. Krasilovsky, that old guy at the end of my street? He's missing," Xander said. "My parents were in bed, but my dad said something woke him up and he went to the window. He says he was sleepwalking."

"God, Xander," Cordelia whispered. "If Angel was right, and your father saw them, then . . ."

"Yeah." Xander nodded, but didn't look at any of them. "I checked the window. There's this big tree right in the middle of it. If you really wanted to see the street, you could. But you'd have to work at it."

Cordelia reached over and took his hand, moved closer to him at the table, for once not caring who saw her.

"It's so typical," Cordelia said. "I mean, we have some spooky horse guys snatching people and . . . and killing babies, and no one notices? Everybody goes like, 'Huh, why am I awake at this hour of the night? Gee, I must be sleepwalking.' What's up with that?"

"Typical Sunnydale denial," Willow ventured.

"But was it all luck, like with Xander's dad not looking?" Buffy asked. "I mean, did the ones who were taken get taken for a reason, or just by chance? And what about Roland? I mean, phantom night riders stealing people away, okay. But how does that turn an abused runaway into a pile of dirt?"

No response.

"Willow, hit the computer lab. Get me whatever

you can find on the Wild Hunt off the Net." Buffy paused, focused on Willow more pointedly. "When's the full moon?"

"Not until next weekend," Willow replied. "Don't worry. Oz is in. I talked to him this morning and he figured we'd be doing something. He had a dentist appointment this afternoon."

Xander opened his mouth as if to speak, but all three girls shot him a warning glance, and he thought better of it.

"Xander, keep trying Giles's phone whenever you're free. Otherwise, everybody go to class and meet up at the library after school. If Giles doesn't show by then, we'll wait until Mrs. Winston leaves, and then we'll break in. We need his books."

"We need Giles, Buffy," Xander said. "A lot of those books aren't even in English. We're not going to have much luck without him."

Buffy took a breath, looked at him.

"Then we won't rely on luck."

Outside, the sun still shone brightly, but the temperature had begun to drop precipitously. Nearly fifteen degrees in an hour. It was sixty-three degrees now, and still falling.

Out past Route 17, the Los Viejos forest rose in the chill air. The National Park Service had saved it from development decades earlier, and though its edges had been chipped away in favor of "progress," it was one of the largest forests in the area.

Deep inside the forest, there was a clearing. In the center of the clearing, something shimmered. All around it, the meager light that managed to leak through the canopy of trees had been absorbed, sucked away like the marrow from a bone. Only darkness remained. Darkness and cold, and it emanated out from that clearing through the forest.

None of the people who passed by in their cars on Route 17 noticed anything out of place. The darkness that now crept across the forest, claiming it tree by tree, could not be seen from the outside. It was as if the forest itself had grown somehow deeper. As if it existed both in this world, and in some other.

No, passersby did not notice anything amiss. But of the few people who stepped into the forest that afternoon—a boy and girl skipping school to spend the day together; an aging professor out for a walk, careful not to let his pipe ash fall where it could endanger the woods; a conservationist who'd appointed herself guardian of this particular stretch of trees—none of them were ever heard from again.

There are those who would believe, ever after, that these four were still lost in the forest; that their cries for help could still be heard.

At the center of the clearing, something shimmered. Across the forest floor, over roots and stones and twigs, the darkness spread.

It was half past three when Giles guided his faithful and expensively repaired Citroën into the parking lot at Sunnydale High. He was greatly relieved to note that Principal Snyder's car was not in the nearly empty lot. They'd taken forever at the garage. When he'd finally returned to his own apartment, a multitude of messages from Buffy and her friends awaited him on his answering machine. Unfortunately, he had no way to reach them at the time, but was greatly relieved to hear all their voices. He imagined that

Angel had found Buffy, and Buffy had been able to warn the others about the Hunt.

He expected that last night they had likely gone off on some brave but ill-informed errand or other. Perhaps, given the problems they all seemed to be having with their parents—a product, Giles believed, of the fact that they would soon graduate and no longer be within the province of their parents' authority—they might have gone home after all. In that case, he could surely manufacture some excuse to ring them at home.

Giles reminded himself that, with Buffy, he needed no excuse. Joyce Summers was not pleased with her daughter's status, but she was aware of it.

He pulled his jacket more tightly around him as he walked toward the school. The temperature had dropped at least twenty degrees since morning, and though the meteorologists continued to deny it, Giles was certain there would be rain. One did not generally have this kind of weather disturbance without some precipitation.

Under the burden of all that had happened in the past day and night, Giles used his keys to let himself into the school. He nodded at the kindly fellow who had taken George's place on the maintenance crew, and idly wiped his glasses with a handkerchief before returning them to their resting place atop his nose.

Light footsteps echoed from around the corner, and as Giles arrived at the doors to the library, Oz stepped into view.

"Ah, perfect timing, Oz," Giles said happily, and with Oz at his side, pushed open the library door. "I may need your assistance in locating . . ."

"Giles!"

The Watcher looked up into the angry face of the Chosen One.

"Where the hell have you been?" Buffy demanded, hands on hips.

In spite of it all, Giles couldn't help but smile.

"It is a shame that Angel wasn't more forthcoming," Giles said with his usual distracted air as he searched through the papers on his desk. "I did however, receive some information from a colleague which might prove useful. And Jamie and his son dropped by to add more pieces to the puzzle."

He emerged from his office and handed a sheet of paper to Buffy, who sat on top of the library counter next to Willow. Buffy scanned the fax sheet, frowned, and handed the paper to Willow.

"Without going into the value of dead art forms and all, how exactly is a poem going to help us figure this out and help Roland?" Buffy asked, raising an eyebrow as she looked expectantly at Giles.

Xander and Cordelia sat at the study table, where Cordy was painting her nails by the light of a banker's lamp. Oz had turned one of the chairs around and now straddled it, leaning his chin on his crossed arms. Buffy thought he looked adorable, and knew that meant they'd probably receive no help from Willow. She'd be too busy also noticing how adorable Oz was.

"Yes, well, it's more than a poem, you see," Giles said. "According to my colleague, it's an actual account. Nonfiction, if you will. This 'elfin king' or Erl King was apparently the commander of a large group of such creatures. According to legend, the Erl King led the elves and dark faerie—Angel's 'wee folk'—on a Wild Hunt across the countryside, appearing almost as phantoms at night. The souls of dead hunters rode with them, and wild animals ran at their sides as well."

Giles drew breath to continue, but Oz interrupted him.

"It's Odin."

They all looked over at Oz, who never interrupted.

"Beg pardon, Oz?" Giles said.

"From Norse mythology," Oz explained, then tilted his head to one side as if in apology. "It's sort of an interest of mine. When I was in fourth grade, I read this one book, *Thunder of the Gods,* about fifty times."

"Odin was the king and the father of all the gods," Xander added.

Buffy shot him a doubtful look.

"Hey, I study my mythology," he said angrily, then bit his lip as they all continued to stare at him, waiting for a truthful response. "Okay, okay. So I read it in a *Thor* comic book. That's kind of like studying."

"Yeah," Willow agreed. "If, you know, the test is to name all the members of the Justice League."

"Which I can do." Xander smiled with self-satisfaction.

"Yes, Xander, perhaps another time," Giles said, and turned back to Oz. "Now, Oz, I'm quite familiar with Norse mythology, but I can't say I recall any connection to the Wild Hunt."

Oz rocked a bit in his chair. "It's also known as the Great Hunt. The Vikings believed that on stormy nights, Odin rode ahead of a pack of mounted hunters, with these sort of ghost dogs tracking their prey. They pretty much partied and trashed the area until sunup," he explained.

"Also, the legend said that if you got to see the faces

of the Huntsmen, you would be, like, teleported away or something. And if you talked to them, you would just die."

Buffy felt a chill run through her.

"That fits," Cordelia said idly, looking up from her nail painting. "Angel didn't let Buffy look at these guys."

"Indeed," Giles said thoughtfully, and nodded at Oz. "Well done, Oz. Thank you. It occurs to me, however, that there are any number of similar legends, from all across Europe. Spectral, nocturnal processions of huntsmen, horses and hounds, ghosts and witches, that sort of thing appears in many different tales.

"One such myth said the goddess Diana led the Hunt, punishing the lazy and the wicked. Another had Hecate as the leader. My friend in Germany pointed out a local Wild Hunt legend about a rather benevolent goddess called Holda, who seems almost heroic until one notes that the souls of unbaptized children were snatched away as her Hunt passed by."

There was a moment of uncomfortable silence then, as Giles paused, blinked, and glanced at Buffy. She knew they were all thinking about the large number of crib deaths the night before. Buffy met Giles's gaze for a moment, and then turned away.

"What about . . . ?" Oz began, then frowned, searching his memory.

"Oz?" Willow slid off the library counter and went to pull up a chair by his side.

Oz smiled thinly at her. "I'm trying to remember the name of . . . Hern!"

"Gesundheit," Xander said weakly, obviously unable to stop himself.

None of them even acknowledged that he had spoken.

"Hern the Hunter," Oz went on. "The Norse mythology books talk about him as the major alternate for Odin in those stories."

"Indeed," Giles agreed. "Hern the Hunter is perhaps the most common among the mythological figures presumed to lead the Wild Hunt. They rounded up the souls of the unbaptized, the hopeless, and were particularly fond of the souls of those who'd taken their own lives. And, of course, anyone foolhardy enough to gaze directly upon the Hunters themselves. Legends describe Hern as a shaggy man with antlers like a great stag. Though some note that local British legends claim he was one of the huntsmen of Henry the Eighth, who betrayed the crown and hung himself for his own crimes."

"Antlers," Buffy repeated. "You said Jamie Anderson saw a guy with antlers last night."

Giles nodded. "Which would lead one to presume it is this Hern fellow."

"But that wouldn't explain the little faerie guys who attacked Angel and Buffy. Unless your Horny man was also the Erl King," Cordelia said without looking up from her nails.

"The two were never connected in any of my research thus far," Giles replied.

"So, more research then?" Xander said.

Giles offered a weak smile. "Thank you for volunteering, Xander."

Xander balked, held up both hands. "Who volunteered? Did anyone hear me volunteering?"

"It sounded like volunteering to me," Willow said.

"I'm not sure exactly what volunteering sounds

like," Oz added. "But it wasn't your usual mockery-of-all-things, so, yeah, volunteering."

Xander sulked.

"Okay, but I still don't see how more research is going to help Roland right now," Buffy said.

"This would be Dirt Boy," Xander noted. "Who needs, I'd guess, watering at this point."

Buffy glared at him. "He wasn't always dirt. He was definitely flesh before. Kind of weird flesh, but, y'know, human. Flesh."

"I've been thinking about that, actually," Giles said. "It is possible that he could be a homunculus or golem of some kind."

"Gollum?" Willow asked. "Like in *The Hobbit?*"

"A golem is a mindless creature created as a servant from lifeless materials, such as stone, wood, or . . ."

"Dirt." Buffy glanced toward the door, both because she wanted to get moving, but also because she was sad for Roland and didn't want any sympathy from her friends.

"While the golem comes mainly from Hebrew mythology, there are legends of homunculi, creatures of similar creation, which have their origins in many other cultures," Giles explained.

"Well, Roland has a mind of his own," Buffy said defensively. "That is, when he isn't, y'know . . ."

"Dirt, yes," Giles agreed. "Well, while it's possible that the passing of the Wild Hunt stole whatever spark of life your friend Roland had, it's also quite possible that whatever spell gives him the appearance of life only works at night. Which would mean that—"

"He'll come back to life at sundown!" Willow said excitedly.

"Precisely."

Buffy chewed the inside of her lip a moment, glanced at the skylight in the ceiling and saw that it was nearly dark already, then turned to regard her friends.

"I don't know what's going on with these Wild Hunters, or whatever," she said. "But I know there's a connection to Roland and to that Faire. It might be that the troupe putting on the show are the Huntsmen themselves.

"I'm going to go home and get Roland. If he does come around when the sun goes down, I'll bring him back here. Even if he doesn't, I'll bring . . . part of him, for Giles to examine."

She looked at Willow. "You and Oz, take the van and go get Angel. Soon as the sun goes down, we're going to need him."

At Xander. "You and Cordelia, help Giles with the research."

Finally, to Giles. "Whatever happens, we can't let the Wild Hunt ride through Sunnydale again. Too many people are dead already. Too many mothers are crying today."

A short time later the library was silent. Cordelia had long since finished painting her nails, and was scanning through dusty old leather-bound books for any references to the Erl King or the Wild Hunt or Hernia man or whatever. She reached the end of one book and dropped it to the oak table with a heavy thump.

"Ah, Cordelia," Giles said, glancing up at her over the tops of his glasses. "Would you mind taking a look in the world religion section for a text on Hebrew mysticism? I've been concentrating on the mythology rather than the magic. In fact, if you'd look that one over, I can move on to the Watchers' Journals for some mention of a homunculus or of the Hunt."

Cordelia had tuned him out as soon as she knew what he wanted. Relieved to get up and stretch a bit, she walked up to the second level of the library and into the stacks. She hadn't gone very far down the first aisle before she realized that she was in the wrong section. Cordelia started to turn around, and then she heard the whimpering, low and pathetic.

"Hello?" she said softly. "Who's there?"

"Cordy?" Xander called from down below. "Are you talking to yourself again?"

She walked to the end of the long aisle, toward the back of the library, and the whimpering was louder there.

"Cordelia?" Xander's tone had changed from teasing to concern, but not quite yet to alarm.

She rounded the end of the aisle, glanced to her left, and froze, a harsh gasp of breath all she could manage in that moment.

At the rear of the library was a second door which led into the other side of the school. It was usually locked, but when they'd thought Giles might be missing, Buffy had broken the lock to get them in.

Against that door sat a man who held a gun to his own temple.

"Please," he whispered, fresh tears rolling down his cheeks. "You've got to help me do it. It's the only way."

Chapter 9

As THE LAST BIT OF SUNLIGHT BEGAN TO LEAK FROM
the sky, Buffy had first begun to jog, and then to run
through the neighborhoods of Sunnydale. Though
Mrs. Cantwell had actually yelled at her once for
doing it, she cut through backyards on her way home.
The Cantwell poodle barked ineffectually from behind their sliding glass door, but Buffy didn't even
look back.

When she hit the pavement on Revello Drive, the
streetlights had come on.

The sun was gone.

Buffy narrowed her eyes, trying to see her front
door, but the pines her mother had loved so much
when they bought the house blocked her view. Her
legs hurt from the exertion, but Buffy began to sprint.
Three houses away, she heard a scream and the sound
of glass shattering. There came a loud crash.

"Mom!" Buffy yelled.

She cut across the lawn, bursting between two of the pine trees. The front door was splintered into pieces, one large chunk still hanging by a hinge.

Buffy scanned her yard, looked around the entire area, but didn't see anything out of the ordinary. On guard, she stepped over the threshold into her house, and called her mother's name again.

From the living room she heard sobbing.

The room was trashed. Not completely. A lot of the furniture would be saved. But there were several crates of things her mother had been unpacking for the gallery, and those were pretty much kindling. A pair of crystal lamps had gone over, and no amount of Krazy Glue was going to fix them.

"Mom?" Buffy asked, tenderly, crouching by her weeping mother and reaching out for her.

"I wish . . ." Joyce Summers croaked, then swallowed and spoke again, wiping her eyes and lifting her chin. "I wish you'd told me we had a guest. He scared the hell out of me."

"Roland did this?" Buffy asked, horrified.

"No. It was the others. Not monsters this time, Buffy, just people. They said they were here to pick him up. And then all hell broke loose." She looked at her again. "All you had to do was tell me, Buffy. Did he hide in the basement all day?"

"Um, the basement. Yes," Buffy ventured. "He was . . . moving?"

"What?" Joyce stared at her. "Moving! Buffy, I'm not an idiot. He wasn't hiding in our basement because he was moving."

"No. I mean, *was* he moving?" Buffy knew she was losing precious seconds. She switched gears. "The people, Mom. Tell me about the people. Were they just regular people?"

"Buffy, I don't understand."

Her mother tried to regain her composure, but now she dropped her eyes and brought a hand to her forehead. Joyce had a small cut on her forehead, and as she brushed her dirty blond hair away from her face, the blood smeared just a bit. After all they'd talked about this week, this was the last thing her mother needed.

Buffy knew she had to persist. "The people. They came to get Roland, and he fought, and they took him anyway?"

"It happened so fast," Joyce said. "Just before you got here."

Just as the sun had gone down.

"And there were no . . . horses?"

Her mother just stared at her.

"It wasn't supposed to be this way," Joyce said, and Buffy wondered if her mother was even speaking to her anymore, or to herself.

Buffy reached for her, pulled her mother close and held her there, biting her lip to keep her own tears back. At the same time, she knew that time was wasting. If the people from the Faire had come to claim Roland, they might not be sticking around in Sunnydale very long. She would need to call to have someone fix the door right away, but her mother should be safe, she reasoned, as long as Roland wasn't in the house.

"I love you, Mom," Buffy said, though she felt the distance that still separated her from Joyce. "I . . . I know you wanted me to be a doctor or something."

Joyce stiffened. Sniffled, then drew a hand across

her eyes as she stared hard at her daughter. Buffy focused on the small crow's feet at the edges of her mother's eyes.

"I never put that kind of pressure on you, Buffy," Joyce said, her face flushed from the panic of the past few minutes.

"I know, Mom, you know what I—"

"No matter what you think, I never had any grand scheme for you," her mother went on. "I would have supported anything you wanted to do with your life. Anything. You're my daughter, Buffy, and I love you. All I ever wanted was for you to be happy."

Joyce stared at her intently.

"You don't look very happy to me, Buffy."

Buffy couldn't breathe for a moment. She swallowed hard, then stood up and moved back from her mother. She looked at the shattered lamp again. Something crunched under her foot. An antique mirror that had hung on the wall in their old house in L.A.—something Buffy couldn't ever remember not having in their home, lay on the floor, little more than reflective splinters in a beautiful frame.

"Mom, I . . ."

"I know," Joyce said. "Go. I'll take care of the door, and the mess."

"Mom, stay in the house. Don't . . . look outside. Promise me." She clenched her fists. "Mom, promise me!"

"I . . . promise," Joyce said dully.

Buffy moved toward the door. Before she was out of her yard, she was running again, her mother's words fresh in her mind.

It wasn't supposed to be like this.

* * *

"Jamie, please . . . put the gun down." Giles held up a hand as if he could reach out and snatch the weapon away. If only that were possible, he thought.

The police officer held his service revolver against the side of his head, his face contorted with desperation and an eerie attempt at a smile.

"I'm sorry, Rupert, I can't do that," Jamie Anderson said. "This is the only way, don't you see? You said yourself, these things . . ." For a moment, the man was overwhelmed by emotion and could not speak.

"After you had that talk with Brian about what he'd seen, I knew you were into this kind of thing. I could never have imagined how deep. But any idiot could have seen that you knew more than you would tell me, Rupert. I'm a cop. Give me a little credit. I thought if I followed you, maybe I could figure out what to do.

"Somebody had already broken the lock on that door," Jamie said, and gestured toward the rear door of the library. "I came in and heard you talking about . . . God, this is insane."

Giles took a step toward Jamie, but the officer held up a hand to warn him off.

"Jamie, it's still possible we might be able to get Brian back," Giles insisted. "You can't give up like this."

The man chuckled dryly. It was an awful sound, full of cynicism and surrender.

"You don't get it, Rupert," Jamie said. "I heard you. That man with the horns, the Hunter, whatever you called him. He's got my son. I don't have a chance in hell of tracking him down, but there is one way I can make him come and get me, isn't there?"

Giles blinked several times, then ran a hand through his hair.

"That's . . . my God, Jamie, that's only a legend."

"So is this Hunter of yours," Jamie snapped. "But he was real enough to steal my son from me."

Giles glanced at Cordelia, nodded slightly.

"Please, Mr. Anderson, don't do this," she begged. "Mr. Giles is right. You don't even know if it would work. We've gone up against way more nasty guys than this."

Jamie narrowed his eyes. "You're lying."

"Excuse me, but, no," Cordelia said angrily. "I'm not saying we haven't had our tragedies, okay? All I'm saying is, unless you know for sure that you're doing the right thing, all killing yourself does is make you a coward. Is that what you want?"

"Cordelia!" Giles snapped, glaring at her, afraid that she had gone too far.

"What?" She threw up her hands. "It's true."

Giles watched as Jamie Anderson seemed to physically deflate, as if he had been suspended by some unseen force, and had now been released, only to crumble down into himself. The gun wavered, but did not move completely away from his head.

"It's not what Brian would want, Jamie." Giles spoke slowly, but did not move any closer. The moment was crucial. Anything could happen.

Which was when the rear door of the library was roughly yanked open, and Xander dove through the door, grabbing at Jamie's gun with both hands.

"Xander, no!" Cordelia cried.

But Xander had already wrested the gun from the man's hand, leaving Jamie to collapse in a silent mass of grief. After examining the gun for a moment, Xander handed the weapon over to Giles.

"Try not to hurt anyone with that," Xander said in a low voice. "Gun, in case you didn't notice."

Then Cordelia pulled him to her, and the students embraced openly, one of the first times Giles had seen them show their affection in public. If the stacks of the library could be considered public.

"I just got him back," Jamie said suddenly, his voice tortured and desperate. "I can't lose him again. I can't."

Giles crouched down in front of the man and managed to get him to make eye contact.

"Listen to me, old man," the Watcher said. "There was a time when I might have made a promise to you. I'm not very good with promises anymore. But I will tell you this. *If* there is a way to save your son, I will find it. We will get Brian home to you."

Jamie Anderson searched Giles's eyes for a moment, then nodded silently.

Giles looked up at the others. "Cordelia, would you drive Mr. Anderson home, please?" he asked, then pressed on before she could protest. "Xander and I will stay here and continue our research. I'd like you to stay with Jamie and wait to hear from one of us."

Cordelia opened her mouth again, then closed it quickly. She raised one eyebrow and looked at him in doubt. Giles hoped she understood what he was asking of her. Not merely to play chauffeur, but to keep this man from falling again into the madness of grief. A part of him railed at the idea of giving her that responsibility, but at the same time, Giles wondered if Cordelia weren't, of all of them, the best suited for the job.

After all, she might offer Jamie Anderson her sympathy, but she wasn't going to coddle him, that was certain. She might be just what was necessary to keep him focused.

Finally she sighed, and rolled her eyes. "Fine," she huffed. "I just did my nails anyway. Going after evil guys on horses is not good for the manicure."

"Thank you," Giles said, putting real feeling into the words.

It was apparently lost on Cordelia.

"The moon's bright tonight," Willow said in a voice little more than a whisper.

"I can feel it." Oz glanced at her, shrugged a little. The full moon wasn't until the end of next week, but sometimes the weird attraction he felt toward it was more powerful than others. Tonight, he almost felt as though it were following him. Threatening, somehow.

He steered the van up the long drive to Angel's. The huge house seemed to glow in the moonlight. For some reason Oz had the weird sense that there was nobody home. No life inside. But in a way, he supposed that was true.

They got out of the van and started up the walk toward the front of the house. It had grown very cold, and Oz had given Willow a leather jacket he'd found after rifling through the mess in the back of the van. Oz was freezing, actually, but he didn't want Willow to feel badly that she was wearing his jacket, so he tried not to shiver. It was fall, sure, but it wasn't supposed to be this cold.

Not ever, as far as Oz was concerned.

As they approached the front door, Willow seemed to hesitate. Oz reached out and took her hand, thinking she was simply anxious about being here, where so much had happened in the past six months. Instead, she frowned and glanced at him.

"Do you hear anything?" Willow looked around, scanning the area.

"Like what?" Oz asked, trying to figure out what had gotten her attention.

"That's what I mean," she said. "I don't hear anything. Not even crickets. Do you remember how loud the crickets were last time we were up here at night? Now . . . nothing. Isn't that weird?"

"Weird," Oz agreed.

They looked at each other. Several seconds ticked by, and then, in unison, they shrugged. Willow went up the steps and pounded on the door with the palm of her hand.

In the eerie silence, they waited, but received no response. Oz began to whistle "Somewhere Over the Rainbow," and his eyes started to wander away from the house. There was some overgrown scrubgrass down the drive near where he'd parked the van, and he thought he saw some kind of animal moving down there. He sighed, hoping it wasn't another skunk. Seemed like the van got sprayed at least once a month.

Willow pounded on the door again. "Angel! Anybody home?"

"I don't think anybody's home," Oz said simply. "Maybe it's too early for him to be up and about. Either that, or he thinks we're Jehovah's Witnesses."

Willow looked at him, glanced once more at the door, and they stepped away from the house and began walking down the path toward the van.

Above them, an explosion of glass.

"Man, Willow, get back!" Oz shouted, grabbing her by the hand and pulling her along the path.

Together they turned and looked up, holding their hands up to guard against the shower of broken glass that stabbed the ground where they'd been standing moments before.

It was Angel.

He pivoted in the air, roaring with anger, his limbs flailing, and crashed to the ground with a sickening thud. As he rose, they could see the tiny goblin creatures that tore at Angel's clothes and flesh. Their laughter was horrible as their mouths and talons dug in.

Dark faerie. They had to be.

Willow shrieked as more of them tumbled out the window after Angel. Oz was already moving. He pulled out his keys and forced them into Willow's hand.

"Get the van!"

Then, against every instinct, he rushed forward and began grabbing at the little things, flinging them away from Angel. Oz managed to stomp one of them beneath his shoe and it screamed before he felt it give way to fluid and gristle.

He tried not to think about it.

"Angel, come on!" he shouted. "We've got to get out of here!"

The vampire rounded on him, eyes blazing yellow, fangs distended, and snarled. "Why? The little bastards hurt like hell, but they can't kill me. I'm not running until I get some payback!"

Oz cried out as he felt sharp pains in his leg and back simultaneously. He thought about rolling on the ground to crush them, but then realized he would just be an easier target. Instead he ripped the one off his leg, quite painfully, and just rammed his back up against the side of the house, crushing the other behind him. Several of them were on the ground, spreading out, coming toward him as if they were a pack of stalking wolves.

"Angel!" Oz shouted again.

The van rumbled over the grass toward them.

Angel kicked one of the faerie hard from behind, and Oz heard something in it snap as it sailed out over the yard. The other two scattered to avoid a similar fate. Though he was still in vamp-face, Angel seemed to have calmed down somewhat.

"Sorry," he said. "Just got a bit carried away."

Oz howled in pain again and batted away a faerie that had dropped from the window above and landed on his shoulder, claws out.

"I can see how that might happen." Oz ran for the van, with Angel close behind. The faerie gave chase at first, but most of them quickly abandoned the idea. One tried to scramble into the van after Angel, but the vampire slid the door shut with all his strength, cutting the thing neatly in half. The part of the tiny corpse on the inside shriveled almost immediately to a dry husk. Oz didn't like the idea of having to pick it up to remove it later.

The van bounced over the grass and back onto the driveway. Soon they were rolling back into town and toward the school.

"Please drive carefully," Oz asked Willow, who smiled painfully.

"Where's Buffy?" Angel asked, his face finally human again.

"She went back to her house to get Roland. We're all supposed to meet back at the library," Willow explained.

Angel swore. "Stop the van."

Buffy crept as silently as she could onto the fairgrounds. There had been a sign by the entrance that the Faire was closed for the night due to illness, and all tickets would be refunded. She doubted that, however. They were going to pack up and run. No question in her mind.

But they were not leaving here with Roland. She'd thought a lot about Giles's many theories, and Buffy had decided one thing for certain. Whatever Roland was, he had a soul. There was something in there, something she could see in his eyes. She'd had plenty of experience with the cold empty gaze of the soulless. Roland had a mind and a heart and a soul. She was going to do whatever it took to get him out of here.

Though most of the fairground was dark and creepy, including the tents and trailers where the troupe lived while camped, she could hear voices coming from up ahead, and there was a flicker of light there. Buffy figured the troupe had gathered around the small dramatic stage where they performed Shakespeare for their customers.

She came to a long line of stripped wooden stands, which she assumed had been the food stalls. Her back to the wood, Buffy moved slowly toward the stage area. The voices became more distinct, and the light grew brighter. She recognized the booming voice of the actor who played King Richard.

"Got to be out of here by dawn!" the King bellowed. "Somehow, there are people in this place who know the truth, or at least suspect. No one must ever know that we have Roland with us. And after the riders last night . . . the Hunt is here at last, and we must be gone."

A great deal of shouting and murmuring followed, but Buffy could make out very little of it. She was also having difficulty deciphering the King's words. Obviously they were hiding Roland, but she didn't understand why. She wished she knew as much of the truth as the big man obviously thought she did. And what did he say about the Hunt . . .

"You just don't know how to leave well enough alone, do you, young miss?" a soft voice said behind her.

Buffy turned with a start, hands up in a defensive stance. A pair of dimly burning green lights crackled in the shadows back the way she'd come. They came closer.

It was Robin Hood. Or, at least, the member of the troupe who was supposed to represent Robin Hood to the masses. But this was no hero, Buffy thought. No kind of hero she had ever seen. His eyes were too white and his fingers too long, and she thought it odd that she hadn't noticed that before.

But how could she fail to notice those fingers now, Buffy thought. Now, when they were surrounded by crackling green fire that swirled like storm clouds about his hands.

"Magic," Buffy whispered.

"Magic indeed," Robin Hood replied. "There's a great deal of magic in this place. Magic, and far, far worse. We've a lot to do before sunup, my dear, and I sense there's more to you than meets the eye. You're an odd one, no doubt. So I'll give you this chance, pretty. Leave now."

"Not without Roland," Buffy replied sharply.

"After what Richard went through to acquire that fool, he'll never let the boy leave. Last chance, girl. Leave now, and don't turn back, or there'll be trouble all around."

"Trouble and me," she said wickedly, crossing two fingers of her right hand and holding them up for Robin to see, "we're like this."

"So be it, girl. You'll be a slave by daybreak. I'll wager you'll look especially fine in the costume of a serving wench," Robin Hood said, eyes narrowing with lust. "Just remember, you had a chance."

With that, he lifted his hands and magic began to swirl above them. He chanted, low and guttural, in a language Buffy didn't even recognize, much less understand.

Buffy ran around the other side of the food stalls. They were all closed now, heavy wooden canopies down over the open counters. But also hanging there were the wooden poles that were used to prop them open. Five steps, the earth soft under her heels, and she held a long, thick piece of oak in her hand. There was a soft laugh behind her, and Buffy turned, holding the long pole like a fighting staff.

Robin Hood was there behind her, the magic no longer flickering above his hands. Instead, it had begun to swirl on the ground, a crackling green dust devil, a three-foot tornado of dark sorcery.

Inside it, something was beginning to take form. It was monstrous, uglier even than some of the demons Buffy had fought.

"It will consume you, girl, body and soul," Robin Hood said. "Your heart will burn and then you will beg to pledge your life to me. I'm not much of a warlock. I nearly had to sell my own soul to learn this spell. But you have no idea how many times it has proven invaluable to me."

Buffy took a step back and stared at him. "Yeah," she agreed. "Especially on date night."

She moved to the right, the dust devil followed. A hand had begun to emerge from it. Buffy moved left, and it followed her again.

"Too late for you to leave, girl, if that's what you're thinking," Robin said, a smug smile turning his face ever more evil in the flickering green light.

"Not quite," Buffy muttered.

She took two steps back, and ran directly at the dust devil, even as a second hand emerged, and a pair of horns to go with them. Using the pole as a spring, Buffy launched herself into the air, rolled into a flip, and landed on both feet directly in front of Robin Hood.

As he opened his mouth to protest, she brought the staff across his skull hard enough to crack the wood in two. Robin fell to the ground in a heap, without so much as a whimper. Behind her, the dust devil disappeared in a sudden rush of air, as if someone had blown out a candle. She thought she could even smell sulphur left behind.

"Moron," Buffy whispered, then turned to look for Roland.

He was right in front of her. Less than twenty feet away. At his side, King Richard stood, tall in his arrogance and not the least bit clownish, despite his girth.

"Buffy, run, please," Roland pleaded.

Good advice, considering that the rest of the troupe had appeared now. Some of them crackled with oddly colored energy, just as Robin Hood had. Several, including a woman with round black eyes, didn't even seem to be human. Buffy was surrounded, but she was confident she could get away if that was what she wanted.

She took a quick glance back at Roland, saw the desperation there. He'd given up on himself. He wanted her to run. But now that Buffy had seen him again, had looked into his eyes again, she could never leave. No matter what he was, she knew for certain now that there was a soul in there.

"I'm not going anywhere without you," she told him.

King Richard laughed, deep and cruel.

"Kill her."

Chapter 10

JAMIE ANDERSON SMELLED LIKE WHISKEY. OR, AT LEAST, Cordelia guessed that was the smell. It was all generic booze stench to her, and it wasn't at all pleasant. She prayed silently that the odor wouldn't linger in her car too long.

"It's just ahead," Mr. Anderson told her.

Cordelia guided the car to the curb, and kept her mouth shut. Whacked out or not, he was still a cop. She didn't think it was a good idea for people to know that some of Mr. Giles's female students were quite familiar with the way to his house. As had so frequently been pointed out, Cordelia was born without tact. She had no use for the gentle untruths that protected fragile egos. She didn't lie.

But she had found that there were times when it was best to say nothing.

Mr. Anderson got out of the car, but Cordelia paused with one leg out. She debated a moment, then thumbed the button to lower the window just an inch. She didn't want to have the car stolen, or the stereo, or the airbag. Anything. But she wanted to air out the stink as much as possible before getting back into the car.

She managed to wedge her keys into her pocket, then followed the man up the walkway to his building. He hadn't so much as glanced at her the entire ride over, and that didn't change now. Without a word, he held the gate for her, and Cordelia started up the steps to his apartment, letting Mr. Anderson follow her up.

At the top of the stairs, they turned right, and came to the door to Jamie's apartment. His big mass of keys jangled as he worked all three locks on the door, and then the door swung wide. Mr. Anderson stood aside to let Cordelia enter.

When she crossed the threshold, she felt a sudden and overwhelming sense of discomfort. It was one thing to have given him a ride in her car. It was another thing entirely to be in his home. She felt like she had walked right into his life in a way she didn't have any desire to do. She was in his living room, now. Not a stranger, but, at the very least, a new acquaintance.

Cordelia was smart enough to know when she was being selfish. Most of the time, like now, she didn't really care. Here was a man who, just a short while ago, had very seriously contemplated blasting his brains all over the ancient history section of the school library. He'd been chugging along toward death full speed ahead. The rest of them had gotten in the way, because that's what you were supposed to do.

But Cordelia didn't want to have to watch out for

him now. He was nothing to her. Some cop who lived in Giles's building. And in a less than immaculate apartment, to say the least. The place needed a serious hosing down, or a sandblasting, or whatever. The curtains were dingy, the carpet spotted, and the coffee table had so many condensation ring stains from bottles of beer and glasses of booze that it almost looked like the pattern was intentional.

She felt a bit queasy for a moment, and was very glad Giles had locked up Jamie Anderson's gun for the night. The guy seemed okay for the moment, but if he was still bent on taking his own life, Cordelia wasn't going to be able to stop him alone.

Creepy didn't even begin to describe the feeling that washed over her now. She didn't want to be there, didn't want to be personal with this man. Didn't want to know him or be concerned for him. She had enough people she'd foolishly allowed herself to become concerned about. Besides, he was obviously a bit unhinged. There was no way to know exactly what he'd do now.

He made them tea.

Cordelia stood by the window looking out, wondering if Xander and the others were all right. She sipped her chamomile and tried to focus on keeping the tangible distance that existed between herself and Mr. Anderson.

"Listen, I just wanted to say thank you," Jamie said, breaking a silence of several minutes.

"Hey, no problem," Cordelia replied. "It's not much of a drive."

"You know I'm not just talking about the ride," the man said.

Cordelia didn't want to hear the pathetic tone in his voice, the aching sadness there. But she couldn't help it. She'd so hoped that he would just try to be macho, and keep up a tough facade. *Maybe he just hurts too much,* she thought. To have his son back, and then lose him again so horribly.

She turned from the window and faced him. "You're welcome," she said, and walked over to sit by him and drink her tea. Cordelia put on a happy face and sat forward to give him her full attention.

"Tell me about your son," she said.

Jamie Anderson's red, bleary eyes widened and a weak smile played at the corners of his mouth.

"Ever since he could walk, he's always wanted to go out and have adventures," Mr. Anderson began.

Cordelia really listened.

The woods on the outskirts of Sunnydale were lined with pathways. Some were wide and well-trodden, others overgrown with disuse. Brian Anderson had rambled through these woods hundreds of times in his life, and yet somehow, when they'd brought him here, he'd recognized nothing.

There were still paths, he noted. But none of them were familiar. The air seemed lighter, like they were on top of a mountain, or something, and Brian found himself gasping for breath several times. Just something odd about the air. About the dark, and the way it kind of floated there, swirling in and out of trees that seemed about to bend over and grab him up with their gnarled limbs.

Brian was relieved that the weird swirling darkness, the . . . breathing dark, was only in the trees, up in the branches, and not flowing over the paths. He felt as if it were watching him somehow, that if it wanted to, it could reach out for him and . . . brrrr. He didn't want to be a prisoner, thrown across the saddle of a huge snorting horse. But Brian felt that there were other things out there in the forest that were even more dangerous, more savage.

Thankfully, he noticed that not all of the trees looked, well, evil. Several times, as they rode through the wood, they'd passed trees he recognized, including a particularly thick one he and his friends had always called "Big Ugly," and in which they'd once built a fort out of wood stolen from a new home construction site in Sunnydale.

And the clearing. He knew this clearing.

But it had never looked like this.

It was a wide field in the middle of the wood, with rock formations and a massive old oak spiking toward the sky. They'd made up wonderful fantasies when they were kids about the many reasons why ancient civilizations might have designed such a place. It did seem to have been made by design, actually. Carved, somehow, from the rest of the forest.

Now the clearing was overrun by creatures so dark they absorbed the light of the moon. Brian stood inside a large cage, fashioned from thick bamboo, with Treasure lying at his feet. She was unconscious, and no amount of trying to wake her had worked. Neither did he have any idea how the cage with them inside had been transported, but it wasn't as though he'd had much opportunity to ask questions.

Treasure looked horrible. The clothes she wore—what was left of them—were filthy rags. Her nails were broken and bleeding. He wasn't sure she had had anything to eat. Through the strips of fabric, he could see her ribs.

In spite of the unnatural darkness, Brian could see by the light of three large fires being tended by looming black figures. These were the things the English librarian dude had been talking about with him and his father. The Wild Hunt. They were the things that had thrown a net over him and dragged him away from his father.

It was real. It was true. It was happening.

To him.

The shadowy figures who were nurturing the fires around the clearing were Huntsmen. At the edges of the clearing, black dogs sniffed the dirt, tiny jets of flame spouting from their snouts with each breath. It had taken Brian some time to realize it, but their paws never touched the ground. Those were the hellhounds. The horses were much the same, with dark, glowing eyes and plumes of fire erupting from their nostrils. They were eerily tame, as if they merely awaited their master's command. Brian also saw at least seven different black deer, all huge bucks with massive racks of antlers.

And then there was the leader: the Erl King, who himself had antlers. It was a disturbing sight, once Brian realized that it wasn't merely some decorative head gear. There were few points, nothing like the bucks that ran with them, but the Lord of the Wild Hunt had horns growing from the sides of his head.

It wasn't enough that Brian saw it all, he had to smell it all as well. Ghosts or specters they might be, but the animals smelled real enough. So did the humans who were with the Hunt. Some rode horses, while others walked by the cage. Several who passed had given him and Treasure a look of great sadness, but most of them either laughed or took no notice of their situation at all.

"Shock?" the small voice said beside him.

Brian glanced over to see that Treasure had finally woken up completely. Her eyes looked like two bruises.

"It's Brian," he said. "My name's Brian."

Shock had seemed like such a cool name at the time. He was a rebel, living on the edge. Now all he wanted was to be home again, to put all that time on the streets behind him. But it didn't look like he was ever going to get a chance. Or a chance to work things out with his dad.

"What are they gonna do to us?" Treasure asked. When he looked into her wide, blackened eyes, he reminded himself how young she was.

"I don't know" was all he said.

Around them the riders of the Hunt began to stir, as if in response to some inaudible call to action. Brian had caught sight of several things that, even more so than the rest, terrified him.

The terror had begun when the Erl King grabbed him away from his father, but that had been only the beginning. Lurking in the woods, sliding in and out of tree branches, behind horses and Huntsmen, there were dozens of wraith-like things. Ghosts. They had to be, because they had form. They had faces. And they were quite obviously tied here, no less prisoners of the Erl King than Brian and Treasure were.

There were monsters. He couldn't think of any other way to describe them. Several abominable creatures. Maybe worse were the little green men. Savage little creatures the librarian had referred to as "dark faerie," whatever that meant. What was important, however, was that a short while ago, the Erl King had issued commands in a language Brian had never heard before, and nearly all of the little beasts had run off.

All but the few who capered about on the Erl King's face and horns, dropping down to his shoulders and onto the head of his horse, and cackling as if it were all a game.

In spite of it all, most of Brian's terror centered around the Erl King himself. He was huge, shoulders wider than his horse, and he had fur on his arms and face in great abundance. He was draped in layer after layer of fur, and hefted a large battleaxe in his hand.

The Erl King whistled. His many huntsmen mounted their horses and managed to form a rough semicircle, with him at the center. Once they had all gathered, the king opened his mouth, and for the first time, Brian heard him speak.

"Soon we will have what we came for. And our vengeance as well," the Erl King said. His voice was low, but it seemed to carry, filling every corner of the clearing, rising to the highest branch of the tallest tree. When he spoke, his words sounded as though they were layered over another sound, a low, deep growling that might have come from the throat of an angry wolf, but certainly not from a man.

More than ever, Brian was convinced the Erl King had never been a man.

"We ride now," the king said. "My own lash on the shoulders of any glutton. This place called to us, we belong here, and we have the ever-unfolding night in which to hunt here.

"First, though, to our captives."

Then the Erl King did something Brian had been praying he would never do. The horned man turned his burning gaze on Brian Anderson and, through a veil of thick, scraggly beard, the Erl King grinned.

"Now, let us see," the growling voice said, as the king rode toward them.

"Oh, my God!" Treasure shrieked. She got to her feet and threw herself against the cage, scrabbling mindlessly to get away.

Brian flailed for her, but he was rooted to the spot. He wanted to look at her, to tell her not to give up, that people would be looking for them. The cops had her locket. This Giles dude knew about occult things.

And his own father was looking for them, and his father would find him and save him.

He wanted to tell her all these things, but he couldn't tear his gaze away from the Erl King's blazing red eyes.

"I will speak plainly," the Erl King said, in a guttural snarl that caused Brian to gasp, then breathe quickly, in ragged intakes of air. "There is magic all around you here. Dark magic the likes of which the human mind cannot comprehend. If you would live, you may ride with the Hunt."

Brian stared in awe. "Ride? With the . . . Oh, God. You've gotta be kidding me."

The Erl King stared.

"Swear your fealty to me, forever, and with dark magic, you will be bound by that vow. Only then can I trust anyone to join the Hunt. But it is your only choice, children. Hunter, or hunted?"

Treasure began to cry in great, sobbing gasps for air. Tears streamed down her face as she tumbled to the floor of the cage and huddled facedown in the dirt.

"Please, just let us go," Brian begged. "We haven't done anything to you."

The Erl King's horse whinnied, sending a jet of flame spouting over Brian's head. It almost seemed as though the beast was laughing. Brian cried out in anger and fear and frustration and embarrassment, and then began to slam his forearms against the bamboo posts of the cage, though he hadn't a prayer of breaking them by himself.

"Very well," the Erl King rasped. "You stay in the cage."

Brian felt a wave of relief wash over him. He'd half expected to be set free and hunted, or just executed right there. It had bought him some time, he figured. Time to think. To plan.

"I'll . . . I'll go with you," Treasure whispered, so low that Brian hoped, prayed that the king had not heard it.

"Connie, no!" Brian said desperately, knowing that tone in her voice was the sound of despair and surrender.

Treasure was still crying, but the tears streamed silently down her cheeks now. The time for sobbing was done. When all hope was gone, there was no need for shouting and discord. Despair was quiet.

"Come, then, my pretty girl," the Erl King said, and the animal in his heart, some fundamental link to all that was savage in nature, roared its pleasure with each syllable.

Several of the horned man's servants came and removed Treasure from the cage, shoving Brian roughly to the hard bamboo bars on the ground. He smelled the cloying earth through the bars, and he smelled people. The filthy, terrified people who'd been in this cage before him, Treasure included.

He tried not to wonder where they all had gone.

After the door was shut behind her, Treasure was led to a horse, which she quickly mounted. He could hear her sniffling, putting away her tears.

She looked horrible. Her hair was greasy and stringy, her face a bruised, muddy mess. She looked like a little girl thrown away in a dumpster. Not a Treasure at all, but an object to be pitied.

"Do you swear your fealty to me, Lord of the Wild Hunt, bound by the laws of magic and nature, forevermore, young one?" the Erl King demanded.

"Y-yeah," Treasure stammered. "Yes, I do."

"What is your name?"

She paused a moment, as if she understood that what she said now would be her name for all eternity. Finally she spoke. "Treasure," she said, and Connie DeMarco was gone forever.

"Excellent," said the King. "Now, let us ride. And when we return, if the wee ones have done their job, perhaps there will be a wedding."

With the thunder of a thousand hooves, far too great a noise for the thirty-odd horses and bucks who ran through the night, the Wild Hunt had begun again.

As Brian watched, the trees seemed almost to open up, to swallow the Hunt, guiding their path toward Sunnydale. Treasure was gone. Brian had only one thought, now, as the dark creatures rushed toward town. He worried for his father.

The troupe of performers who surrounded Buffy— now revealed as witches and warlocks and monsters—were the same people who had run the Faire, but they looked quite different. Their clothes were contemporary—jeans and shirts, skirts and blouses—but old and faded. And where before they had seemed menacing, they now looked purely evil.

"Poor Robin tried to warn you off," fat King Richard said angrily. "He was the only one among us who might have given you that chance."

"Just my luck," Buffy said, and then ducked as a pair of muscular men who had previously been dressed for the Faire as knights rushed at her.

A sweep of her leg brought one of them down. Buffy followed through, coming up with her back to King Richard and her other attacker. She brought up her right hand, which held half of a broken wooden staff. It connected solidly with the knight's face, pulping nose and cracking bone.

There were too many of them, though. They circled warily now, but if they rushed her together, she wouldn't stand a chance. Buffy glanced around quickly, counted those who seemed to emanate any kind of weird energy. Three. Two women and a man.

Magic users first, she thought.

She ran at a woman to her left. From behind her, a man whose hair was blazing orange fire and whose hands were smoldering, with blue smoke billowing from his pores, came after her. His hands were raised, and Buffy smelled something awful, and realized she definitely did not want him touching her under any circumstances.

The woman straight ahead had a lavender glow in her eyes, and Buffy was ready to attack, prepared to duck whatever she might try. But the man with the blue, smoking hands was coming too close.

Buffy stopped short, spun, cocked back her arm, and let the broken pole fly from her hand in a perfect trajectory at the throat of the warlock with smoking hands. Only when the wooden shaft hit, and the man's eyes went wide, did Buffy recognize him as the thirsty man in the stocks whom she had tried to help. The man reached for his own throat, trying to understand how she had crushed his windpipe.

Whatever poisonous magic seeped from his own hands killed him instantly.

As the others looked on in horror, Buffy rushed suddenly back toward the woman with lavender eyes. She leaped, spun in the air, and kicked her in the side of the head hard enough to knock her unconscious. Then she had a clear field, or at least, an open path to the food stalls where she'd hidden out before. Buffy started to sprint, but her path was blocked suddenly by the old crone from whom Cordelia had bought her dress.

Except she wasn't quite human anymore. The old woman's skin was scaly and had a green hue. A forked tongue darted from her mouth and her fangs glistened with venom. One of her eyes remained the color of sour milk. The other, good eye was slitted like a lizard's.

"All is not what it seems, girl," she hissed.

"Nothing is what it seems, Granny," Buffy snapped.

She had to stay away from those venomous fangs, she knew. Buffy dove forward into a handspring, let her momentum carry her almost over, then used her upper body strength to drive both feet up into the snake woman's gut hard enough to pop some ribs.

Then she froze, focused, dropped to a crouch and

leaped straight up to land on the roof of the nearest of the food stalls.

Already they were moving in around her. She chanced a glance around, trying to spot Roland again. Incredibly, he was still standing by King Richard, tethered by a thin line, almost like a leash. The sight enraged her further. Buffy had been holding back, unsure what she was dealing with. It would be so much easier if they were just monsters, but she was pretty sure that at least most of them had been human once upon a time.

"Enough!" King Richard bellowed. "I'll kill her myself."

Now it was the obese ruler's turn to begin burning like a candle. A white light, tainted with a blood red, began to radiate from his chest as if he had a little bit of the sun there, coated with his own viscera. King Richard started to chant, and the light grew brighter.

Buffy kicked a serving wench in the head as the woman tried to climb onto the food stall's roof.

Richard chanted louder.

Then he cried out in pain.

Buffy narrowed her eyes, looking into the glare from the dimming glow of Richard's chest as the warlock stumbled. There, behind him, was Angel. He looked like hell, very ragged, and very pissed off.

Angel held a long aluminum baseball bat in both hands, and swung again at King Richard's back. The bat connected with a crack and the leader of this coven—or whatever it was—went down on his knees. Angel gave him a solid backhand to the side of his head. Richard went down on his belly, unconscious.

"Buffy!" Roland cried out in fear, shying away from Angel.

"He's a friend," Buffy confirmed, even as Angel snapped the leash that had been around Roland's neck.

A pair of serving wenches and three brawny men were on Angel almost instantly. But these were merely human, no magic there, and the vampire was more than strong enough to throw them off.

Buffy dropped down from the food stalls and whipped a roundhouse kick into the jaw of the man who'd sold them the tickets to the Faire. Then she scanned the grounds quickly. If she'd counted right, there was still someone conscious who was a magic user. Witch or warlock, she couldn't recall, and so she looked for anything that glowed. Anything at all, out of the ordinary.

There was a soft laugh, and Buffy spun to see the woman behind her. She lifted her hand and tiny sprigs of lightning seemed to web between her fingers and spread out from there, reaching for Buffy. Reaching for—

The woman began to scream and beat at her clothing. Buffy blinked and looked more closely. The ground around the witch was crawling with dark faerie. They swarmed over her, biting and clawing her until she fell under the sheer number of them. The onslaught was horrible.

"Angel!" Buffy shouted. "Take Roland and get out of here!"

She turned to run, batting at a pair of dark faerie who tried to latch onto her clothes. With the flickering light from the stage area behind, and the dim moonlight above, Buffy could see the members of the Faire troupe flailing at the creatures that tore into their flesh, going for their throats and other tender parts.

Buffy froze. She couldn't see Angel at all.

On the ground not far from her was an undulating mass of dark faerie. Their laughter was a cacophony that chilled the soul, and Buffy shivered. Then the mass rose, almost erupting from the ground, and she saw that it was Angel. He was almost completely covered with the creatures.

Somebody called her name, and Buffy turned to see that Roland had somehow been bound, and even now the faerie were carting him away. It must have taken dozens of them just to hold him up, but Roland was bound well. He wasn't going to escape without help.

But then there was Angel.

Buffy cursed loudly and began ripping the vicious little creatures off Angel, leaving small wounds and splashes of blood behind. She heard a bellow of rage behind her, and turned to see that King Richard had risen to his feet once more, covered in dark faerie. The bloody white light from his chest—*heart magic,* Buffy thought suddenly—burned at least a dozen of them to nothing but cinder and ash.

Sensing that threat, the faerie swarming over Angel began to withdraw, some attacking Richard, others running for the safety of the fence and the trees beyond.

"Are you all right?" Buffy asked Angel, staring at him intently.

"Not even close," he said, teeth gritted in pain. "But I will be. Meantime, we'd better catch up with your friend."

They started off after the dark faerie and Roland as fast as Angel could move.

Chapter 11

VIENNA WAS ONLY A LITTLE DRUNK WHEN SHE WALKED out of the Bronze. Bruno was on the door tonight, and she stumbled over to plant a wet and very deep kiss on his mouth. He shook his head and laughed when she was done.

"You're crazy, girl," he said. "Go home."

"I hate going home alone," Vienna replied, batting her lashes at him.

"Stick around an hour and I'll walk you," Bruno offered.

Vienna smiled, shrugged. Bruno was a nice guy. He was a little older than she was, but who was she kidding. At twenty-two, Vienna was over the hill compared to most of the girls at the Bronze. And her whole goth thing was very much over. Still, she liked the look. The straight black Morticia Addams hair, pale skin and bright red lipstick suited her. Plenty of guys had thought so, too.

Bruno thought so. She could see it in his eyes.

"You know where I live?" she asked him.

"Yeah."

"I'll be up if you want to come by, Bruno. That'd be nice," she said, and touched him on the arm lightly. He really was a nice guy.

Vienna pushed past him, walked off with long strides that showed off her long pale legs under the too-short skirt. She didn't look back, but she knew Bruno was watching. Vienna smiled to herself. *Tomorrow*, she thought, *I'll start the job search again*.

After she made Bruno breakfast.

"Evening, little lady."

In the shadows beyond the dumpster, a gaunt old man leered at her. She ignored him, keeping her eyes straight ahead and walking a little faster. *Homeless old pervo,* she thought.

Then something clicked in her head, and she realized that she'd recognized him. It was Old Man Sayre. He lived just a few doors down from her grandmother. She almost stopped, wondering if something was wrong with him, but then her self-preservation instinct kicked in. If he was whispering to girls a quarter his age—okay, maybe a third—from shadowy corners . . . well he might not be homeless, but he was still probably an old pervo.

Vienna rolled her eyes. Was she going to have a story to tell Gramma. She chuckled softly.

A powerful hand clamped down on her shoulder tightly enough to crack bone.

"Dammit! Let go of me!" Vienna shouted, and turned, fingers bent into claws, to tear into her attacker's face. But Old Man Sayre's face had changed. His yellow eyes glowed, and his teeth . . .

The better to eat you with my dear.

Vienna screamed.

Old Man Sayre grabbed her by the hair and stared into her eyes as he moved his mouth down toward her neck. Then she saw only the white hair on his head, and felt teeth sharp as needles punching through the flesh of her throat.

Her legs went weak, but Old Man Sayre held her up. Sucked on her.

Bruno was shouting her name, his voice coming closer.

At first she thought the thundering, the rhythmic pounding, was his boots on the pavement. She was losing blood, her mind growing fuzzy and dim, but the sound wasn't just footsteps. It was more like an old-time train pumping along at full speed, like in the old westerns.

Westerns.

Not a train, then. Horses.

Old Man Sayre dropped her to the ground. She heard Bruno shouting at him, telling him to back off, asking her if she was okay. The thing that used to be Old Man Sayre told Bruno he was going to die for interfering with dinner.

Vienna wanted to cry, but she couldn't. And her head hurt from all the pounding. Didn't they hear the horses?

Bruno said, "Ohmigod," real quiet.

Old Man Sayre started to whimper like a frightened animal.

Vienna had just started to get up, still disoriented, and she looked up to see the terror on the old man's misshapen face. The fanged mouth made a huge *O*, and then a thick shaft of wood with feathers on one end—an arrow, impossible as it was—punched through Old Man Sayre's chest.

She watched him explode in a cloud of dust, and the arrow clattered to the ground. A wave of nausea swept over her, and Vienna fell to her knees again.

By the time she was able to stand and turn around, the sound of the horses had moved on, far down the street.

Bruno was gone.

Vienna stumbled back to the Bronze and waited while someone called an ambulance. She had a horrible feeling she was never going to see Bruno again.

It was the last time she ever went to the Bronze.

Most of Sunnydale was already asleep when the Hunt rode through the center of town. Hooves thundered and spectral flames burned. The hounds bayed. The Erl King roared his supremacy, and sang the song of the hopeless. And the hopeless came to him.

He was pleased.

Some of them would become Huntsmen. Few of those would last until the next hunt. He would kill them himself if they displeased him, or send them back to the Lodge with the others they'd collected, the suicides and the unloved children whose souls he'd stolen. And the ones foolish enough to dare to look upon the Wild Hunt, instead of showing the proper respect. All those would go, this very night, to the Lodge, where they would forever remain, to suffer eternal despair and misery.

But the hopeless, they were given a chance. Hunt or serve. Or die.

Hooves pounded pavement. The stench of sulphur spread from street to street. The dark faerie gabbled and the horses snorted. And the Hunters rode as if eternity had no meaning and held no fear for them.

Though the hunting in this place was excellent, most of the townspeople survived the night. Perhaps they turned over in their sleep and groaned. Perhaps they dreamed of shapes passing by their windows and galloping on their roofs. Perhaps in the morning, they felt exhausted and anxious. But more than anyplace the Hunt had ever visited, the people of Sunnydale paid little attention to the Hunt. As if, in some unconscious way, they understood what was out there on the streets. As if they knew they were better off keeping their doors locked and their eyes closed.

Better for them. Most of them would still be alive in the morning.

Still, though the Hunting was thin, the resident vampires proved great sport, and a handful of the Huntsmen diverted themselves for several hours by running many to ground and destroying them. That's all it was, however. Sport.

Once, long ago, a human girl had told the Erl King the true nature of vampires. They didn't belong to any world, not this one nor the world beyond where the Wild Hunt traveled eternally. The undead were soulless, and as such, abominations in the eyes of the Erl King and his Huntsmen. When they were found, they were killed as a matter of course.

As the Wild Hunt rode, the Erl King went to the new girl, Treasure, and offered her his hunting horn. She placed it to her lips, and trumpeted her new life with every bit of breath she could muster.

The King thought that this Treasure might survive the night. The more he watched her, the more he began to wonder if he might not make even greater use of her.

"Giles."

"Hmm."

"Giles."

"Hmm?"

"Buffy is on a runaway train barreling headlong toward a horrible, fiery demise. While, given the choice, I wouldn't want to trade places with her, I'd really like to help her get off the train. And as opposed to sitting here in the library being as useful as a confessional in Congress, it'd be a toss up, honestly. Fiery demise. Watching Giles read. Definite coin toss. And you're not listening to a word I'm saying."

Without warning, Xander began to sing. Loudly and badly. The theme from *Friends*. It was apparently the most annoying song he could think of on the spur of the moment.

"Xander?" Giles asked, horrified. "What is . . . did you say something about a train?"

The Watcher was saved Xander's reply by Oz and Willow, who pushed hurriedly through the library doors. Giles looked up and instantly noted the frustration on their faces. And for the first time since Giles had met Oz, the young man seemed positively galvanized. Face flushed to match his hair—which was reddish orange this month—he held Willow's hand tightly, fingers laced through hers, as if he might never let her go.

"No luck with Angel?" Giles asked.

"Luck. Sort of," Oz replied.

"We found Angel . . . and a hundred and one ugly little green guys who tried to eat us. And him,"

Willow said breathily, eyes darting around with a realistic paranoia about her surroundings they had all become familiar with, and fallen victim to at one time or another. She paused, tilted her head slightly, and added, "We got away."

"Indeed," Giles said.

"And the part where you found Angel?" Xander asked.

"When we told him where Buffy went, he had us stop the van and just took off," Willow said. "Without, y'know, bothering to tell us anything useful."

"We're wondering if he figured out some connection between those little faerie guys and the people at King Richard's," Oz suggested. "Buffy was on that riff. When we told him so, he booked big-time."

"In case anyone wanted to know, my brain is a mass of melted gray slag," Xander volunteered. "I still don't have any idea where there's a connection between the hungry critters, the crazy Faire people, the dirt boy, this Wild Hunt thing, and well, anything."

"Well, we do live on . . ." Willow began.

"Okay, just stop now, Will," Xander snapped. "The old we-live-on-the-Hellmouth excuse is handy, but sometimes it just isn't enough, you know?"

"Witness me stopping with the handy dandy excuse," Willow said, without much self-recrimination, then looked at Giles. "Have you heard from Buffy?"

"I called and spoke to her mother," Giles said. "It seems Buffy's new friend, Roland, was forcibly taken from her home. One would assume by the actors from the Faire who had mistreated him."

"Actors," Xander sniffed.

"So Angel's on a wild Buffy chase?" Oz asked.

"He's always been rather successful at tracking her in the past," Giles said. "We've had to assume that Buffy would have gone after Roland and were merely waiting for the rest of you to return before deciding upon a course of action. I daresay I'm relieved to know that Angel is likely to be with her, but we should move along now and try to catch up with them. We'll take my car," Giles added.

"Really, no," Xander said.

"Why doesn't Oz drive?" Willow suggested simultaneously.

Giles sighed.

In the van Willow glanced at Giles. "So," she said, "have you come up with anything we can use?"

Giles raised his eyebrows and removed his glasses. "In fact, I've learned a great deal these past few hours. This isn't the first time a Slayer has crossed paths with the Wild Hunt. It's happened several times, most recently in 1865, with a girl named Lucy Hanover. According to the journal of her Watcher, Miss Hanover spent several nights slaughtering many of the dark faerie before the Hunt itself rode through the small town in Virginia where she was living at that time. It lasted only a single night. Deaths and disappearances in the town that night were nearly as high as for the entire rest of the year."

"Which doesn't add much at all to what we already knew," Xander said, as he and Willow bounced around in the back of the van.

"But it only lasted one night," Oz pointed out. "So we're in the clear, right?"

"It's possible, but I doubt it," Giles replied. "Not if you were all attacked again tonight."

Oz only nodded at that, taking it in as he watched for the turnoff for Route 17, streetlights flashing across the windshield in syncopated rhythm.

"And this other Slayer, Lucy, couldn't stop them?" Willow asked, disturbed. "She couldn't do anything?"

"She was the first Chosen One who was a slacker," Xander suggested.

"No, actually," Giles said regretfully. "Lucy Hanover, though short-lived, was quite an effective Slayer." He paused, weighing his words. "Apparently, the night the Wild Hunt rode through, she disappeared and did not appear again for several weeks. When she returned, she told her Watcher that she had been taken and that she had later escaped by slaying several of the Huntsmen while the Erl King was away from their camp, which she called 'the Lodge.'"

"But that's good, right?" Willow asked. "They can be killed."

"Unfortunately, according to his journal, Lucy's Watcher thought that the Slayer was lying, though he never knew why," Giles said, and wondered if his features revealed how deeply distressing he found this information.

"Miss Hanover did, however, confirm that the Erl King is indeed also known as Hern the Hunter, so perhaps we have a bit more to go on," Giles added.

There was a silence of several seconds as each of them looked to the other. Xander ran out of patience first.

"All right," he said, and paused. "And now that we've exhausted our research angles, we're going to . . . ?"

"First we must get to the bottom of this situation with Roland," Giles said. "I've never seen a homunculus before. It should be fascinating. When that is done, I suppose we try to find the nest of these dark faerie or the camp of the Wild Hunt."

"Is that really a smart thing to do?" Willow ventured.

"I don't see what other choice we have." Giles wouldn't meet her gaze.

"Guys," Oz said slowly. "Don't look now, but . . . man . . . hold on!"

He cut the wheel violently to the right and the van slewed sideways across the road, momentarily tilting on to two wheels. Willow and Xander, in the back of the van, tumbled against each other. The front wheels bumped up over the sidewalk and the fender bent a street sign back to a ninety-degree angle before the van came to a stop.

From beneath the hood came the hiss of several ruptured hoses and who knew what else. The odd ringing of metal on pavement reached the van as a hubcap that had originally been on a Cadillac rolled away and then spun to a halt on the street.

But beyond that, there were other sounds.

Giles had struck his head on the dash, and a small trickle of blood flowed down through his eyebrow and onto the bridge of his nose. He blinked several times, looked up, and through the windshield he saw them.

"Good God," he whispered, but could not turn away.

Behind him, he heard Willow and Xander muttering and was about to tell them not to look when both of them swore.

"I told you not to look," Oz said, rubbing his shoulder where the seat belt had cut in.

"Get us out of here!" Giles said.

But it was too late. The Wild Hunt had turned and was coming toward them. The Erl King, Hern the Hunter, led the way. There were at least a dozen horses, perhaps ten bucks, but the way the ground shook beneath them it might have been a herd of buffalo. A panama hat none of them had ever seen before tumbled off a stack of Oz's things and slid to the floor of the van. The van trembled as if it were caught in an earthquake.

This was worse.

Oz turned the key, there was a grinding sound, but the engine wouldn't turn over. *This is going to cost,* he thought absurdly, and then he forgot all about the van. The passenger window shattered, and the rear doors were torn open as if they were made of soggy cardboard.

Fear seemed to wash over the van, to electrify and paralyze all those inside it. But Oz couldn't afford to freeze. Willow needed him. Then Willow screamed.

That did it.

Oz popped his seat belt, turned and was about to lunge into the backseat. Giles grabbed him by the shoulder and pinned him back to the driver's seat with one arm, covering Oz's eyes with the other.

"Did you *look?*" Giles shouted.

"I saw them!" Oz said angrily, trying to pry him off. Giles was grabbed from behind.

"But only for a moment, and you turned away!" Giles yelled in desperation. "You paid obeisance, by their rules. You turned your head and did not *look.*"

Oz tried to say something. He couldn't see into the back of the van. Xander was cursing and then gave out a shout of pain. Willow shouted for Oz. Giles grunted and his hands dragged against Oz's body.

"Don't open your eyes!" Giles said.

What? Oz's heart nearly stopped. "But Willow . . ."

"If you want to save her, keep your bloody eyes shut!" Giles roared. "Find Angel and Buffy. It's the only way to save us now!"

Then Giles's voice was gone. There was shouting, and a horrible smell, and a kind of howling that made even Oz's skin crawl. He thought he heard Willow calling his name, and he bit his lip hard enough to make it bleed.

Silence now. The van was empty.

Oz growled. "Bastards."

Cordelia thought for sure that Jamie Anderson was asleep. His eyes were closed and his mouth was open, his head back, and though he wasn't snoring, the rhythm of his breathing was slow and even. She envied him. Even if she wasn't so wired after the past couple of days' weirdness, there was no way she would have been able to sleep. Not here. Cordelia had a hard time going to sleep anywhere but her own bed.

Or a very expensive hotel room, preferably one her parents had paid for, somewhere the real tourist rabble had yet to discover.

Sigh. The thought of clear, ice blue Aegean Sea water gave her pause. She fantasized a moment, and then moved on. For now, there was senior year to think of. After that . . . Cordelia could almost envision a permanent Mediterranean vacation, maybe with Xander as her cabana boy. But for now, there was school, and the tremendously inconvenient Hellmouth.

Meanwhile, she was planted in a reclining leather chair, sipping a mug of tea, and waiting for the cabana boy or Giles to call and tell her what was going on. She wondered if they'd forgotten about her, or if things had simply gotten as chaotic as usual and they hadn't had a chance to clue her in. If that was the case, Cordy really didn't mind. Sure, Mr. Anderson had every cable channel ever invented, including one that made Cordelia blush deeply, and sure, all she kept doing was switching from channel to channel trying to find something to hold her attention.

But that was better than battling—or more than likely, running from—the forces of darkness any day of the week.

She clicked over to Nickelodeon, and caught the very beginning of a "first Darrin" episode of *Bewitched,* a series she and her mother had bonded over while Cordelia was growing up. Sure, it had been canceled back in the Stone Age, but that was what cable was for. Why else was Xander always talking about Scooby Doo?

"You tell 'im, Endora," Cordy whispered to the TV, as Samantha's scheming mother tried to get first-Darrin to toe the line. Endora always said exactly what she thought. And she was right, too. Here was this beautiful, smart, funny, captivating woman with magical powers who'd fallen in love with a decent-looking but otherwise totally inept and skinny geek.

Boy, could she relate.

Cordelia had the volume on low because she didn't want to wake up Mr. Anderson. The window was open, and every once in a while, the sound of a car passing by would drown out the TV, but she didn't bother to turn it up. She heard the sound of a truck rumbling down the street, and she strained to hear, even though a commercial had come on. The truck was incredibly loud, rumbling, annoying her enough to make her think about actually rising from the chair long enough to close the window. But, no, it would pass.

Only it didn't.

Her tea mug trembled, was jostled to the edge of the end table, and then fell over, shattering on the hard wood floor.

Jamie Anderson sat up straight, eyes wide, staring around in confusion. He probably thought it was an earthquake.

Cordelia had already figured out what it wasn't.

It wasn't a truck. And it wasn't an earthquake.

The hounds began to howl and she could even hear some of the horses snorting and whinnying. Someone blew a hunting horn—Cordelia had heard them before when her father had gone fox hunting with a duke or somebody in England. But this was no fox hunt.

"It's them, isn't it?" Mr. Anderson asked, staring at her with wide eyes and a sweaty sheen on his forehead, though it was kind of chilly in the apartment.

Cordelia nodded, trying desperately to pretend that she wasn't terrified. Maybe if she could convince herself, then the drunken officer would believe her as well.

"I think if we just stay here, we should be all right," she said, hoping she was right. "Giles was pretty clear; there are rules these hunters have to follow. Just stay put. We'll be all right as long as we don't look at them."

The hounds barked and howled as they went by, and the horses' hooves were like a brutal drum roll on the street outside. *They're passing by right now,* Cordelia thought. A few seconds more, and she could actually begin to breathe again. Maybe her heart would start to beat. Maybe she could open her eyes.

At the moment, she had them tightly closed. No need to take chances.

So it wasn't until she heard a thump and the sound of Jamie Anderson cursing under his breath after barking his shin on the coffee table that she realized he was moving. He was up. He was headed for the window.

He was going to look.

"No!" Cordelia yelled.

She was up from the chair and after him in an instant. He was a big man, much bigger than Cordy, and he knew how to fight. But it was as though every ounce of fight that had ever been in the man was long gone. The wind could have sucked him right out the window, then. As Cordelia lunged after him, he reached for the dingy curtains covering the window that looked down on the street. He never made it. She'd never tackled anybody before, but Cordelia did a fine job of it, locking her hands tightly around his chest and using momentum to tumble the man off his feet.

"What are you doing?" Jamie shouted. "If I look at them, they'll take me! I'll still be alive, and I can see Brian! Maybe I can rescue him!"

"You're just going to get yourself killed," Cordelia shouted at him. "Trust me when I say that is not the best plan if you want to see your son again. We'll find another way, all right? If there's a way to do it, Buffy and Giles will figure it out. Just give them time. Just tonight!"

Jamie looked at her, eyes red and puffy, and he shook his head sheepishly. He opened his mouth to say something, perhaps to apologize, Cordelia thought. But he never managed to come out with those words. From outside, there came a loud wailing like dozens of people crying and shouting in pain and calling for help. The sound of horses was fading, but the cries of the Hunt's captives still echoed their complaints.

"Do you hear it?" Mr. Anderson asked cautiously, as though afraid Cordelia might not have heard the chorus of agony and fear after all.

But she heard it all too well, and wished she didn't. For among the screams and shouts and cries, there was a voice Cordelia thought she recognized.

"Xander?" she whispered to the darkness outside the open window.

The thunder of hooves was fading. Cordelia buried her face in her hands, wiping tears from her cheeks.

"Oh, God, Xander."

"Lions and tigers and bears," Buffy said in a low voice.

"Oh my." Angel smiled thinly. He liked surprising her, and he was certain that an affection for *The Wizard of Oz* wasn't among the list of things she knew about him for fact.

They hurried as fast as possible, pursuing the dark faerie who had literally stolen Roland out from under their noses at the Faire. That made sense to Buffy. He was a runaway, so the Hunt would want him. But where were the Hunters? And where were the faerie taking him?

It was less than a mile and a half to Route 17 from the fairgrounds. Buffy and Angel, despite their injuries and exhaustion, made it in record time.

There were no cars on the highway at this time of night. Buffy thought they would have to turn east, but Angel was tracking Roland, and instead of turning one way or the other, he simply continued across the highway and dropped down the embankment into a gulley on the other side.

"Not far now," Angel said quietly.

They stood at the edge of a thick forest, so dark within that it was hard for Buffy to see past the first few trees. Beyond the first few trees, the forest seemed to undulate with a darkness more profound than mere night. Almost as if it were breathing.

"Next we're going to have talking trees and flying monkeys," Buffy said dejectedly, wishing they could avoid the creepy, dark forest altogether.

"How about werewolves?" a voice said behind them.

Buffy spun, ready to fight. Up at the edge of Route 17, just where they'd come over the embankment, stood a very human but intense-looking Oz. The tranquility that always seemed to guide him was completely gone. *Nothing ever seems to phase Oz,* Buffy thought.

At least until now.

Chapter 12

CORDELIA HELD HER HAIR AWAY FROM HER FACE WITH one hand, hung her head over the sink in Mr. Anderson's bathroom and splashed water on her face. She had cried so hard that her makeup had been completely ruined. Mascara streaks like skid marks had run down her face. After scrabbling through the grimy medicine cabinet, the racks on the inside of the linen closet door, and under the sink—very gross—Cordelia had managed to find one very old, very crusted jar of Pond's cold cream. No, thanks. She'd pass.

She splashed cold water on her face yet again, then reached for a dry handtowel she'd gotten from the linen closet after she'd shaken it to get the dust out. Cordelia pushed her fingers through her hair, then looked at herself in the mirror. Despite the crying jag she'd been on only minutes ago, her eyes were clear and alert. She wore no makeup. Without a scrunchy to pull her hair up into a ponytail, she was forced to use a rubber band she'd taken from the bathroom doorknob. Of course, she rinsed it well in the sink first. And slathered it with the cold cream to prevent hair damage. Everyone knew regular rubber bands could destroy smooth hair follicles . . .

Mr. Anderson was on the phone in the living room when Cordelia came out of the bathroom. She waited patiently for him to notice her. As soon as he had, he nodded politely and told whomever was on the other line that he would see them in the morning.

"That was Liz DeMarco," he said as he settled the handpiece back in its cradle. "Her daughter, Connie, has been missing for a while. Liz runs the local runaway shelter. We're going to have breakfast in the morning. I told her I'd push harder for a special task force at the department. I need to help her, but I can't tell her, can I?"

Cordelia wasn't happy with the fact that she had to appear in public—well, in front of him—without any makeup on, but sacrifices had to be made. "Lots of kids, you know, really do run away," she offered. "Maybe you'll just find her."

"I told her I'd go back through my contacts. See if I can turn anything up."

She sensed that he was desperately seeking some kind of encouragement.

"That's great," Cordelia offered, and meant it. "She didn't mind you calling this late?"

"I called her at the shelter," Jamie explained. "She almost never goes home until after midnight, or so she says. But that husband of hers . . ."

He cleared his throat as if catching himself saying something he shouldn't. "Liz told me your friend's mother is planning a big meeting at the school. Joyce Summers. She wants to try to get the parents more involved with the situation. The runaway situation, I mean."

Oh, that'll help just oodles, Cordelia thought acidly. With great effort, she managed to keep her opinion to herself.

"Liz also said her daughter knew you."

Cordelia went through her mental photo album of everyone who was anyone at school—plus Xander and his friends, of course, *who are now my friends, I guess*—*shudder*—and came up empty.

"Maybe she did," she said, shrugging. "We probably had a class together."

"Well, from what Liz said, Connie admired you."

Cordelia only nodded. No surprise there. It was her responsibility—one she had taken upon herself—to be a role model for other girls.

They sat for a moment in silence. Mr. Anderson looked like he was going to fall back into his depressed mode and she searched for a way to distract him.

"About Brian," she began.

"Don't," Mr. Anderson said, holding up one hand like a traffic cop. "I'm dealing with it as best I can. I'm sorry to have made things more difficult for you. I know Rupert and that girl . . ."

"Buffy."

". . . are doing everything they can. I won't even pretend to understand any of it, but I know you're right about me . . . getting myself killed. I've been a cop for a lot of years, but I've never seen anything like this . . . Hunt, or whatever it is. It isn't something you learn on the job. But I'm smart enough to know it's way out of my league. Rupert knows about this kind of thing, and . . ."

The man trailed off, seemed to deflate a bit, and sank down on the sofa. "Maybe in the morning, when I'm sober, I'll get my head together, figure out a way to explain it to the lieutenant enough to get a search going. For now . . . just thank you, I guess."

Cordelia crossed her arms. "You're welcome."

She studied him closely, saw the exhaustion on his face, and read that as a serious intent to get some sleep and not try to do anything stupid until the sun came up.

"I have to go."

Mr. Anderson blinked. Nodded. "Thanks for staying with me. I'm sure your . . . I'm sure your parents must be worried about you. You should go home."

"Sure," Cordelia agreed. "So you'll be all right, then?"

"Maybe in the morning," Jamie replied sadly. "For now, I'll settle for asleep."

"Can I use your phone?"

Moments later Jamie Anderson had shut the door to his bedroom and left Cordelia to use the phone and let herself out.

She dialed, then listened through four rings until a click indicated someone had picked up on the other end. A sleepy voice said, "Where are you, Cordelia?"

"Hey, Mom!" she said, with a levity she did not feel. "Willow and I just finished studying, and we're totally brain-drained. I'm just gonna crash here, okay?"

There was a long pause on the other end of the line, and for a moment, Cordelia wondered if her mother had fallen back to sleep.

"Are you out with that Harris boy again?"

Cordelia could hear the disdain in her mother's voice. As a rule, she didn't lie, but she'd had to lie to her mother so much since Buffy and the others came into her life. Lies were stupid and hurtful, and Cordelia hated them. But this time she wished desperately that she had a lie to tell.

"No, Mom," she said, fighting the tears that threatened to come again. "I'm not with Xander."

"Do you promise?"

"I promise, Mom, yes. God!"

"This is the last time, Cordelia," her mother said flatly, sounding quite awake now. "From now on, when you want to spend the night at a friend's, I want to know beforehand. When you live on your own, you'll have to live by your own standards, but as long as you live under our roof, your father and I make the rules."

"Don't I know it," Cordelia said, with a venom she hardly felt. The conversation had been repeated so often, it was almost as though the lines simply had to be said.

"Don't get smart with me, Cordelia," her mother snapped.

"Sorry, Mom. I'll be home early, okay?"

"You and Willow have fun, but don't stay up too late. You need your beauty sleep," her mother said.

Cordelia rolled her eyes at the phone.

"Don't we all," she said tersely. " 'Night, Mom."

"Good night, honey."

* * *

Cordelia stumbled as she climbed in through Buffy's bedroom window. It wasn't as easy as the Slayer made it look. She'd have a bruise on her right knee in the morning, no question about that.

On her feet once more, Cordy started by going through Buffy's closet. *Buffy actually has a couple of decent outfits,* Cordelia noted, surprised. *But, ew, what is this on this sweater? Blood?*

Cordelia made it a rule to throw out all the clothes monsters, demons, and other assorted creatures of the night had bled on, drooled on, or in other ways expired on. Bloodstains were next to impossible to get rid of, but let's face it, there was no secret Martha Stewart remedy for any of the various slimey, oozy, gooey things that occasionally got sprayed on her.

Grimacing at the sweater, sparing a moment to wonder if Buffy's knee boots would fit her, she moved to Buffy's bureau. Socks, underwear, stockings, workout clothes. Lots of workout clothes. Knee pads. Shin guards. Ace bandages.

Ah.

In the lower left drawer she found what she was looking for.

Sort of.

There were a few stakes, two crosses, three plastic bottles of what she could only assume was holy water, and a pair of spiked brass knuckles Cordelia had never seen her use. She stared at the odd collection for a few moments before carefully removing the brass knuckles and a container of holy water not much bigger than a bottle of nail polish. That, she slipped into her pocket. The brass knuckles, she had no idea what to do with. She tried to fit them into the other front pocket on her pants, but they were too big, and

Cordelia ended up dropping the hunk of metal on the floor with a loud clank.

She cursed silently and picked them up, just holding on to them for the moment. Cordy glanced around Buffy's room, trying to figure out where the girl kept her major weapons, particularly the crossbow. That was what Cordelia had come in looking for in the first place. Idly, she wondered if she should check the closet again.

The door opened.

"Buffy, I've told you that you don't need to climb through the . . ." Joyce Summers began, then froze when she saw Cordelia standing in the middle of her daughter's bedroom with a pair of brass knuckles in her hand. Buffy's mom wore a bathrobe and carried a paperback book—some tawdry Hollywood romance by the look of the cover.

"Cordelia?"

"I'm sorry, Mrs. Summers," Cordy said quickly. "I just . . . I didn't want to wake you, and . . ."

Joyce's expression changed from surprise to horror and despair, her features crumbling down until she looked almost disoriented.

"She's in trouble, isn't she?" Joyce asked, staring. "If she was . . . if she was dead, you'd have just come to the door. But she's in trouble, right?"

Cordelia shook her head, moved over to put a hand on Mrs. Summers's shoulder as the woman sat down on her daughter's bed.

"No," Cordelia said. "Or, at least, not that I know of. But Xander *is* in trouble and I don't know where Buffy is and I can't just let them . . . I can't wait for her to show up."

Relief washed over the woman's face, followed by

concern, and now it was Joyce's turn to reach out for Cordelia. "Is there anything I can do?" she asked.

"I don't know if there's anything *I* can do," Cordelia replied. "But I can't *not* try."

Joyce paused for several seconds, staring at nothing off in the corner of her daughter's room. When she spoke, she didn't even look up.

"It's really as bad as she says, isn't it?" Mrs. Summers asked. "Here, I mean. Sunnydale."

"Yeah. It is."

"Then why do we stay?" Joyce asked, looking puzzled and slightly overwhelmed. "Why does anyone stay? Why don't you find a way to get your parents out of this place?"

Cordelia pondered that for a moment, but only a moment. In truth, it was a question she'd posed to herself many times.

"This is my home," she answered. "Lame, I know. But I live here. I'm not letting some slimy hell-beast take that away from me. I'm not, like, a hero or something, but I'm not running away, either. Buffy's different, though. You guys moved here, *you* could move away. Except that Buffy can't. Her being the Chosen One and all."

Joyce laughed bitterly. "I told Liz DeMarco I'd organize a big meeting at the school. Mobilize the adults. Oh, I'd never tell them, of course." She pressed a shaky hand against her forehead. "It's really ridiculous, isn't it. Futile."

Cordelia bit her lower lip to keep herself from speaking.

When Buffy's mother stayed silent, Cordelia moved back toward the window.

"You can go out the front door, Cordelia," Joyce Summers said.

Cordelia sighed and walked to the bedroom door. "When you see her, tell her I love her, will you?"

"Sure," Cordy said softly. "No problem."

When she left, Joyce was still sitting on her daughter's bed, staring at nothing.

Brian felt numb. He suspected it was from concentrating so fiercely on trying not to cry. He was too old to cry. The Hunt had returned, pounded into the clearing only moments ago, with captives aplenty and various and sundry wildlife they had killed on their ride. The clearing was drenched with the odors of sweat and fear, sulphur and smoke.

And blood.

They had opened his cage and put him to work instantly. From the back of a frothing, snorting black stallion—an unnatural thing nothing like a real horse—he had pulled the body of a small brown and white deer. As ordered, he cut it open and threw it on the ground near the edge of the clearing.

Of Treasure there was no sign, and he was terrified that they had killed her.

The hounds tore the dead deer to shreds, consuming each bit, even the bones, which were seared by the fire from their nostrils even as they ate.

The horses were fed as well, from supplies that seemed to have come from nowhere. Their feed was a revolting combination of rotting grain and some kind of bloody meat. His mind raced to his missing friend, and he closed his eyes and gagged.

Now he cleaned blood and gristle off an axe one of

the Huntsmen had handed him. Human or animal, he didn't know. Nor did he want to.

Brian heard shouting. He turned, scanned the clearing. One of the fires was out, but the other two provided enough illumination. That, and the glow from the opening at the other end of the clearing. And though it was an opening, it sure didn't look like one. Instead of some kind of portal or door or gate, there was simply a bit of thick dark mist there. Already, he had seen corpses and prisoners trotted through that mist on foot or on horseback, carried or shepherded by a Huntsman. Only the Huntsmen ever returned.

Again he heard shouting. The new prisoners were struggling. Arguing. He was surprised that Hern had not executed them immediately. The Erl King had proven himself terribly impatient.

Then, through the thickening crowd, past the stamping horses, a huge black buck moved out of the way and Brian could see the face of the prisoner who was creating the disturbance.

"Oh, no," he whispered to himself.

Brian felt the weight of the axe in his hands and hefted it, glanced at it, then began walking toward the Huntsmen and their captives. His rage grew, his fear grew, and his despair grew until he began to raise the huge war blade over his head.

A strong hand landed on his shoulder, spun him around hard enough to knock the axe from his hand. It clipped his forehead, slicing into his scalp, as it went down.

"Shock, what are you doing?" Treasure demanded.

She was visibly changed. He stared at her, at the loose linen shirt and brown stitched leather pants that had replaced her old clothes. At the blaze in her eyes, and the way she stood tall. At the flecks of blood that dotted her right cheek and forehead.

"Treasure?" he asked. "Connie?"

"Don't call me that," she said angrily. "And leave the prisoners alone. I want to keep you alive, Shock. You're my friend. I still care about that. But you have to be useful to stay alive around here. And you have to keep your mouth shut."

Brian glanced once in the direction where he'd seen the librarian dude, Mr. Giles. Then he turned away, and went back to work. He paid no attention to the small trickles of blood rolling like tears down the side of his face.

He didn't want to attract attention.

Some of the prisoners were screaming. Some were crying. Many were unconscious. Bleeding. Dying. Wispy things moved just out of sight, caught in peripheral vision a moment before moving on. Ghosts. Spirits. Suicides and worse.

All were being herded toward the thick, dark mist that roiled in and about itself at one end of the clearing. All but a small group who stood off to one side, aimlessly staring at nothing, like patients at an asylum.

They look as though they've already given up all hope of escape, Willow thought. Or, as if it had never occurred to them. Several of them were being moved into a wicker cage, and did not protest at all.

"Move along, now," Hern the Hunter roared. "Take the prisoners to the Lodge and return straight away. There is still work to be done this night. Vengeance to be had."

"Kingdoms to save and women to love," Xander

whispered halfheartedly, rubbing a sizable knot on his forehead.

Willow knew she was meant to laugh, or at least smile, but she couldn't do either. Xander was trying to be funny, but Willow knew that he felt the terror just as strongly as she did—a profound, irrational fear that had swept over them in the van and caused her to sweat and sob as they were carried here to the woods. Something about the Hunt caused it, and not merely the horror at being captured by such creatures. There was something about them, a fear pheromone or something.

It hadn't worn off, but logic could beat it. Sort of. If she could break it down, study the biological reaction, understand what was happening, well . . . the fear wouldn't go away, but she could put it aside enough to focus on what was happening.

The pain helped, too.

She'd been hit in the side several times, and was finding it hard to breathe now. She wondered if they'd broken some of her ribs.

At her side Giles trudged with his head high, eyes darting around, studying the Huntsmen and their animals. It was amazing to Willow that his glasses hadn't been broken or lost. *Just luck,* she guessed.

Then she did smile, wanly, to herself. Some luck.

They all had their hands bound behind their backs with rope. They were herded like cattle, Huntsmen around them with sharp implements of all sorts. Herded toward that mist. Willow didn't understand much about what was going on, but she knew one thing with absolute certainty: she did not want to see the Lodge of the Wild Hunt.

"Giles, we've got to do something," she whispered.

The Erl King continued to snap and bray his orders and all throughout the camp, they were obeyed instantly.

"What can we do, Will?" Xander rasped, his voice low. "I mean, except for waiting for a chance to make a break for it."

"We can't do that, either, Xander," Giles said. "We've got to help these other people as well."

Xander felt like laughing. More than laughing, actually. He felt as though this insane giggle that was building in his gut and in his brain would bubble up and overflow right out of his mouth. His eyes were wide as he glanced around, and he bit his lip to keep the giggle in. If he could keep that laugh down, maybe he wouldn't be so scared, he thought.

And he was scared. No question. The woods just weren't normal. They'd all noticed it, he was sure, but even Giles hadn't said anything about it. The trees were almost leering at them, bent over the path they had followed into this clearing as if they might begin to speak, to move, at any time. Something huge and white had roared off in the forest as they passed, and two Huntsmen had gone off in search of it, but come back empty-handed.

But it wasn't just the trees and it wasn't the weird creatures that roamed all around. Now that they were back at the encampment, the darkness that ebbed and flowed in the trees had receded a bit. The hounds no longer bayed and the horses snorted only from time to time. Only their hooves, soft on a bed of dirt and twigs and stone, made any noise at all.

The silence was worse than the clamor of the Hunt. With the horn and the hounds and the hooves pounding, he had been able to look at them as physical enemies. Somebody he could punch.

Tough guy. What a joke.

In the relative silence now, he looked around and saw the reality. They weren't simple physical things he could fight. The beasts were dead, or they had been dead before something brought them back. And not any vampire, either. This was a whole other kind of living death. Some of the Huntsmen were like that as well. Others were elves or something, but not any kind of nice, sweet, bright, pointy-eared elves like the ones in the fantasy novels he'd read in junior high.

Xander allowed himself to admit, in spite of his fear or perhaps because of it, that whatever this place was, it wasn't really the forest at the edge of Route 17. Oh, it occupied the same space. The clearing was there, but . . . somehow it had all been changed or merged with whatever primeval forest the Wild Hunt made their camp in.

Already, Xander felt as if he was gone from home. Gone from the world he'd known. They were being marched toward the dark, swirling, oily mist at the other end of the clearing, and he knew, as his heart raced with jackhammer terror, that once they passed through that mist, they would truly be gone. He'd never see home again.

To Xander's intense amazement, he realized how badly he wanted to see his home again. His room. X-Men poster on the wall, swim team photo in a drawer somewhere. Dirty socks next to the bed and an array of only slightly preworn clothes scattered about, ready to be worn again.

Home.

Even Mom and Dad. If he had the opportunity to

eat cold shrimp fried rice from a small white carton at three in the morning with his mother again, Xander promised himself he would take it. He might not have the most caring parents in the world, but they were all he had.

He missed them.

He didn't want to die.

A group of Huntsmen were still astride black horses, and they rode alongside the line of prisoners like cattle rustlers. The Erl King followed behind them, overseeing everything that happened in the camp. They had all noted how hairy he was, almost like a huge bear walking like a man. Willow stared at the horns that jutted from his head. There had been some debate over whether they were part of his helmet or came right out of his skull. Willow was convinced they were all natural.

Like the devil's.

The Erl King turned to ride back to the center of camp, eyes blazing. Willow figured it was now or never. She turned, about to step into his path, but Giles nudged her back. Instead, the Watcher turned to the huge beast man on his black horse and stared at him in open disdain.

"King of the Elves and Lord of the Wild Hunt, Horned Man and Hunter, know me and my name," Giles shouted.

The Erl King drew his horse to a stop. It snorted flames down at Giles, but the Watcher did not turn away.

"You are Hern," Giles said. "My name is Rupert Giles. I am the Watcher, and you are not my liege. I defy you."

From his hip, Hern the Hunter slowly drew a long ebony blade.

"How dare you?" he drawled angrily, voice and hand quaking with his rage.

Willow had no idea what Giles was doing. Had no idea if even he knew what he was doing and was terrified that he was going to get them all eviscerated immediately, but she had demanded that he do something, and here it was. She had to back him up.

"My name is Willow Rosenberg, and you are not my liege!" Willow yelled. "I defy you!"

She glanced at Xander quickly. His eyes darted from her to Giles and back again, and he looked like he might throw up. But he stepped forward.

"My name is Alexander Harris, and you are not my liege!" Xander said, his voice uncertain. But then his eyes narrowed and he raised his voice louder. "I defy you!"

The Erl King began to laugh, loud and deep and long. His laugh was cruel, and when he stopped, it was with a suddenness that Willow took to mean he had not truly been amused at all. Fire snorted from his nostrils, just as it did from the horses' and hounds', and Willow knew for certain then that he had never really been human.

"Feed them to the hounds," the Erl King said.

"Oh, dear," Giles muttered.

Whatever he'd hoped would happen obviously hadn't panned out. But now that they had the Erl King's attention, there was no way Willow was going to let it go at that.

The hounds began to bark and howl and run across the clearing, several of them snuffling the ground as if their prey had to be tracked. Long rivulets of saliva fell from their hanging tongues. Willow shivered as she saw that their paws did not throw dirt up from the ground. Their paws did not even touch the ground, but floated spectrally above the soil.

"Run!" Xander yelled.

Willow intercepted him, forcing him to stand his ground, and looked up at the Erl King. Her refusal to flee had gotten her noticed. The King stared down at her.

"Lucy Hanover sends her best," Willow said in a low, even voice.

In the blazing, pupil-less eyes of the Lord of the Wild Hunt, Willow saw surprise. For a moment, the face seemed to soften.

Willow prayed.

The forest seemed different, somehow. Buffy couldn't quite put her finger on it, and she hadn't ever really explored the woods here, but the whole place seemed somehow more . . . wild than she'd expected. The floor of the perimeter was littered with tangled roots and brambles that seemed to grab hold of her as she walked past. They hadn't really even entered yet. Instead, they were walking around the outer edges, trying to find or glimpse something even remotely resembling a path.

It smelled different. Forests generally had many smells—pungent, moist earth; growing things; and yes, a few dying things, but this was something that, when she inhaled it, warned her to stay away. It was a primitive, atavistic reaction, one she had to fight to ignore.

There was also the issue of the darkness. Just beyond the first line of trees, the darkness in the forest looked different. More textured, somehow, as if it floated there through some illusion. As though it had been placed there with purpose.

She shivered and tried not to think about it.

"They had to have had a path in order to carry Roland through this tangle," Oz said, his concern for Willow plain in every word.

A moment later Angel pointed. "Here."

They joined him twenty yards ahead, and Buffy saw instantly what he was talking about. Not only were the trees much less crowded here, but there were signs that something had been dragged or carried over the ground there not long before. A little army of dark faerie would do the trick.

"Stay together," Buffy said.

And they went in.

Less than twenty feet into the forest, the trees thinned and an actual path presented itself. It wasn't well trodden, but it was open and obvious enough to indicate that it led somewhere.

"Now we're getting some place," Angel said quietly.

Buffy blinked in surprise. His voice had a familiar and quite discomforting growl to it, and she looked over to see that his face had changed. Yellow eyes blazed and fangs gleamed: the vampire was ascendant.

"What?" he asked. But he saw the look in her eyes. Angel reached up to run the fingers of his right hand over his features. He looked puzzled. Clearly he hadn't brought the change on himself. That worried Buffy.

"I don't get it," he said.

"Something about this place," she replied. "There's

magic here. I can almost sense it. It's leaking all through the forest, like radiation out of a nuclear accident."

"Welcome to the supernatural Chernobyl, kids," Oz said quietly and without humor.

They walked on another thirty yards or so. Things moved in the woods, and several times Buffy thought she saw shapes moving deep in the forest. A tall white creature far off moved in a rolling apelike gait through the green. They heard the thump of hooves once, but it was nothing like the Hunt and it moved away quickly.

Buffy thought she heard a flute.

Then Oz grunted in pain and doubled over, holding on to his stomach as though he'd been shot in the gut. She called his name, and Angel knelt down beside him.

"What is it?" the vampire asked.

"I . . . don't know," Oz stammered. "But I think I'm . . . okay . . . I'm okay now."

When he stood up, Oz looked even angrier than before. His face seemed to be curled into a snarl, and Buffy wasn't sure she liked that at all. She kept an eye on him as they walked, but a few yards farther up the path, Oz stopped and pointed into the woods.

"This way," he said. "They took Roland this way."

"How can you tell?" she asked.

"I can smell them."

Buffy's heart leaped, but she didn't question. Instead, they followed Oz as he forged his way through the thick undergrowth. After a short time he knelt and sniffed the ground.

"They're close," Oz growled.

"Do you think they know we're following them?"

Angel asked quietly. He looked at Buffy, and then at Oz. She shook her head. She didn't know what was up with Oz either.

"Maybe they don't care," Oz replied.

Buffy felt a small drop on her cheek and wiped it away. She glanced up, trying to see the clouds through the branches, and her eyes widened.

"Uh, guys?" she whispered. "They care."

The dark faerie began raining down on them from the trees.

Oz tore into them. He could never remember moving this fast, but then, he'd never been so frightened for another person before. He loved Willow, and he wasn't going to let anything get in the way of his getting her back. Especially not these annoying little critters.

Angel tore off into the woods, bashing himself against one tree after another, scraping them off his body. Stamping them beneath his feet. After a moment, Oz couldn't see him anymore.

Buffy was in trouble. They were tangled in her hair, beating and slashing at her with talons. Oz tore as many of them off of her as he could, but then she was on her own. He had his own troubles. But Oz knew how to deal with these things.

He ignored the ones that were on him. Ignored the pain, focused away from it. Instead, he started to hunt them. He pulled them from the trees and stomped them on the ground. He chased after several, and a number of them fell away from him as he ran.

Some of them screamed as he chased them. They were frightened of him. Good. That was how he would beat them. Terrify the nasty little cowards. Oz chased them farther and farther into the woods. From somewhere far off, he heard a high pitched whistle, and all at once, the dark faerie retreated in a single effort, moving up into the trees and across the forest floor and heading north through the forest. They were a horrible sight, a tiny army of screaming and laughing green goblins scurrying over roots and underbrush—and all Oz could think of was a pack of rats swarming through a sewer.

Oz grabbed one last faerie in his fist, and pulped it with a squeeze.

Then they were gone.

He laughed, and the laugh came out as a choking snarl. He felt the sharpness of his teeth against his lips. Questioned the glee with which he had killed the things, and the ease of it as well.

Saw the fur on the back of his hands.

It wasn't the full moon. Not for a week. Yet somehow, Oz had begun to change. Begun, and stopped, somewhere between human and werewolf.

He opened his mouth and tried to tell himself that it was impossible.

What came out was a howl.

Chapter 13

A S THE SNARLING HOUNDS BORE DOWN ON THEM, Xander turned to run. He tugged as hard as he could at his bonds, and the rope cut into his wrists. But if he couldn't get his hands free enough to climb a tree or grab a stick to defend himself—or something—he didn't stand a chance of saving himself. Never mind Willow and Giles.

Speaking of whom, Xander couldn't help but notice that they weren't keeping up with him. He risked a quick glance over his shoulder.

He caught his foot on an exposed tree root and went down hard on the packed earth of the clearing, a stone scratching his cheek and soil sliding up his left nostril.

The hounds moved in.

Xander closed his eyes. Their searing breath burned the skin on the back of his neck. Their stench was unbelievable. He heard the clack of their fangs and then—

"Wait!" the Erl King roared. "Away the hounds!"

Xander opened his eyes in shock, wondering why he wasn't dead. Reluctantly, at the Erl King's command, the ghost dogs crept back toward the fire on the other side of the clearing. Xander rolled and awkwardly got to his feet.

Giles and Willow drifted toward him, and he toward them, until the three were more or less a unit again. The Erl King held the reins of his fire-breathing stallion and the beast carried him toward them. The king stopped just in front of them, and then he lowered his sword so that its tip was not far from Willow's right eye.

"What do you know of Lucy Hanover?" Hern the Hunter asked.

Willow seemed surprised and opened her mouth to respond.

"Don't tell him anything, Will!" Xander snapped.

Giles cleared his throat, but Xander shot him a look that he hoped said, *Trust me, I know what I'm doing.* In reality, of course, he had no idea what he was doing, but he did have a hunch. The Erl King would kill them, no doubt. And Xander had no idea where Willow had come up with that Lucy Hanover line, just grasping at straws same as he was, he figured. But it had bought them a few minutes of life.

Xander hoped he could buy some more.

"Still your tongue, whelp," the Erl King sneered, eyes burning as he leaned out of the saddle a bit. "Or I'll fry it for my dinner with . . ."

"Yeah, I know, some fava beans and a nice Chianti," Xander said, his voice sounding a bit crazed, even to him.

Good. Maybe the king would think he was completely nuts and have pity on him. Maybe, but not freakin' likely.

The king slipped from his horse with the sound of leather on leather, and landed heavily on the ground. He was huge. Over seven feet tall, not counting the horns. Around his eyes, one of the few places where the thick fur did not grow, the Hunter's skin was oily black and raw as a wound. Xander thought there was blood on his horns. Then he didn't want to look anymore.

"What do you know of Lucy Hanover?" the Erl King demanded once more. "Speak, now, or you will die."

Xander swallowed, hesitated. But only for a moment.

"Go on, then, kill us!" he said, and then he did something that took every ounce of control he had over his own body: he stepped toward the Erl King.

"Xander!" Giles hissed.

Willow glanced at him, eyes wide with terror. He couldn't hear the whimper in her throat over the pounding of his heart, but he knew that it was there.

The Erl King swung his sword toward Xander. Flame blew from the man-beast's nostrils and he lifted the blade into the air.

"You were gonna kill us anyway," Xander said hurriedly. "What difference does it make? We've got a message for you from Lucy Hanover, big fella. You want it, you've got to let us go."

The sword wavered in the air. The Erl King growled, "Lucy Hanover has been dead for a century."

"I know plenty of dead people," Xander said dismissively. "What, you never talk to dead people?"

Giles and Willow stared at him as though he were insane. Xander shrugged, still smirking arrogantly. Whatever worked.

"If your words please me, I will let you live," said the Erl King.

"I don't think so, Hernie." Xander shook his head and rolled his eyes, and reminded himself not to push it. "Whatever honor is worth to you, we need your word that you'll free us. In fact, I think you better let my friends go right now, and I'll give you the message myself."

The Erl King began to laugh, and then Xander knew he had pushed it too far. Asked for too much, and in doing so, as well as admitted he was bluffing.

"Fine," he said, scrambling for something, anything, to distract the Lord of the Hunt. "I guess you don't want her back, then."

Hern the Hunter stopped laughing. Xander blinked. It was the reaction he was hoping for, but he sensed something he hadn't expected at all. The King wanted the long dead Lucy Hanover back, but not because she had escaped from him. It was obvious that he wanted her back because, somehow, incredibly, he missed her.

As the huge creature stared down at Xander, silence blanketed the clearing. Then, suddenly, it was broken by a murmur and the loud cackling of a hundred tiny voices. The Erl King turned, glanced across the clearing, then seemed to rise up and stand even taller, if that were possible.

"Ah," he said, "Roland is returned. We shall let him decide."

"Thank God," Xander whispered, allowing himself to relax the tiniest bit.

"But, why Roland—" Giles began, then realized he was revealing his own ignorance. He clamped his mouth shut.

It was too late. The Watcher had managed to get the Erl King's attention again. The king looked at them, narrowed his eyes, and laughed.

"You know nothing," he said in a snarl. "But I will tell you because it pleases me to speak of my son." He leaned foward over the saddle of his mount and regarded each of them in turn.

"Though she could never have borne him in the natural way, the Slayer gave up part of her essence, her soul, what makes her human, so that Roland could be born."

They watched as Roland shook free of the dark faerie and, staring petulantly at the ground, walked toward the Erl King without any fear.

"In every way that matters," the king said quietly, "Lucy Hanover was Roland's mother."

The sad-looking boy stopped in front of the Erl King. He glanced at Willow and Xander and Giles, nodded to acknowledge that he had recognized them, and looked up at Hern briefly before turning his eyes down once more.

"If you run away again, I shall kill you," the Erl King warned grimly.

Roland glared at him.

"Yes, Father."

Ira Rosenberg missed Johnny Carson. All these other late-night faces seemed like hucksters to him. Johnny had been like a friend of the family. When he'd laughed, you knew it was real. Now there was nothing like that on TV, particularly late at night. Though he hated the smut, Ira had gotten cable just so he'd have something to watch on the nights when he couldn't sleep. Reruns of *The Dick Van Dyke Show* were a particular favorite. That Morey Amsterdam got him laughing every time.

"Ira?"

He turned in his La-Z-Boy to see that his wife had come in, rubbing sleep from her eyes. She pulled her robe tight around herself.

"Willow still hasn't come in?"

"Not yet, dear," Ira said. "Didn't she say she was going to be studying late at Buffy's?"

"That's what she said," Mrs. Rosenberg confirmed, then clucked her tongue as she sat on the arm of the La-Z-Boy. "It isn't that I don't trust her, Ira. She's a good girl. But with this Oz, and those crucifixes a while ago . . . and after all the trouble the Summers girl has been in, I just worry. She used to talk to me."

Ira patted his wife's hand. "Willow's a good girl, sweetheart," he said. "She's just growing up. She's almost an adult now. When she goes away to college, we won't be able to watch out for her anymore. She'll have to make these choices for herself."

She sighed. "Maybe we've come down too hard on her lately. Her first boyfriend, a musician." She gave him a look. "Maybe she's rebelling."

He paused, looked into the eyes of his wife. "I was hard on that boy. Fathers are supposed to be."

"Yes." She sighed. "But it seems like it's all gone by so fast."

He nodded. "I miss it too. The way she depended on us. The way her eyes lit up when I came home from work. But that's what happens. Kids grow up. Their eyes don't get quite as bright. They start to question whether or not their parents are actually the wisest people in the world."

"I know," she replied. "I know it happens, I've felt

it happening from the day she was born. I've been preparing myself for Willow leaving for a long time. But sometimes it just feels like she's already gone, and I'm not ready yet."

"Not ready for her to grow up, you mean?" Ira asked, head bowed with sympathy.

"I suppose that's what it is," his wife admitted, smiling a bit sheepishly.

"I don't think I'll ever be ready for that," Ira confessed, and smiled broadly. "And, yes, I'm worried that she's out so late. And, yes, I'm going to yell at her if I'm still awake when she comes home, because that's what parents do. And she's going to get defensive, because that's what teenagers do. And you know what? I'm going to enjoy it, because even that's something I'm going to miss."

Mrs. Rosenberg laughed. "You know, Ira? You should have been a rabbi."

"True. Very true."

She laughed again, then slid off the arm into the chair with her husband, where they kept each other warm, and laughed together as they watched Dick Van Dyke in black and white, and thought about simpler days.

During the attack, Angel had gotten separated from Oz and Buffy. Oz, in his changed form, had matched the dark faerie in their savagery, routing them and running them down. He was not very worried about Oz. But Buffy . . .

He reminded himself that she was the Slayer, and she would want him to stay on the trail of the Hunt. It was most likely that she would too, and he would probably meet up with her somewhere soon. At least, that was what he kept telling himself.

Angel stood waist-high in clinging nettles and tangled undergrowth, nothing like a forest in southern California, inhaling a strange scent that reminded him all too well of the grave. This place was . . . touched, as they used to say in Galway. It was not right. Something had blanketed it with dark magics; something had come forth and possessed it.

"Buffy!" he called. "Oz!"

Silence.

He moved forward slowly, searching for the path, refusing to be distracted by wondering about the others. Refusing to be distracted by the feeling of eyes on him, watching with predator's eyes. He didn't smell anything nearby, nothing but the trees. Angel wondered if the darkness itself were watching him from where it slithered in and out of tree branches above his head.

With a shudder, Angel pushed his way through a low spread of branches, and glanced ahead, trying to orient himself. Without Oz to lead the way, Angel simply had to follow his instincts. They'd always worked for him before, and this time was no different. It wasn't long before he knew he was on the trail of the dark faerie again.

Alert to any movement around him, he moved as silently as his sense of urgency would allow. Though the dark faerie were a problem, mainly because of their numbers, he had no other recourse. It might already be too late to save Giles and Willow and Xander, but he had to try. And there was still no telling what had become of Oz and Buffy.

But as surely as he had found the path, Angel felt it was all going to come together when they finally found the Erl King and the Wild Hunt.

His mind was on that and focused on looking for

any little things that might jump from the trees to attack him, when he heard a growl from the deep woods off to his right. Angel crouched and grabbed a long tree branch, splintered and sharp on one end. He stared into the trees, the forest dark even to his eyes.

"Come out, whatever you are!" he snarled.

The growl came again, followed by a single word.

"Relax." Oz stepped out of the trees, but Angel only knew him because of his voice. And the fact that he didn't know any other werewolves.

"New look for you," Angel noted. "But it isn't your time of the month, is it?"

"I stopped myself halfway. Even brought myself part of the way back. It helps to be able to talk. Don't know why it's happening, though. It must be this place," Oz said, his voice a low rumble. "There's magic in the air," he added, a whimsical note in his growl.

"Yeah," Angel agreed. "It's Disneyland."

In silence, they fell into step together, following the trail of the dark faerie. It occurred to Angel what an odd team they made, but he decided not to mention it. He didn't know Oz that well, and he might be sensitive about the whole werewolf thing. Angel had had plenty of time to get used to being a vampire. Oz had been a werewolf for less than a year.

"You hear something?" Oz asked.

Angel listened, and was about to say no, when a howl split the darkness like lightning. Angel strained to figure out the direction it had come from, but it seemed to echo, bouncing off the night, off the trees.

Then it didn't matter where it had come from. Because the howl was replaced by a chorus of growling and barking and baying that was all around them. For the second time in minutes, they were surrounded.

This time, by six huge black hounds whose eyes burned with fire. Smoke rose from their mouths as they panted eagerly and growled deep in their throats.

"There are too many," Oz snarled.

Angel tensed. "Kill them quick."

The hounds lunged as one, moving in, jaws snapping, nostrils blazing.

"If they can be . . ." Oz began.

Angel didn't hear the rest. The dogs were upon them. He launched himself forward, and kicked with all his strength up into the throat of the hound closest to him. The thing yelped, flying backward, and rolled into the trees.

"They can be hurt!" Angel shouted over the growling, though he had no idea if Oz would hear him.

Powerful jaws clamped onto his left arm, razor fangs sinking deep into his flesh. He was already ravaged, flesh torn over every part of his body from several run-ins with the dark faerie. But this was something else. Angel let out a cry of agony, and turned in time to see a third hound leaping for him. Even as the other hung from his arm, worrying the flesh with its teeth, he grabbed the newcomer, mid-leap, around the throat. He roared in pain and fury, choking it, then threw it against a tree. He was gratified by the sounds of bones snapping.

Angel grabbed the snout of the beast whose jaws were locked onto his forearm. He pulled, trying to tear it off him, and the pain was horrible. Teeth scraped bone. It wasn't working.

He heard Oz growling and turned to see that he'd changed a bit more, become more of the wolf, and was even now gutting a black hound with his claws. Fire blazed up from the belly of the beast.

Then he knew the things could die.

Lifting the thing by the same arm it was tearing up, Angel used his free hand to choke it, driving his fingers deep into the flesh of its throat. Its grip weakened, but it still did not give up. He bared his fangs, hissing in pain, and gave in almost completely to the vampire inside. Angel dipped his head and sank his own teeth into the dog's throat.

Fire spurted from its veins and burned his mouth and tongue, shot down his throat. The hellhound let go. With both hands, he brought it down over his knee, shattering its back.

Even as he let it go, one of the others bit into his right leg. He didn't waste any time, but used both hands to tear its jaws away. Then another was there, snapping at him, and then he couldn't focus on one long enough to kill it.

"Oz, can I get a hand?" he rasped through his scorched throat.

Oz only growled. Angel risked a glance over and saw that the werewolf was busy with two huge hounds of his own. Two down, four to go, and from Angel's perspective, the home team was losing ground fast. He batted one of the hounds away, but the other had leaped high, snapping for his throat. Angel turned, lost his balance, and went down.

The hounds were on him, then. He felt teeth through his jacket, and the tug of its bite, as he lost a bit of flesh to the animal.

"Get off!" Angel snarled, and threw one of them aside.

It was back too quickly. He cursed under his breath. Things were not going well.

He looked into the fiery eyes of the hounds as he

held them back, barely. He felt the blaze of their breath on his face, singeing his eyebrows and hair. Angel knew he had to think of something fast.

Without warning, a spurt of water splashed across the hounds, and they howled in pain. A second splash, part of which dappled Angel's face, and he knew what had hurt them.

Holy water. It burned his face in several spots like acid.

But the hounds were running off into the woods. Oz, bloodied but a bit more human looking than before, was just climbing to his knees several feet away. A hand clamped to his savaged arm—he'd have to wrap that up good, get it to heal faster—Angel looked into the darkness of the trees on the other side, eyebrows raised.

"Man, Buffy, you sure know how to make an entrance," he said.

"Please," Cordelia said, stepping out of the dark. "I dress way better than her."

Buffy had picked up the trail of the dark faerie several minutes after they'd run off. She was hurting pretty badly, and still bleeding in several places from superficial wounds she'd received from the nasty little creatures. She wished that she hadn't been separated from Angel and Oz. Angel, at least, could take care of himself. But Willow would kill her if she let anything happen to Oz.

Still, he'd seemed to have access to his lycanthropic senses in these woods, so Buffy had to just move on and hope that they'd all be reunited as they kept on after the dark faerie.

As she moved through the woods, and the pain

from her wounds began to numb, she started to think about the actual danger the faerie represented. She had no real weapons and would probably have to face the savage little things as well as the Huntsmen, and the Erl King himself. Buffy was realistic. Those were absurd odds.

She glanced around and saw a thick branch that had been broken off a nearby oak tree. After snapping off the smaller branches that jutted from it, she broke several feet off one end. When she was done, she held five feet of thick oak in her hand. It would serve as both spear and fighting staff, if necessary. Not much of a weapon, but in her hands, capable of doing a great deal of damage.

The path left by the dark faerie had grown erratic. Almost as if there were more of them, or they were more spread out. It had changed somehow, but she followed it anyway. She'd run out of other options. In truth, she had begun to lose hope when she heard a rustling in the woods ahead.

As quietly as she was able, she quickened her pace, the length of wood at the ready. The darkness was thick in the trees, almost as though it had been painted onto the air itself. Eyes narrowed, she peered ahead, trying to see what had made the rustling noise.

Suddenly the sound of hooves trampling underbrush shook the ground. Buffy turned the broken end of the branch up, held it as a spear, waited for the Wild Hunt. A face appeared from the darkness, a Huntsman, astride a short horse. It looked fierce and barely human, and it reared back and Buffy drew back the spear.

And froze, staring in astonishment.

This was not the Wild Hunt, but a single creature. Not horse and rider, but one being. *A centaur?* she thought. Half man and half horse, it reared up and struck her down with its forelegs. A heavy hoof slammed her shoulder and Buffy fell hard to the ground, crying out.

"You'll not have my hide, Huntsman!" the centaur said in a high-pitched, angry voice as it pranced threateningly close again.

"Wait!" Buffy cried, holding up a hand. "I'm not one of them. I'm not part of the Hunt!"

The centaur reared back again, but then let its hooves drop to the forest floor again. It backed up several paces, all four hooves on the ground, and Buffy got a good look at it for the first time. A horse, yes. But from the point where the horse's neck would rise grew the upper torso, arms, and head of a man. It scratched its head with one hand, and Buffy almost laughed, so normal was the action.

"No, you don't look like one of them, do you?" it said to itself. "What are you, then?"

"Just human," she said, standing painfully, keeping her distance.

It had brown hair and eyes, and a great deal of hair on its chest, and thick, muscular arms most human guys would have killed for. Buffy blinked, then shook her head in wonder. She'd seen a lot of things since she became the Slayer, weird things. But most of them had been horrible, evil things. It was a relief to see, for once, something beyond the natural world that was not trying to destroy humanity.

The centaur studied Buffy as it shifted its weight, then gave a stamp with its right rear leg. "No," it said. "Not just human. Something a bit more, but I can't quite put my hoof down on it."

Buffy raised her eyebrows. "So, you're not part of

the Wild Hunt? Then what are you doing here? Sunnydale isn't exactly known for its mythological creatures. At least, it isn't in the tourist brochure."

"You speak very strangely, girl, but you presume correctly. I am not of the Hunt. Rather, I am trying to stay ahead of them and out of the way. I don't want my head hung on the wall of the Lodge, like so many of my brothers and sisters." It stamped the earth again, took a step back and a rear hoof pawed the dirt.

"But how did you get here?" Buffy asked. "I don't understand."

The centaur smiled, shaking its head the way a horse shakes its mane. "It isn't for you to understand," it told her. "The Wild Hunt rides the night, as the first forest, the dark magic place of times past, rolls out across the wood along with them. There are a great many strange and wonderful creatures in this wood tonight, you can be sure. Things running from the Hunt. But we cannot pass outside the edges of the magic. We cannot leave the forest.

"And you? What do you want here, more than human girl?" it asked.

"The Hunt has taken my friends. I want to get them back. And make sure the Erl King leaves here," she said truthfully.

The centaur laughed, deep in its belly.

"One girl against the Wild Hunt?" it asked.

Far away, the sound of a horn tore through the night, set things flying in the trees above, set things moving in the darkness around them. Buffy glanced around, thought she saw several other strange things, but couldn't focus on any of them.

When she looked back at the centaur, there was fear on its face.

"You want to find them, there they are," it said, nodding to indicate the sound of the horn. "They camp in a clearing due north of here. But if you want to catch them, you'd better hurry. That horn means they've one more Hunt tonight."

Then it ran off, crashing through low branches without another word, to hide from the Erl King and his Huntsmen. Buffy watched it go in fascination and awe, and with a little bit of sadness as well. So much of her life of late had been dark and cruel magic, demons and spells, that it was a little piece of bliss for her to know that there was a simple and innocent side to magic as well.

After the centaur was gone, she wondered if she would ever see anything like it again. Wondered if anyone, even Giles, would believe her. Of course, she couldn't ever tell him about it if he didn't live through the night. Buffy set off due north, determined to stop this last Hunt, for old friends and new acquaintances alike.

But she decided that, no matter what happened, she'd keep this little meeting in the woods to herself.

Nobody was going to buy it. Not even for a minute.

She thought about what the centaur had said, about the Lodge, and grew angry. Buffy didn't know what Hern the Hunter looked like, but if he'd harmed any of her friends, or hurt Roland, who'd already suffered so much . . . well, there was a big spot on her bedroom wall where the Erl King's head was going to hang.

Chapter 14

FOR A MOMENT GILES SAW THE ENTIRE SCENE AROUND him as some horrible tableau—the Erl King triumphant, his poor, strange son in his tattered and ruined motley costume, defeated, as Giles and the others stood helplessly by. Then he closed ranks with the others as they were herded toward the large bamboo cage. Firelight flickered on the faces inside it, and he was reminded of Buffy's thirsty man in the stocks at the Faire: cracked lips, dull eyes, and so much suffering.

Dear Lord, that Faire seemed another world away. Another lifetime ago.

An eerie hunting horn sounded, and Giles slowed his pace and turned to see what would happen—what it signified.

"Move!" a dead-eyed Huntsman grunted, and shoved the Watcher from behind.

Giles stumbled and went down hard to his knees.

With his wrists tied painfully behind his back, there was little he could do in retaliation, even if he thought it was a viable option. Which, for the moment, it most certainly was not.

"Stop that at once!" Roland snapped at the Huntsman. "Get him up."

The Hunstman grunted and grabbed Giles's arm, nearly breaking it. Giles bit his lip to keep from crying out.

His captor looked—and smelled—like a dead man.

The Hunters were of two breeds. Perhaps a dozen of them were tall and thin, olive-skinned elfin creatures with dark hair and eyes, thin lips, and angular features. They had never been human, that was clear. The other Huntsmen had obviously been human, once upon a time. Their eyes glowed with scarlet malice. They were all different, one from the other. Men and women of various races, from vastly differing periods in history—from barbarians to samurai to modern day.

The man who towered over Giles had a long, filthy, shaggy beard and matted hair, but there were others who were clean-shaven, and Giles had seen a woman who was completely bald, with ugly tattoos marking her skull and talismans dangling from piercings all over her face and ears.

The Hunter looked at Roland and his eyes blazed a bright crimson a moment before he turned back to Giles. He leaned over and lifted Giles, one-handed, by his bound wrists, back to his feet. Giles couldn't stop himself from letting out a small cry of pain as the rope bit into his flesh.

This time, Roland said nothing, but he walked next to them until they came to a large bamboo cage inside which Willow and Xander stood with Jamie Anderson's son, Brian.

"Giles, are you all right?" Willow asked.

"Considering the circumstances? We're all still alive," he replied.

The Huntsman locked the cage behind Giles, glared at Roland again, and then moved away. Brian Anderson started to ask Giles something, but Giles shushed him and watched the Huntsman move off. Roland stood just outside the cage, his face both bitter and sad, and quite inhuman in the flickering of the firelight.

"Thank you for your intervention," Giles said cautiously.

Roland opened his mouth to reply, but closed it again as he was interrupted.

"Not that I'm not supremely grateful, pal," Xander said, moving against the bars of the cage to get as close as he could to Roland. "It's just, okay we're alive, but we're still here. And from what I gather, your horny pappy over there has no intention of letting us go."

The sadness on the boy's face was difficult to watch, and Giles glanced away a moment. He only looked back when Roland began to speak.

"You are to serve the Hunt," Roland explained, and looked at Willow and Xander particularly. "I'm . . . I truly am sorry. You and Buffy helped me without even being asked, came to my rescue when I had already started to believe I didn't deserve to be rescued."

"Okay, but now *we* need to be rescued," Xander pointed out, anger and desperation in his voice.

Giles shot a harsh glance at him. "You do have a talent for stating the obvious."

Willow wrapped her fingers around the bamboo bars, her face smeared with dirt and a streak of dried blood from a cut on her cheek. Brian Anderson had never seen Roland before, but he also came close to the edge of the cage. His hair was completely white now, his clothes tattered, spattered with blood Giles hoped was not the boy's own. *We are all quite pitiful,* Giles thought, himself included.

Roland only hung his head once more, soft brown eyes downcast. "I've done all I can," he said. "However I can help you, I will. But I am as much a captive here, in my way, as you are. I ran away, don't you understand? I wanted to know what kind of life the lightworlders led."

"Then the actors found you," Willow said. "The people from the Renaissance Faire?"

Roland nodded. "They were so nice at first. My friends. But they were never my friends. It was no accident that they found me. They're witches and warlocks . . . and worse, some of them. There's power in me. Not that I can use, not in any real way, except just to live. But having me around seemed to increase whatever magic they used."

"A kind of supernatural battery," Giles muttered, fascinated. He'd never heard of anything like it, but it seemed eminently plausible. "Since you are a homunculus, you're built to contain things, a vessel of sorts, yes? You must have accumulated magic from traveling with the Hunt all these years, a kind of reserve. It's only a theory of course, but it makes a certain amount of sense."

Xander was staring at him. "Could you stay on the issue, here?" he said desperately.

"Yes, sorry," Giles muttered, and looked back to

Roland, whose face was etched with pain and regret. "What is it?" he asked. "I'm sorry, have I said something . . ."

He let his words trail off. Giles had been tactless, and he knew it.

"A hamunkli?" Roland asked, softly. "I . . . I never knew there was a word for what I am. Are there . . . others like me?"

There was a bit of hope in the boy's eyes, and Giles couldn't bring himself to crush that hope.

"I don't know," he said. "I don't really know how you came to be. You have a soul, or spirit of some kind, yet no human parents, at least not in the sense of natural biology."

"I don't really understand it either," Roland admitted, uncomfortably shifting his weight. "My mother . . . gave part of herself, some of her life. Some of her dreams, my father said. He gave some of his own dreams and combined them, and then he put them in me."

"Your mother was Lucy Hanover?" Willow asked gently.

"I never knew her," Roland said.

"She was a Slayer, like Buffy," Willow explained.

"Just tell everyone, Will," Xander said, exasperated, and nodded toward Brian Anderson.

"Ignore me," Brian said. "I just want to get out of here. I'd like to get Treasure out of here, too. I mean Connie. Connie DeMarco. She rides with them now."

Roland sighed. "Treasure is to be my wife. Father has decreed it. He is the king and so it shall be. Upon our return to the Lodge, there will be a wedding. One day she will be Queen of the Hunt. My father would never let her go. He will never set any of you free. It just isn't done," Roland said regretfully.

"Then we'll free ourselves," Xander said.

Giles watched the prince of the Hunt carefully. Saw the tiny smile that played at the edges of Roland's lips.

"Nothing would make me happier," Roland said.

Then he turned and walked away, leaving them to whisper among themselves a dozen ideas for an escape attempt, none of which seemed remotely feasible. The camp was controlled chaos, but a chaos that contained dozens of beasts and men and supernatural beings whose only talent, only purpose, and only joy was hunting and killing their prey.

This is insane, Giles thought. A primitive asylum of caprice and bloodlust. Several horses snorted fire where they grazed nearby. Hounds bayed. Huntsmen grunted and roared battle cries. The fires crackled. The dark faerie cackled madly and capered, staging violent battles with one another that took them in a horde back and forth across the clearing.

Still, he would not give up. Somehow, they would find a way out.

The filthy, bearded Huntsman was called Lars. His stomach rumbling, Lars tore barely cooked flesh off a boar's leg with his teeth. He grunted, but was otherwise silent. The horn had been blown, a signal. The final Hunt in this place would commence soon, but it wasn't just the Hunt this time. No, there was vengeance to be had. Murder to be committed for a purpose. A novel event, to be sure. He looked forward to it.

He sat by the fire, enjoying the gristly meat, the way the flesh slid off the bone, the way bits of muscle hung on and had to be torn away. It was almost as pleasurable as the Hunt itself. A sound off in the trees distracted him, the snapping of a branch. Lars paused in his chewing. Glanced into the woods.

A smelly little dark faerie tore the boar's leg from his hands and scurried off toward the trees. *Little vermin,* he thought angrily. Distract him and steal his food. They were doing it all the time.

Lars shouted at the vicious green rodent to stop, to bring back his dinner, but the faerie ran into the forest where two others joined it. With a war cry, Lars snatched the battle axe from his belt and lurched into the forest after them, swinging toward the ground, but never even coming close to catching them. They moved swiftly through the dense tangle of undergrowth and into the trees, and then were gone, too fast for Lars.

Dejected, Lars sighed, and turned to walk back to the clearing. His eyes glowed red in the dark, and he reminded himself that he didn't really have to eat. He'd died centuries ago, by any human concept of the word. It was part of the ritual, part of the Hunt. But it was the part he liked best. Lars hated to miss dinner.

Another branch snapped off to his right. Lars lifted the axe, thinking the faerie had come back. Something moved behind him. Lars turned, and someone clubbed him in the face, shattering his nose and cracking his skull. The club slammed down on his head again and again, but Lars kept trying to rise, trying to lift his axe. The Erl King had promised him that once he joined the Hunt, he would hunt forever.

Then the club became a spear, its pointed end

slammed through his chest and pure, oily, roiling darkness came out in a thick mist, like blood on the water.

Lars would never hunt again.

Buffy hefted the axe for weight, nodded grimly, then relieved the Huntsman of his dagger as well. Or what was left of the Huntsman. The body had collapsed, almost caving in on itself to become a dry husk. The dark mist that came out of him floated up into trees and joined the seething, almost living darkness there, like mercury flowing together.

"Okay, that's creepy," Buffy said to herself.

But quietly.

She wouldn't want to ruin the surprise.

Moments later she stood at the edge of the clearing, behind a huge tree, and scanned the area, trying to decide on her first move. Too many Huntsmen. Too many dark faerie. Too many hounds. Even the big deer looked dangerous. She spotted the Erl King. He'd mounted his horse and was riding across the clearing toward a girl Buffy's age who seemed relatively normal except for her clothes. Not far away, Roland was running his hands over the mane of a black, fire-eyed stallion. He seemed to be whispering to it. Like the teenaged girl, Roland was dressed, now, like the Huntsmen, in leather and fur. But nothing so elegant as those words implied. These garments looked handmade, roughly tanned and sewn.

A slave again, Buffy thought. *Poor guy.*

Then she saw the cage. Her heart leaped as she realized Giles, Willow, and Xander were alive. But that was just the first step. The easy part. The hard part was keeping them that way. As stealthily as she was able, Buffy made her way through the trees around the clearing.

As she took another step forward, something crunched beneath her foot. She looked down, grimacing, at the crushed body of a dark faerie. After a second's hesitation, she reached down and smeared some of the creature's fluids on her clothes and face in an effort to mask her scent. She wrinkled her nose in disgust at the stench, like skunk spray, only worse.

She passed the horses where they were grazing in front of a stand of trees, and several of them started snorting and stamping. Buffy caught her breath and froze behind a tree trunk, waiting for the shouts of discovery. Nothing happened.

Then she crept foward, abandoning the safety of the trees and began to run.

One of the hounds started to bay, and she figured this time the jig was up.

There was nothing to do but go forward. If she stood out in the open like this, she would be noticed. But as she jogged on, the beast calmed and the moment passed.

She reached a clump of bushes and counted to one hundred before sprinting across the few feet to the back of the cage.

"Buffy!" Willow said in a hoarse whisper.

They were all there, with a guy she didn't recognize. Yeow. Pale face, white hair . . . for a split-second she almost thought it was Spike, a vampire who'd tried more than once to kill them all. Then she realized he was a human. A terrified human.

Willow looked as though she'd been crying, streaks on her grimy face. Xander had a big bruise on his forehead. Giles seemed supremely relieved. They were all bruised and bloody, but appeared otherwise intact. She glanced at the guy she didn't know, wondering how much she should say in front of him. Then she realized how stupid that thought was.

He was here. He knew the world wasn't what he'd thought it was.

"Buffy, thank God," Giles whispered.

"What happened to everyone else they captured?" Buffy asked in a low voice. "I don't see any other prisoners but you guys."

"The others were all taken through that mist," Willow explained, and Buffy looked over at the black fog that enshrouded the east end of the clearing. "It leads to wherever they come from, I guess. They call it the Lodge."

The guy Buffy didn't recognize came a bit closer to the bars. "I'm Brian."

"Buffy."

"There were a few others who were taken as servants, like me," he said. "Treasure . . . I mean, Connie, she joined the Hunt."

Connie DeMarco? Buffy blinked in surprise. That must have been the girl she'd seen.

"Why?"

He shook his head, his haunted eyes drifting away. "I don't know. They told us if we swore our loyalty, we could ride with them. That we wouldn't be prisoners." He moved his shoulders and sighed raggedly. "I figured out there, in here, what's the difference?"

Buffy agreed. She didn't understand how anyone could willingly join, could want to be a part of the Wild Hunt. But then she thought about Billy Fordham and his loser friends, all of whom had wanted to be vampires, and some had died for that fantasy.

"But you're a slave," she said. "Right? And she's a Hunter." And if slavery was the other alternative, maybe she could understand Connie's choice a little bit.

"Yeah." He looked hard at Buffy. "Listen, there were other people in here with me and Connie at first. But they . . . they didn't make it. The Erl King told us we're only allowed one mistake, and they already made theirs."

"Then we won't make any," Buffy said grimly, pushing her hair away from her eyes.

"Have you got anything you can use to get us out of here?" Giles asked her.

"I could break you out myself, I think," she said quickly, eyeing the bamboo. "But it's gonna make a lot of noise. If I can create some kind of distraction . . ."

Giles frowned. "You must be careful. The odds are too great. The Huntsmen and the Erl King are bad enough, but with the hounds and the dark faerie, you might as well be fighting an army."

"I'll stay clear of them," Buffy said, and pulled out the dagger she'd stolen from the Hunter she'd destroyed. She handed it through the bars to Giles. "Use this to break the lock or even cut through the bars. I'll draw them away, and then . . ."

"Buffy, what is it?" Willow asked.

The Slayer let out a long breath as she realized her plan wasn't going to work. "Nothing. It just occurred to me that I've got to wait until Roland is out of the center of the clearing. Do they put him in here with you?"

"What, the little dirt prince?" Xander asked, almost under his breath. "Sorry, Buff. He's one of them.

Let's concentrate on getting the actual humans out and let the evil fairy tale creatures fend for themselves, okay?"

Buffy stared at him, then glanced at Willow, who looked away. Giles adjusted the way his glasses sat on the bridge of his nose.

"It's a long story, Buffy," he said, "but Roland is the Erl King's son. It's only thanks to him that we weren't also taken to the Lodge. He had run away, and now . . ."

"Now they've taken him back," Buffy finished for him. "So he's still a prisoner, family or not, right?"

"Well, it's clear he'd rather be somewhere else, but he seems to be staying of his own free will. Though it's obvious there is some fear involved in that decision," Giles explained.

"Typical teenager," Xander said dismissively. "Parents are a little tough, so take off. Then the real world turns out to be tougher than you think and, hey, the parents don't seem so bad."

"The real world *is* tougher than you think," Brian said. He seemed to have folded in on himself. This discussion was personal for him, that much was obvious. Then Buffy realized who he was. Brian Anderson. The runaway.

"Sometimes Xander talks without putting much thought into it," Buffy told Brian, her tone gentle. "Sometimes he forgets who he's talking to. I left for a while, too. But this isn't like my life, or your life. Roland's father is evil for real, not just in his head. I'm not leaving here without hearing from him that he wants to stay."

Giles ran a hand through his hair, winced as he touched a bruise he had obviously forgotten. "I'm not certain that's at all wise," he said. "Trying to get to Roland could cost us all our lives, yours included, Buffy."

"Just be ready for my distraction," she said, and faded back into the trees.

When she was back on the south side of the clearing, as far away from the cage as she could get, Buffy surveyed the area once more. She noted the locations of the Huntsmen, the hounds, Roland, and the Erl King.

She thought about going deeper into the woods and shouting, drawing their attention, running through the trees. Imagined herself maybe taking one of the horses. *That might work,* she thought. She'd need one to outrun them. But she had no idea if the horses would let her ride, or try to throw her. Plus, that plan didn't leave any room for her to talk to Roland.

To create a distraction and get to Roland, Buffy thought, *there's really only one possible course of action.* Buffy braced herself, took a deep breath, crouched low, and ran into the clearing with the axe clutched in her right hand. She leaped over an exposed root and paused behind a stone formation that jutted from the earth.

Three Huntsmen were cleaning viscera from their weapons, grunting to each other as they sat around a flickering fire only a few yards away. Buffy headed directly for them. A hound spotted her and started toward her, growling loudly. She spooked a buck as she passed it, and the animal quickly moved away from her.

Buffy ignored the hound.

She was ten feet from the Hunters when the hound's growls attracted their attention. Then they saw her. All three of them stood at once, weapons rising. Buffy stopped, planted her feet, held the axe above her head with both hands, and threw it. The double-bladed battle axe spun through the air and buried itself in the chest of a dark elfin Huntsman with a splinter of bone and a blast of black mist that shot from its chest cavity, with a sickening hiss.

The Hunter went down. The other two glanced at their dead comrade with wide eyes, as if Buffy was going to wait for them to comment on what she'd just done. The Slayer didn't wait. She pressed the attack. Even as one of the Huntsmen raised a wicked-looking sword, its blade flickering in the firelight, Buffy spun, kicked the sword from his hand and into the dirt. Another swift kick, directly to the gut, and the Huntsman fell back into the fire and stayed there, screaming. The blaze ate him like a voracious beast, consuming him instantly, leather and fur bursting into flames along with his hair and scraggly beard. Fire exploded from his eyes, and then from the empty sockets black mist spurted as though from a wound.

"Ick," Buffy muttered.

It was his screams that finally got the camp in motion.

The third Hunter was a woman she'd noticed before, bald head and talismans dangling from her many piercings like a horrible S&M Christmas tree. Already Buffy heard the pounding of hooves, heard shouting. The bald woman lifted her hand and Buffy's eyes widened as she saw the weapon there. It was a Swiss morningstar mace, something Giles had shown her only in books. A long metal shaft with a chain at one end, and attached to the chain a huge spiked metal ball.

The woman's eyes blazed as she began to swing the ball on the end of the chain. No fancy kicks, no flips, nothing from a distance would work, Buffy knew. Before the Huntress could even aim an attack on Buffy, the Slayer moved in close. She drove the fingers of her right hand into the bald woman's throat, crushing her larynx. The Hunter faltered, tried to bring the morningstar down on Buffy's head. The Slayer grabbed her left arm, ducked behind her, breaking the arm, then reached up and grabbed the hand that held the mace.

With the chain that held the spiked ball to the metal shaft, Buffy broke her neck. Black mist escaped from her mouth.

Hooves pounded earth. Buffy glanced up, saw a Hunter bearing down on her with a sword raised to hack at her. She swung the morningstar, whipped it around the blade as the Huntsman passed by and the sword was pulled from his hand.

Buffy dropped the morningstar, lifted the heavy, gleaming sword, and turned to face the rush of Huntsmen moving toward her. The dark faerie were there as well, but only a few of them. The others hung back, laughing madly. The Huntsmen paused as three hounds rushed through their ranks to attack Buffy.

She turned and ran. Three of them at once would be a deadly distraction.

The girl was behind her. Connie DeMarco. Treasure, Brian had called her. She was on a horse, and she had a sword. But she wasn't really one of them, not yet. She was still alive. Buffy wasn't about to kill her.

But maybe that meant Connie was also not quite ready to kill indiscriminately.

Buffy rushed at her.

Connie raised the sword.

"Your mother misses you," Buffy said loudly.

The girl's eyes went wide, the sword faltered, and Buffy grabbed her leg and flipped her off the horse's back. She leaped into the saddle just in time to escape the hounds. She saw Connie's wide eyes staring at her, and Buffy felt horrible for manipulating her. But too many lives depended on her success to worry about it overmuch.

She dug her heels into the horse's flanks, and to her surprise, it began to move, following her commands. Buffy raised her sword, and rode directly at the knot of Hunters who had been about to attack her. Dark faerie ran around under the horse's feet, trying to get to her, but the horse ignored them, even stamping on one of them.

"Roland!" Buffy screamed. "Where are you?"

She spared a moment to wonder if the others had succeeded in escaping. With every fiber of her being, she prayed they had.

A Huntsman on foot tried to block her path. Buffy bent low over the horse and rode the man down, trampling him under the beast's hooves. Two more on horseback galloped directly in front of her and Buffy rode right at them.

"Roland!" she cried.

Buffy reined her horse to one side, so both Hunters were to her right. Her sword flashed out, and the nearest Hunter's head flew from his shoulders, neatly decapitated in a splash of thick black gas. Quickly, she turned to face the other.

Her horse reared. Buffy was nearly thrown from its back, but managed just barely to hold on. When she looked up again, the Erl King was bearing down on her. He was a horrible sight, flames burning in his eyes and nostrils, horns crusted with gore . . . and he was huge.

Buffy raised her sword and spurred her horse on toward him. In her heart, she said goodbye to her mother.

The Erl King turned his horse at the last moment, and barked something in a guttural language. Buffy's horse stopped too fast, almost slammed into the King's horse. Buffy rocked forward.

With a backhand, Hern the Hunter knocked her from the saddle.

Buffy hit the ground hard enough to knock the breath out of her. Her head spun from the force of the Erl King's blow, and she tasted blood in her mouth. She thought she might have swallowed a tooth. She wondered if her nose was broken. Disoriented, she looked up at Hern as he dismounted, and approached her, sword in hand. The others crowded around behind him.

Then Roland pushed through them.

"Father, no!" he said. "She rescued me. From the warlocks. She was the one who saved me."

The Erl King stared at him, spoke sternly: "*I* saved you, Roland."

"Yes, Father, but . . . Buffy's my friend," he said. "Please!"

"Buffy?" the Erl King said, and a laugh bubbled up inside his chest. Fire spouted from his eyes as he turned to look at her.

"What kind of a name is Buffy?" he asked, his voice like stones scraping together.

She stared at him defiantly. "What kind of a name is *Hern?*"

Buffy wanted to close her eyes, to wait for the death she knew was coming. But she didn't. She only glared at him. Then, as it seemed death was not going to be immediate, she climbed painfully to her feet, her wounds finally beginning to catch up with her, the ache and burn of the many cuts and bites and bruises sapping her strength. Still, better to die standing, with some dignity, she thought.

"You aren't an ordinary girl," the Erl King said. "What are you, then?"

"I'm the Chosen One," she said simply. "The Slayer."

The Erl King actually took a step back. The fire dimmed in his eyes. Buffy knew it wasn't fear, but she had no idea what it was. Then Hern the Hunter did the most unexpected, most extraordinary thing Buffy could ever have imagined. He lifted his sword, point down, both hands on the hilt, and drove it into the ground between them.

And he knelt on one knee.

"You honor us with your presence, Chosen One," he said. "You are not the first Slayer to walk among us. The Hunt also strikes down the soulless vampire wherever he slinks through filthy alleys to steal his nightly bit of life. They are abominations. We have much in common, you see. Though this will not stop me from taking your life any more than my son's misguided pleas. Instead, however, I ask you this.

"Ride with us. Grace the Wild Hunt by becoming

one of us. The girl Treasure was to be Roland's bride, but you . . . you are the Slayer. Wed my son, join the Hunt, and one day, you will be its queen."

Buffy opened her mouth to say something obnoxious and insulting. Then she closed it again, and thought a moment. This wasn't the time. This needed to be played a different way.

"I'm honored by your request," she said. "But I'm the Slayer. There are duties that go along with that, that I can't just walk away from."

Hern the Hunter barked orders in that guttural language, and the crowd of Huntsmen split again. Beyond the circle, several Huntsmen and a horde of dark faerie surrounded Giles, Xander, Willow, and Brian. They looked even worse than before.

"I'm sorry, Buffy," Giles said. "We almost made it, but the faerie caught on . . . they gave us away."

Buffy hung her head.

"Join us and they will live," the Erl King said. "Refuse me, and I will kill them. Slowly. They will die cursing your name." He locked gazes with her. "Join us."

She stared at him, not looking at her friends. She didn't want to see them. It would make her choice all the more agonizing.

"Set them free. When I know they're safe, I'll join you," she said.

"Buffy, it isn't worth it!" Xander shouted. "Please, don't."

"Run him through!" the Erl King thundered, and pointed a long, taloned finger toward her friends.

Instantly a mounted Hunter bore down on Xander. He held a sword, and he angled it toward Xander's heart.

"No!" Buffy shouted. "Stop!"

"Halt!" the Erl King commanded, but not before the Hunter's sword had pierced Xander's left arm. Xander cried out in pain and fell to his knees. Willow ran to him and threw her arms around him.

"Buffy, don't," Xander panted, eyes wide and imploring. "Don't."

Tears spilled down Willow's face as she draped her body over Xander, trying to protect him. "Buffy, don't."

His own eyes welling, Buffy's Watcher raised his chin. "Buffy," he said, "don't."

Buffy ignored them all. *If I look at them, look in their eyes, I will never have the strength to go through with this,* she thought.

The Huntsman on horseback wheeled his mount around and waited for the Erl King's orders. The king raised his arm. The Huntsman raised his sword.

The Erl King looked hard at Buffy. "So, Chosen One. Do you consent?"

She tried to speak, but her throat closed up.

The king lowered his arm, and the Huntsman trotted toward her friends with his sword extended. Xander's blood dripped from the tip.

"Yes!" she shouted. "Yes, I consent!"

"No," Xander groaned. "Oh, Buffy."

"You will be loyal always to the Erl King's commands. You will become Roland's bride," Hern growled.

"Yes."

"Swear it by the light of Hecate's moon, under the lost eye of Odin," the Erl King demanded.

"Buffy, don't do it!" Giles snapped. "It's a magical oath. It can never be broken."

"I swear by the light of Hecate's moon, under the lost eye of Odin, that I will be loyal always to the Erl King's commands," Buffy said.

"Set them free!" the Erl King announced happily, fire snorting from his nostrils, blood smeared across his widely grinning teeth.

Willow began to sob loudly. Giles swore. Xander was silent. Still, Buffy would not look at them.

She had never been any good at saying goodbye.

Chapter 15

As Brian Anderson and his new friends were taken to the edge of the clearing, the Erl King grabbed the reins of Buffy's horse and led her away. She did not look back.

Brian could relate. Looking back hurt something fierce. Mr. Giles had taken off his tie and wrapped it tightly around Xander's arm. Xander had said something about a field dressing, nodding, insisting that he felt fine. He insisted that the sword had only grazed him, and that he had cried out more from surprise than pain. Brian wasn't sure of that. On the other hand, Xander didn't look great, but he didn't look like he was going to die.

It was almost as though Brian and the other three were invisible to the Hunt now. The hounds didn't growl at them. Hunters rode by as if they were trees.

Even the dark faerie ignored them. Brian was free. He could go back to his father now.

Buffy had given up everything for her friends, and he had just been fortunate enough to be along for the ride. He was free.

But he couldn't leave yet.

"Brian, we must go now," Giles whispered. "We've got to find a way to save Buffy and we can't do it here."

"Just . . . hold on," Brian said, staring at Connie DeMarco, the girl he knew as Treasure.

She wouldn't look at him.

Brian cupped his hands to his face and called out to her. "Treasure! Come with us, please!"

Treasure did not turn.

"Treasure!"

"Brian," Xander said, his expression dead serious. "I know it's hard, but you've gotta let her go, man. There's probably a time limit on our ticket out of here, and I, for one, do not want Buffy's sacrifice to be in vain. We need to get the hell out of Dodge."

Brian stared hard at Treasure. He hadn't realized until that moment that he had come to love her, in his way. Not as a boyfriend, but maybe as a close friend.

Was this the same kind of pain he'd caused his father?

How did you make up for a wound like this?

Connie DeMarco kept her back to Shock, and she wept human tears. She was still human, still alive. She knew that. But she also knew that wouldn't be the case for very long.

There was nothing she wanted more than to go back to the world with Shock . . . with Brian. Connie missed her mom terribly. She wished now that she had never run away. It was a horribly immature thing to do. Sure, her mom could be a raving bitch sometimes, and they didn't ever seem to be able to understand each other. And her dad, hell, he was just a mean old bastard. But she could've tried harder to get Mom to see him for what he was. Tried to really talk to her.

Now it was too late.

Her mother would never forgive her for what she'd done, for riding with the Hunt. She hadn't taken a life yet, not really. But she had stood by while the others did so. She was a part of it. Even if her mother said she forgave her, Connie didn't think she could ever forgive herself. She belonged here, now. She was one of them.

If she wasn't going to be Roland's bride, she would be just another Huntsman. They would be her family.

She cried all through Brian's attempts to get her to look at him, to talk to him. After a while, her tears dried up, though she continued to cry. A small bit of dark mist floated in front of her face, and Treasure stared at it. It might have just floated by, of course.

But she had to wonder if it had come from inside her. From her tears.

The horn blew. She hefted the sword she'd received, and then sheathed it. Treasure mounted her horse, and prepared to go on the Hunt again. She understood something at last. She was already dying, just by being here. Just by wanting to be part of the Hunt. It was killing her.

She was becoming something else. Becoming a Hunter.

Though it was difficult, through her tears, to admit it, Treasure liked it. Her father had hit her sometimes, called her a tramp. Her mother, in their worst fights, had always told her she was a waste. That she'd amount to nothing.

Treasure was something now.

Treasure was something horrible.

Willow wiped the tears from her eyes as she followed Xander through the trees and away from the clearing. Despite his arm, he was keeping a steady pace with Giles and Brian Anderson. Soon they would reach Route 17.

She kept trying to slow down, but every time Giles and Xander would urge her on. Finally she just stopped.

Xander went on a few more strides before he noticed she wasn't keeping up.

"Come on, Will," he said anxiously.

"We can't," Willow said. "We can't leave her like this."

Xander stared at her. Giles moved to her, put a hand on her shoulder.

"Of course not," he said softly. "We're not going anywhere without Buffy."

"But that oath," Willow argued. "You said . . ."

"I know what I said," Giles snapped, then shook his head in tacit apology. "I only wish we had time to research a way to break that oath. I'm afraid we're going to have to improvise."

"Improvising is good," Willow said encouragingly.

"Guys, this is not the place to stop," Xander said. "Let's put some distance between us and tiny little ears."

Finally Willow understood. The dark faerie might well be following them. Or there might be other things in the forest. Xander wanted to get some distance before they began to plan.

"Agreed, Xander," Giles said. "But not too much distance. There probably isn't much time before the last Hunt begins."

They began moving again, and Willow felt a bit better. Not about the odds, and not about their chances. But she knew that if they'd left there without at least trying to rescue Buffy, no matter the cost, she would never be able to forgive herself.

A short while later they came to a broad path that led south. Willow had been trying to gauge their location, and she thought that, more than likely, the path would take them out to Route 17. If they wanted to go that way. But they weren't. They were staying.

"Brian," Willow said quietly. "We're stopping now. You should probably go on."

"Yes, Brian. You really should go," Giles agreed.

Brian stood fast. "Buffy saved my life too."

Willow thought about Brian's father, about him trying to kill himself. Drunk. Wallowing in despair. She didn't want to think about what her own parents would do if she went missing, or Xander's. But Buffy was their friend, and she had come to rescue them. Not only tonight, but time and again. They had to go back. Brian didn't.

Obviously, they were all thinking the same thing, but Xander spoke up first.

"Your dad's waiting for you, man. Get out of here," he said, holding his wounded arm close to his abdomen, obviously trying not to let anyone see just how badly hurt he was.

Brian looked at them in turn, saving Giles for last.

Finally he just said, "Thank you," and turned away down the path.

"Brian?" Willow asked.

He stopped, turned to regard her.

"If we never come back, try to explain to our parents, okay? And tell my mom and dad . . ." Her voice trailed off then, and she bit her lip, eyes moist.

But Brian understood. He nodded. "I'll tell them," he said, and looked at Xander. "For both of you."

They watched him until he took a turn in the path, then the living darkness in the trees blocked him from sight.

"Right," Giles said, taking his glasses off and rubbing the bridge of his nose. "Let's think. What do we know?"

"That Buffy swore an oath to Hecate which is unbreakable and just about now Papa's calling a wedding consultant," Xander said, "and don't tell me not to make jokes because it's what I do."

"Hecate is the queen of the witches," Giles said. "Perhaps there's a parallel here to the Holda Hunt legend. But then, we don't really have a comfortable fit, seeing as our Lord of the Hunt is male . . ."

"What about the Odin thing? She had to swear on his eye."

He slipped his glasses back on. "It's a common ritual, swearing on a body part. In some cultures, one swears by one's thigh. According to myth, Odin lost an eye on a quest for wisdom. It likely has to do with the severity of the oath."

"Look, all this talk is nice," Xander said, "but it isn't getting us anywhere. I figure the only thing we can do is get back to the clearing, watch the path they take on the way out, then wait for them on the way back. If we can ambush Horny the Hunter, take him out, maybe we can throw the rest of them off enough for us to get away."

"That isn't much of a plan," Willow said hesitantly.

"It isn't a plan at all," Giles sniffed. "Particularly when one considers the hounds and the dark faerie. Many of them have been killed, but there are still a great many to deal with. Too many. The faerie alone could kill us if we tried to escape with Buffy."

"So we take the faerie out of the game too," Xander declared.

"How do you propose we do that, exactly?" Giles asked.

The answer came, not from Xander, but from the deep shadows of the woods beyond the path.

From the darkness, a dead faerie flew through the air and landed, twisted and limp as a rag doll.

"We might have an idea or two about that," a voice said.

Angel stepped onto the path, followed by Cordelia. Willow's heart quickened as she peered into the shadows for a third new arrival.

"Oz?" she asked.

"I'm here," he said, his voice a growl.

"Oh, Oz," she whispered, as he emerged from the dark woods. He was slightly stooped, his clothing in tatters. Where she could see his skin, there was fur. His ears were pointed and his jaw and nose thrust out unnaturally. When he spoke, his lips curled back to reveal needle sharp yellow fangs.

She said his name again, and moved toward him tentatively.

"It's cool," Oz said. "It's actually sort of like a V.R. computer game. Only, y'know, with consequences."

"That's called life, by the way," Xander pointed out.

A silence descended upon them, as Willow went cautiously to Oz and then they embraced. Xander and Cordelia joined hands briefly and their eyes met.

"What happened to your arm?" she asked anxiously.

"I gave blood." He shrugged. "Didn't want to." Then he smiled at her concerned expression. "It'll be okay. Promise."

"How'd you find us?" Giles asked Angel.

"Long story," Angel replied. "I'll tell you all about it over a beer sometime."

The two regarded each other. After a beat, Giles gave a quick nod and said, "It had better be a Guinness."

Angel smiled faintly. Then he said, "Cordelia saved my life," he said to Xander. "Oz's, too."

"A big save for Queen C," Xander said, attempting to high-five her with his unpunctured arm.

Cordelia punched him.

It was almost as though everything was all right again. Which, of course, it wasn't.

"All right," Willow said, looking at Angel and Giles, "let's hear the plan. I want to know exactly how we're going to pull this off."

Buffy had been offered new clothing. She declined. They offered her meat that was cooking over a fire, but she remembered the centaur in the forest, and shook her head. There was a little Summers policy she hadn't had to institute very often, but it had to do with not eating anything that could hold a conversation.

The hunting horn blew, but this time there was a keening, almost mournful note to it that was different from the triumphant ring of before. All the bodies of the Huntsmen Buffy had killed were thrown on the fire and burned quickly. Amazingly, none of the others seemed hostile to her. She had just slaughtered half a dozen of them, and they didn't seem to care.

But then, what was their life but hunting and killing? They were already dead. And she had been chosen to marry Roland, which would one day make her Queen of the Hunt. If they wanted to continue with the illusion of life that they had, they would have to treat her with respect.

If the chance came, she might be able to use that. If the chance came.

She looked for Roland, her only friend among these nightmarish beings. What would it be like, to have him as a husband? To ride through the night forever with him at her side? Would his kindness drain away? Would that soul she had come to admire mutate into an oily cloud of smoke?

Finally the horn sounded again. Roland trotted up next to her on a fire-snorting, stamping mare, and Buffy looked closely at him. *He hates this,* she thought.

"Mount your horse, Buffy," he told her gently. "And take your weapons. This is the final Hunt before we return to the Lodge. My father wants vengeance on the Faire."

Buffy picked up the sword she'd acquired and carried the morningstar as well. There was a sort of holster for it on the horse she had chosen, and it had made an effective weapon.

"Why do you stay?" she asked Roland as she mounted her horse.

When he didn't answer, she looked at him, searched his eyes, saw the pain there.

"Why are you the Slayer?" Roland asked.

Buffy was about to answer, when she understood that there was no need to. It had been a rhetorical question. Buffy had not chosen the life of the Slayer. She had been chosen. But she understood how vital the obligations were that had been conferred upon her, and she accepted them.

Roland was to be the Erl King.

"I never would have guessed we were in the same situation," she said to him.

"Not the same," Roland corrected. "But similar."

"You know if I figure out a way, I'm going to get out of this," Buffy told him.

"If I could find a way, you would already be home in your bed," he replied.

"You have a good soul, Roland," Buffy said. "Guard it carefully."

Roland did not reply, but Buffy thought his eyes welled with tears. Then the horn sounded again, incredibly loud and deep. The Erl King sat astride his fierce stallion at the center of the clearing, and he spoke loudly so that they could all hear him.

"Enjoy the final Hunt of this cycle," he said. "Exotic beasts for food are our primary goal. Also, reach your spirits out over the area to find the truly hopeless. Our numbers have decreased and we must add to our ranks."

He looked at his son. "First, however, we ride to what remains of the actors' encampment. As you know, when our prince lost his way in the lightworld, these wretches pretended to befriend him. Sensing his power, they made him their slave.

"Then, in an effort to come back to us, he ran from them. Our princess offered him shelter, and for this, we thank her."

He made a courtly bow in Buffy's direction. She gave no response.

He continued, "But these same blackguards desecrated her dwelling and forcibly took him back to their encampments. The chief of the faerie reports that several of the warlocks, those who disgraced our prince and the Hunt itself, still live. The Lodge closes its doors to anyone who does not have the blood of these, our enemies, on his lips when we return."

"Promise?" Buffy muttered.

Then the horn was blown a final time, and the Erl King led the charge out of the clearing and into the woods. Instantly, Buffy felt the world change. She had been in horrifying, surreal situations, more times than even she could believe. But this was something else. She was part of the Hunt now, on the other side of that veil of mysticism and predation. The very air seemed different, tasted different. The forest seemed to part before them as if it served the Hunt willingly, and perhaps it did.

The ends of Buffy's hair crackled, sparks flicked from the ends of her reins as they streamed in the growing wind. She shivered with a deathly cold.

She wondered if she would ever be warm again.

One of the huge black bucks ran alongside her horse. She wondered if it had once been a target, the prey, rather than a creature of the Hunt.

Her horse breathed fire. Its eyes were ablaze. Yet it was cold as ice under her thighs. It knew without her encouragement precisely where it fell in the procession. Hooves pounded, the hounds bayed as they nipped at the horses' heels, their own paws never quite touching the ground. Buffy couldn't help herself. For a moment, she felt an electric jolt of power. Of hunger and bloodlust. As the Slayer, she knew what it was to be a hunter, to stalk a thing and kill it, to prey on an enemy. But this was something else completely. For as the Slayer, she was sadly outmatched and outnumbered by her enemies. It was a war.

What the Wild Hunt did was pure slaughter. Plunder. They were barbarians, but for just a moment Buffy thought there was a certain freedom in barbarism.

Buffy shivered in horror as she pushed the thought away. She would not become part of this, not become one of them, even if it meant her death. Somehow, she would break her oath to the Erl King. For the moment, however, she could think of nothing but holding on to her horse's reins.

They thundered through the woods, black mist in the trees dissipating as they passed. The air pulsed with energy; at times trees and bushes shimmered with a blue aura. The Hunters shimmered with black.

Despite the darkness that flowed through the branches of the forest, Buffy glimpsed, in the distance off to her left, a flash of white fur. It had to be something very big to be seen so far away. A sasquatch or something? she wondered. After the centaur, she was willing to credit anything she might see in these woods.

A pair of Huntsmen, who'd obviously seen it as well, tore off through the trees in pursuit. A moment later, she heard a roar of almost human agony, and a whooping cry of triumph from the Huntsmen.

Buffy thought about the people from the Renaissance Faire. She had no sympathy for what was going to happen to the ones the dark faerie had left alive. They were evil, no question, and deserved what they got. Buffy herself would have killed them in self defense. But murder? Cold-blooded, hunt them down and kill them murder? She didn't think she could do that.

She also couldn't think of a single thing she could do to stop it from happening.

The horse snorted beneath her. Buffy looked next to the path as one of the hounds rocketed through the trees. Its paws traveled well above the forest floor and it turned and glanced at her with its burning eyes. It snarled a moment. Maybe it was her scent, but the hounds still regarded her as the enemy.

There was an inhuman roar ahead. *The Erl King,* Buffy thought. Horses began to whinny and there was a great deal of shouting. Buffy pulled up on the reins of her horse as Roland slowed his mount and dropped back beside her on the wide path.

For the first time Buffy noticed that all around them the forest had somehow become less dark. The black mist that had enshrouded the woods was gone, at least in this spot. She could even see the stars, and the moon.

"What happened?" she asked.

Then the Erl King shouted again, and Buffy looked ahead. Past the mounted Huntsmen who had crowded around each other, many of them getting down from their horses. Past the trees. For the first time, Buffy saw what had stopped them.

At the end of the path there was a wall. An undulating mass of black mist, but much thicker than what had swirled through the forest before. Somehow it had been drawn in, coagulated, and formed a hardened mass that now prevented them from moving forward. The wall was at least thirty feet high, and from the look of the flowing morass ahead of them, quite thick.

The Erl King screamed in fury and brought his sword down with all his might on the black wall. Its oily surface was moving, swirling, and the sword cut through the mass a ways before it was trapped. The wall was like tar. It was a chore for the king to remove his sword, and when he had, the wall was no worse for his attack.

"What is it?" Buffy asked Roland.

"I was about to ask you that," Roland replied. "I thought your friends might have had something to do with it."

Buffy thought about that, but neither Giles nor Willow had enough knowledge of magic to do something like this so quickly. She looked at Roland and shook her head.

"Are we trapped here?" she asked.

"It certainly seems that way," he replied. "I've never seen anything like this before. My father has never been defied like this. His will is very powerful."

Buffy looked back at the wall, completely baffled. The Erl King and several Huntsmen were still attacking the thick, swirling magic of the wall. They weren't giving up yet. Buffy's concern was what might happen when they did give up. Her oath was magic, as Giles had told her. She could think disloyally, but if she tried to move toward the king in a hostile fashion, or ride off and leave the Hunt, her body would not respond.

She'd tested it, of course.

But as long as they stayed in this forest, or even in Sunnydale, there was hope that somehow she would figure out a way to free herself.

If they returned to the Lodge, however, left the world Buffy knew completely, then all of her hope would die. And in order for her truly to be part of the Hunt, to become one of them, Buffy would have to die too. To die, and live on with black magic in her veins. She wouldn't be human anymore.

If that happened, she had already decided what she would have to do. Her only recourse.

She would ask Roland to kill her.

Though he felt horribly guilty for leaving the others behind, Brian was ecstatic when the darkness around him began to abate. It was still night, but it was his night. Real and tangible. Nothing magical at all about it. He wanted to shout his relief. Instead, he picked up the pace even more, despite his injuries and his exhaustion.

He couldn't wait to see his father.

Then he rounded a corner in the path, and saw the inky black mass at the edge of the trees.

Brian stared at it for a moment, then he ran toward it and came to a stop only inches away. He reached out his hand, but found himself too terrified to touch it. A short mental war ended with him admitting his fear, giving in to it. He fell to his knees, brought his hands to his face, and began to cry. He sobbed loudly.

Then he heard a voice.

"He's not one of them, then?" the voice said. It was deep and hearty.

"No, just a boy," the other replied.

Brian looked around but saw no one. Thought he must be going mad.

Then a hand shot through the inky blackness as if it weren't there, gripped him by the wrist, and hauled him through the black wall as if it weren't there at all.

He fell to the grass, stumbled, and rolled partway down a short hill into a gulley that separated the embankment of Route 17 from the forest. From the bottom of the gulley, he looked up at his saviors. A hugely fat man in tattered clothing held his hands up to the black wall that blocked the woods from sight completely. Only the tops of the trees were visible. The man's chest shone with light, almost white, but tainted somehow with a pinkish glow.

There was another man there as well, dressed in green. The green man's hands glowed with crackling energy that flew from his fingers to the wall and back.

"You escaped, then?" the green man asked. "How did you manage that?"

"What are you doing?" Brian asked, stunned by what he saw, but too emotionally drained to be afraid.

"Keeping them inside," the fat man said. "What does it look like, boy?"

"Like magic," Brian said softly.

Both men laughed.

"King Richard and I are going to be here until morning, son," the green man said. "If the wall falls, we're both dead men. We'd be grateful to you if you could run up the road to that twenty-four-hour diner and get us some coffee."

Brian stared at them as though they were both insane. Neither of them said another word after that, and he noticed the sweat on both their faces, the strain of keeping the wall intact. Keeping the Wild Hunt trapped within. He watched them for nearly ten minutes, never putting voice to any of the other questions in his head. He didn't really want answers, he decided.

Finally, he got to his feet, felt for his wallet, which was miraculously still in his back pocket, and then started trudging along the empty highway with only one thought in his head.

Coffee. He could do that.

With the combined energy of the Wild Hunt focused on the wall that kept them trapped within the forest, nobody noticed the buck drift away from the main body of the Hunt. It straggled back along the path, feeling hungry and smelling something unusual. Something new. There weren't a great many new things, and it wondered, in its way, if this were a new something it should eat, or something it should fear.

It wandered back far enough that it reached a point where the liquid darkness still filled the trees. It stepped off the path and into the wood. The new thing was close, it knew.

Once, the buck had been something else, something that didn't eat meat. Now, meat was all it could eat. This smelled like good meat.

In the darkness ahead of the buck, something growled.

A pair of wide, glowing yellow eyes loomed ahead in the shadows.

Powerful hands gripped the buck's antlers, and twisted. It fell heavily to the ground, unnoticed. A small cloud of black mist escaped its mouth.

Chapter 16

NOT LONG AFTER THE GRANDFATHER CLOCK CHIMED twice, Mr. Chase pushed aside the heavy floral comforter his wife had insisted upon purchasing on a recent trip to Los Angeles, and rose from the cherry wood sleigh bed they'd bought the year before in Austria. He wrapped himself in his silk robe and descended to the first floor kitchen, where he poured himself a glass of natural spring water.

On the way back to bed, he stood for a moment in the open doorway to his daughter's bedroom. Cordelia had decided to sleep over at some friend or other's house tonight, he recalled.

Outside, a car with a poor exhaust system—obviously not one of the Chases' neighbors—rumbled down the street, rattling the window in Cordelia's room. Mr. Chase listened a moment to see if the noise would wake his wife. When he was sure it hadn't, he walked to the window and gazed out, saw the taillights of the car just before it turned a corner down the street.

Troublemakers. Hoods, they'd called them, when Mr. Chase had been a boy.

He worried about his daughter whenever she wasn't home. But at the very least, he knew that Cordelia's priorities wouldn't allow her to fall into the company of troublemakers. Nope. With very few exceptions, Cordelia steered very clear of kids in the habit of causing trouble, or putting themselves in the way of danger.

Mr. Chase went back to bed. He was disturbed to find that, for the first time since college, he could not sleep.

In the kitchen of the Harris household, at a round Formica table that hadn't been moved from that spot in ten years, Xander's mother sat in the dark, sleep-eating. It was something she did at least once a week. In the unlit kitchen, she smoked a cigarette (something her wide-awake self had quit two years earlier), drank warm Diet Coke, and ate leftover chicken wings from a take-out container. Frequently, members of her family would hold entire conversations with her under these circumstances that Mrs. Harris couldn't for the life of her remember come morning.

When there wasn't any leftover Chinese food, chocolate would do. Cake or cookies or, even better, fudge. She frequently wondered why she just couldn't seem to shed the twenty extra pounds she'd gained when her oldest had finally moved out on his own. Mr. Harris had joked once that she would gain a whole other person when Xander finally moved out.

Once had been enough. After the look she'd given him, her husband had never said anything of the sort again.

She barely blinked when her husband turned on the light. He stood in the kitchen doorway, rubbing his eyes and adjusting his pajama bottoms.

"I suppose you noticed that Xander isn't home yet?" Mr. Harris asked.

"Maybe he's out with that nice Cordelia?" Mrs. Harris replied. Since she was asleep, she was not truly cognizant of the lateness of the hour.

"Not with those parents of hers," Mr. Harris replied. "Not if she wants to live. Nope. He's a senior now, and seniors, as I recall, have a lot of parties. I understand that. But we've got to have some rules in this house or it's all going to be chaos.

"Tomorrow morning, assuming he bothers to come home tonight at all, I'm going to tell him he's grounded," Mr. Harris said.

"Got to have some rules in this house," Mrs. Harris replied happily. Completely asleep, she pulled a drag off her cigarette.

Joyce Summers stood and stared out a window in her living room. In her hands, she cradled a long, very sharp stake. Its weight was a very real connection to reality for her.

Her conversation with Cordelia had been helpful in getting a focus, something she had been dealing with off and on ever since Buffy returned home. Reality had been somewhat subjective for her, as it was for all parents who alternated between wanting to know what their kids were getting into and then wanting desperately not to know. It was just that, in her case, the consequences of that knowledge were so much higher.

She'd managed to get to sleep for a few hours. When she woke, Joyce realized that whatever was going on tonight was very grave. From what little Cordelia had said, just from the fact that Cordelia Chase had come into the house at all . . . Joyce knew the stakes were high. And Buffy was out there fighting. Her little girl faced horrors most people couldn't imagine. She'd insisted that Joyce stay out of it. That she would just be a liability, a distraction that might actually get Buffy killed instead of helping.

But tonight, Joyce felt something odd. Buffy needed all the help she could get. There was something . . . it was as if Buffy was slipping away, being taken from her.

Which was why she had gone into Buffy's drawer and found the stake. She'd put on a jacket and her sneakers, and gone to the front door. Joyce had the front door open before she realized that she had no idea where Buffy was. No idea, even, where Cordelia had gone. There was nothing she could do.

She stood at the window, numb, holding the stake and waited for her daughter to come home.

After the rest of their troupe had been slaughtered by the dark faerie, Robin Hood and King Richard— who had long ago given up any attachment to their real names—had used their magic to heal each other as best they could. Then they had followed the trail of the dark faerie using a tracking spell Robin had been perfecting for years without having any real way to test it.

They'd wanted Roland back, but realized very quickly that there wasn't much chance of that. When they had first discovered that the Hunt had come to Sunnydale, well, there was only one thing to do: survive until morning and then get the hell out.

Easier said than done.

Robin felt the strain horribly. Already he had moved from a standing position to sitting on his wet bum on this dewy grassy slope, elbows on his knees, feeding as much magical energy as he could funnel from the ether into the upkeep of the barrier holding the Wild Hunt within the forest. There was no way they could hope to battle the Erl King openly. But if they couldn't fight him, they could at least try to stop him.

"Wow," said the kid who'd brought them coffee. "This is . . . it's just amazing."

Robin said nothing. Richard only grunted. They had both thanked him for the coffee however. It was that flavored hazelnut crap, but Robin figured beggars couldn't choose. Without the coffee, and the accompanying caffeine, he might have just given up half an hour ago.

It was a futile effort, though. Another fifteen minutes. Even forty-five. It wouldn't make a difference. There was no way he and fat Richard were going to be able to keep this up until morning.

"You guys must know Mr. Giles, huh?" Brian asked. "He knows all about this kind of thing."

"Never heard of him," Robin said, mostly to have something in his brain besides keeping the magic flowing.

"You aren't friends of his?" Brian asked. "Then

how did you know about . . . I mean, why are you doing this?"

Robin smiled thinly, but didn't turn his attention from the barrier. It was Richard who answered the kid's question.

"You misunderstand, lad," Richard said. "We aren't heroic wizards from some fairy tale. We're warlocks. Black magicians. We're only here because the Erl King—I assume you know who we mean, seeing as you were stuck with him inside our barrier—will have our guts for garters if he catches up with us."

The kid, Brian, was quiet. After a moment, he asked. "Why?"

"We kept his son prisoner," Richard replied coolly.

Robin shook his head. "Look, kid, thank you for the coffee," he said. "But maybe you should be getting home now, eh?"

There was no reply. Robin didn't even have to turn around to know that Brian was already moving up the embankment as quickly as he could.

Good for him, Robin thought. *At least one of us will see the sun again.*

But just as he thought this, he felt something else. The barrier had been under intense pressure from the inside for three quarters of an hour, at the very least. Suddenly, that pressure had greatly lessened, as if someone had opened a valve somewhere.

"Richard?" Robin asked tentatively.

"I feel it, Rob," Richard replied. "They've stopped trying. They're giving up. I think they might even be going back. Going home."

"Thank God," Robin whispered.

"It isn't God, Rob," Richard said confidently. "He doesn't owe us any favors, that one. If we live through this, it'll be pure luck. Pure luck."

Buffy pulled on her horse's reins to allow the pair of elfin Huntsmen to pass her by on the path. The Erl King had sent them riding in opposite directions along the perimeter of the forest in search of a break in the magical barrier that was holding them all inside the dense woods.

Roland rode up next to Buffy. Together, they watched the two fur-draped outriders report to the Lord of the Hunt.

"Well?" the Erl King boomed, snorting orange flames, his fury growing with each passing moment.

"We are trapped, my Lord," one of the Huntsmen said.

A tiny smile began to play at the edges of Buffy's lips and she forced it away. The Hunt wouldn't take any more lives in Sunnydale tonight. Her mother was safe. For the moment, at least.

"We cannot leave without having our vengeance on the ones who made Roland suffer so!" the Erl King snarled. "Ride again. We've got to find a way out of here."

Roland led his mare a few paces forward with a regal dignity that surprised Buffy. "Father," he called. "The faerie killed most of them. If some of them yet live, their lives are as good as over. They don't matter. They have been punished and I am back with you now."

"They haven't been punished enough," Hern the Hunter scowled, fire jetting from his nostrils.

"What would be enough? Surely not even death," Roland reasoned.

Hern stared at his son for a moment, then he threw his head back and rumbled laughter from deep within himself, and fire belched from his throat with each note of amusement.

"You are my son," the Erl King said.

More than ever, Buffy felt relieved. The Wild Hunt would be gone from Sunnydale. If they ever came back, it would probably not be for a very long time. Now they would . . .

"Oh, no," Buffy whispered to herself. Her heart raced and for a moment she couldn't take a breath, waiting for the order she feared would now come.

And it did.

The Erl King raised his sword high. "Very well, then, we return to the Lodge for a feast unlike any we have ever known. We celebrate the return of the prince, and we prepare for his wedding to the Slayer!"

"No," Buffy whispered.

But already, she could feel her body responding to the commands of the Erl King. She had sworn her loyalty, after all. Stinging, salty tears began to well up in her eyes and her heart felt like it was trying to escape her chest, so hard and fast was it beating.

Roland looked at her in sympathy. "I'm sorry," he whispered. "I've done all I can."

"Giles, hurry!" Willow snapped.

She kept glancing up at Cordelia, who was standing watch just off the wide path. Nothing so far, but it wouldn't be long. Willow thought they were lucky the Erl King had been so stubborn up until now. But even he would have to give in to futility soon.

"I think I've got it right," Giles said.

Willow looked over at Giles, who sat cross-legged in a pentagram he'd drawn in the dirt with a thick branch. At its five points, little more than furrows in the soil, were pieces of wood whose tips were wound with strips of Oz's shirt, which had been in tatters anyway. Angel had supplied them with an old metal Zippo lighter that he said had belonged to Spike. He'd apparently found it when he'd returned to the house he'd shared with Spike and Drusilla before they'd fled Sunnydale.

For her part, Willow had produced a small, blood-stained note pad and a ballpoint pen from one of the deep pockets of her jacket. Giles was busily scribbling away even now, trying desperately to recall a powerful spell he'd committed to memory some years ago, when studying to become a Watcher.

Xander had contributed a handful of mini Milky Way bars he'd stolen from a bag his mother had bought to give out on Halloween night. Though Giles had tried to explain it to him, he just couldn't seem to grasp the reason why he was forced to give up his personal stash of chocolatey goodness. But Giles had insisted.

Willow was proud of Xander, though. No matter how many jokes he might make, and in spite of the fear they were all feeling, much of the plan they were about to enact had come from Xander. He constantly belittled his own contributions, so much so that Willow wondered at times if he had actually fooled the others into not noticing how often he came through with a plan. Willow was proud of him. The man with the plan. And, almost as important in this case, the snack food.

"Is that going to be enough?" Willow asked now, staring at the candy.

"It will have to be," Giles replied. "We haven't any wine or bread or fruit. And the *loa*—the great spirits to which we communicate in voodoo ritual—are often placated with honey and sweets as well. If it's going to work at all, this should be a sufficient offering."

Willow shook her head. "I still don't understand how it could work. Whatever magic is involved in the Hunt, it's got to be some pretty ancient stuff, right? And culturally, it couldn't be further away from voodoo."

Giles stared at her. "If you must know, it's the only thing I could think of," he admitted. "Let's hope one walking dead man isn't much different from another, hmm?"

Then he stood and handed her two small pieces of note paper. "Make sure you can read it."

Willow glanced down at the scribbled French, trying to decipher it as best she could. A few yards away Cordelia cleared her throat loudly. Then Willow heard the thundering of hooves.

"It would appear to be show time," Giles said calmly.

"Oh," Willow breathed. She had succeeded in pushing her fear away by focusing on the danger Buffy was in. But now it all came rushing back. She'd been afraid before, when they'd faced horrors she'd never imagined. But this was different. This wasn't just some hellish demon ready to rip out their hearts, this was almost an army. The odds were . . . the odds were impossible.

Willow swallowed hard and settled down inside the

pentagram with a dirty and sweating Giles, who was even now lighting the makeshift torches around the circle. If the odds were impossible, they would just have to even them a bit.

"Here goes," she muttered.

The Erl King had moved on. He would not forget what had happened here. Nor would he give up his vendetta against those few who had survived the dark faerie's retrieval of Roland. The warlocks would die one day. But for now, there was a wedding to prepare for. The very thought filled him with pleasure. He had loved a Slayer once, but had not been able to wed her. Now Roland would have what Hern himself had always mourned the loss of—a bride worthy of the Lord of the Hunt.

His sword sheathed, the Erl King signaled for the horn. It sounded deep and clear through the trees. He spurred his stallion forward and the Hunt fell in beside and behind him. The hounds bayed as they ran on ahead, and the dark faerie clung to the horses' manes and saddles, rode the backs of hounds and swung and cavorted in the branches above.

One of the dark faerie landed in his lap. The Erl King glanced down and saw that it had no head. Before the fury that was stoked in the furnace of his chest could even begin to rise, the horse pulled up short and he rocked forward, scrabbling to hold onto his mount.

Across the path in front of him were four black bucks, their gray and rotted viscera strewn across the ground. He hadn't even noticed their absence, and now the extraordinary insult of this affront, this incursion into his territory, made Hern scream with rage and draw his sword. His huge chest billowed with the roar of fury, eyes blazing, sharp teeth flashing in what little moonlight reached down into the wood.

The hounds ran forward and buried their black, fiery snouts in the open guts of the dead bucks. The dark faerie fell from the trees and raced along the path to begin ripping chunks of the bucks out for themselves and gulping them down their gullets as fast as the greedy little creatures could. They began to fight each other, and the hounds, for each bit of flesh.

The Erl King roared his displeasure, commanded them to stop. But they were already in a frenzy. He would have to interfere more directly.

"Huntsmen, stop them!" he ordered, with a chop of his hand, and a nod of his horned head. "And find the ones responsible for this effrontery. I want their teeth for a string of pearls!"

There were seventeen riders of the Hunt left, without counting the Slayer, the girl Treasure, or his son. Five rode ahead to scatter the hounds and the faerie. The Erl King waved for the others to fan out into the woods and bring his enemies to him. He would feel their eyes pop and spurt between his jagged teeth.

He surveyed the wide path, back and front. Behind him, he saw his son and the Slayer holding their counsel together. He wanted to think they were bonding, as a couple about to be wed ought to. But something else struck him.

The Slayer's friends. The ones she had sacrificed herself to free. The way the dark-haired boy had stared him in the face and lied, and held his head high in disrespect.

Hern the Hunter knew.

"My Lord!" one of the Huntsmen called.

The Erl King looked around in astonishment as the Huntsmen began to fall from their mounts, to tumble like stricken children to the ground below. Their own horses trampled them on the path and on the forest floor, with the sound of breaking bones and another sound, like the rush of air through the leaves above. But they felt no pain, that much was obvious. Those who fell were dead before they struck the ground. Closest to the Erl King, a rider named Pontius, whom he'd had with him since he'd stopped the human from hanging himself in the twelfth century, fell from his horse and exploded in a cloud of black mist, leaving only a dry, ragged, shattered husk and a pile of leather and fur.

For the first time in a thousand years, the Erl King felt a tiny twinge of cold in his gut. A feeling he could not name. Whatever it was, however, he did not like it.

"Search the trees!" he roared, sword high. "Find them and bring them to me!"

The nine Hunters who remained were elfin creatures he had conscripted from his own realm. They had never been human. Somehow, the spark, the fire of the Hunt that he had given to those humans who had joined him . . . that spark had been taken away. The life he had granted as a boon to the faithful had been snuffed.

The Erl King growled deep in his chest, and dipped his horns slightly, instinctively, wanting nothing more than his enemy's guts on the points of those antlers. As one, the nine elfin Huntsmen began to crash through the trees on their dark steeds, shouting with a fury that rivaled the King's own.

Only a few feet away from the King's horse, the dark faerie and the hounds still tore into the corpses of the dead bucks. Now some of the faerie had begun to drift over to what little remained of the fallen Huntsmen. Less competition.

The Erl King lowered his sword, just a bit.

Which was when the vampire dropped from the branches above and tore at his throat with razor claws.

"Angel!" Buffy shouted.

He struggled with the Erl King for a moment, gnashing teeth and flashing claws, and then they both tumbled from the back of the king's stallion. Angel rushed at him again, but the Erl King batted him away with a single blow from his huge, taloned hand. Angel slammed against a thick tree trunk and collapsed onto a nest of exposed roots, his forehead slapping the ground.

The Erl King moved toward him.

Buffy raised her sword, urging herself to move forward to protect him, but could not.

"Roland!" she cried, and turned to him in desperation.

The prince of the Hunt hung his head in shame. A tear glistened in his eyes and he seemed to shrink down inside the leather and fur he wore now as the heir to the Erl King. "Your oath binds you, Buffy," he reminded her.

"It's working!" Willow shouted from her post behind a tree. "All the dead guys are . . . dead. We've cut them down by more than half, I think!"

One of the hounds turned its attention to her,

growling and running at her. It leaped, aiming for her throat.

Treasure's eyes darted around. She didn't know what to do. After what happened to Pontius and the others, she wondered why she hadn't just collapsed. Maybe it wasn't too late for her? Maybe she could still get out? Maybe she wasn't really dead yet.

A hand gripped her ankle, hard, and pulled. Treasure slid off the back of the horse and all the air went out of her lungs—she saw a bit of black tinging her breath. She scrambled, trying to get to her feet, reaching for her sword.

Willow screamed as the dog's fiery breath singed her throat.

Oz leaped across the path, muscle and sinew rippling beneath his fur, and grabbed the hound up in both hands, then brought it down hard, breaking its back with a sound like pottery shattering.

"Get the others," Oz growled, then he was off, running at a still-mounted Hunter, leaping up to tear the elfin rider down from his horse, and tearing into the evil thing with his claws.

Willow stared after him a moment. Then a hand clamped on her shoulder. She turned to see Giles offering her a sword. He pointed to the dead bucks, and the faerie and hounds that battled amongst themselves for the spoils.

"Their feeding frenzy won't last forever," Giles said. "They're beginning to notice . . ."

"Tell me about it," Willow said, thinking of the hound.

Without waiting for Giles, she ran toward the mound of faerie, toward the snarling hounds. Summoning all the skill she had acquired since she had asked Giles and Buffy for some self-defense tips, she swung the sword, cleaving a hound into a blast of black mist and twin dead husks. Several faerie turned to see what had happened. Two of them were sliced in half by her next slash. Some of them began to run.

Then Giles was with her, and soon a small cloud of black mist had begun to eddy on the breeze around them. The cloud was growing.

Xander leaped from his perch in the trees. The momentum of his fall took a huge bald Huntsman right off his horse. The two landed hard in the undergrowth and Xander didn't give the dark-skinned elfin man time to even move. He started pounding the Huntsman's face with his fists. The rider's weapon, a straight black iron mace—no ball and chain but one solid piece—lay on the ground two feet away.

When the Huntsman threw him off, Xander landed right next to the mace. He grabbed it with both hands as he rolled to his knees. The Huntsman had drawn a dagger and was diving for him. Xander swung his arms, the mace crashed into the Huntsman's knee from one side and pulped the bone into powder. The hideous elf went down. Xander smashed the hand that held the dagger.

Xander's heart beat a mad, terrified rhythm, but he didn't stop. He raised the mace above his head and brought it down onto the face of the Huntsman. The elf's skull imploded with a burst of oily black mist that was quickly sucked away on a powerful wind which had begun to kick up.

"No, no, no, don't do that," Cordelia said.

Cordelia spun Treasure around with one strong tug. The other girl was still reaching for her sword. She'd hoped to reason with the girl, but it was too late for that. Cordelia hit Treasure in the head with a large rock she'd picked up from the path, closing her eyes as if the pain were her own.

Treasure collapsed in a heap, blood flowing down over her face. She didn't get up again.

"Oh my God, oh my God," Cordelia whispered to herself.

"I can't kill the king," Buffy said angrily, "but until he orders me to stop, the rest of the Hunt is open season."

Roland said nothing, but Buffy didn't wait for a reply. She rode down hard on one of the elfin Huntsmen who had dismounted. Her sword whickered through the air, cleanly severing the rider's head with the sound of a hatchet striking wood. The head tumbled through the air, rolling into the trees as the headless corpse fell under the hooves of Buffy's horse.

A second rider was just ahead, his eyes burning with fire, ears pointed at the tip. His features were thin and cadaverously bony. There was nothing human in him, in any of the elves who still lived. Maybe six, at a glance.

Any trace of fear was gone from her. Now, all she cared about was saving her friends, and stopping these monsters who had preyed so long on the hopeless and helpless and unsuspecting people, the ones who had nowhere to turn. And the babies. She thought about the babies, and she screamed, her lungs seared by a cry of such savagery it frightened her.

Buffy put one foot on the back of her horse and catapulted herself at the Huntsman. She was behind him, and he tried to move his horse around to defend against her attack. Not fast enough. Buffy held her sword in both hands, point down, and landed behind him on his mount, driving her sword down through the Huntsman's back hard enough for the tip to stab the horse through its back.

The stallion screamed in pain and bucked, throwing Buffy to the ground with the corpse. She tried to withdraw her sword, but it was lodged inside the dead elf warrior. She pulled as hard as she was able, but could not free the blade.

Giles saw the Erl King lift Angel off the ground, his sword held high. He was roaring unintelligibly, too infuriated to even pretend at humanity any longer. Instead of slashing at Angel, the King slammed him against the tree again. Then he lowered his head, his horns sharp and gore encrusted. As Giles watched in astonishment and horror, the Erl King reared back and rushed at Angel like a savage bull.

Buffy screamed.

The Erl King's horns gored Angel's abdomen.

Angel's eyes snapped open and he cried out in agony. Blood spurted from the wounds, soaking Angel's clothes, running down the tree bark, splashing the Erl King's face.

Oz leaped onto the Erl King's back.

Giles rushed forward and ran his sword through the Erl King's side, buried it to the hilt and then pulled up as hard as he could, trying to eviscerate the creature but failing as the blade snagged on bone.

The Erl King backhanded him with one taloned hand. Giles's glasses flew off, and he stumbled backward and dropped to the path, barely conscious. Several dark faerie cackled in chaotic madness, and leaped on him.

Then Xander and Willow were there, tearing them off, stomping them into the ground, mashing the creatures beneath their feet.

Oz was slashing the Erl King, but then even he was thrown aside. Hern the Hunter rounded on them all. He snorted like a bull, fire rushing from his eyes and nostrils in long streams. Blood dripped from his horns. Where Angel had torn his throat open, flames licked at the wound, blackening the edges.

Then the Erl King's eyes locked on Buffy. "You!" he roared through his destroyed throat, more than ever sounding like an animal. "This is all because of you!"

He stalked toward Buffy. Oz went after him again and was thrown aside. Angel staggered to his feet, but one of the few remaining Hunters slammed into him from behind and they tussled on the hard-packed dirt of the path.

Buffy turned to face the Erl King. She had lost her sword, but now she brandished the cruelest of weapons, the morningstar mace. Its spiked ball swung menacingly on the iron chain.

"Put it down," the king snarled.

Her oath controlling her movements, Buffy put the weapon down.

"On your knees!"

Buffy fell to her knees on the path.

The Erl King raised his sword.

Willow and Cordelia brushed away the few dark faerie that remained and ran for Buffy, holding weapons they had no hope of using effectively.

The sword began to fall.

And clanged and sparked as the edge of a battleaxe turned it away.

The Erl King turned, enraged, ready to gut whomever had dared interfere. He found himself blazing eyes to blazing eyes with his only son, Roland, prince of the Hunt. Roland held his double-edge axe at the ready.

"I will not let you kill her, Father," Roland said, his voice low and dangerous. "You'll have to kill me first, and I don't believe you would take my life."

Hern the Hunter stared at his son for several moments before lowering his sword. "You're right, Roland. I cannot kill my own son."

Roland seemed to relax a moment. Then his father's burning throat pulsed with bursts of fire as the Erl King began to laugh.

"Slayer," the Erl King said, turning to Buffy. "Kill Roland."

Against her will, Buffy reached for the morningstar.

Chapter 17

IN THE CLEARING, RIDERLESS HORSES TRAMPLED THE dessicated remains of most of the Wild Hunt. A small handful of dark faerie still survived, but they were running about in a blind panic, unable to gather together for any kind of joint action. War cries and screams filled the air, and horses stamped their hooves.

It was not hot, but sweat ran down Buffy's forehead. She was hunched over, the iron handle of the morningstar held tightly in both hands. Her hair had fallen over her face, and she blew it away from her eyes. She gritted her teeth so hard that her jaw hurt. With every fiber of her being, she tried to drop the morningstar, to throw it aside. She thought about using it to strike herself, thinking that perhaps pain would break the magical hold of the oath she had taken.

She could not even do that.

"Kill him, Slayer!" the Erl King roared.

Roland attacked his father again, axe blade scraping sword edge before Roland spun away. He turned to attack again, and the Erl King had rushed at him, head bowed, horns deadly sharp. But the Erl King was huge and heavy, and Roland small and lithe. He easily outmanuevered his father, and hacked a deep wound in the King's side as he passed by.

"Buffy, I command your loyalty," Hern the Hunter declared. "Slay my son!"

Buffy stood a bit straighter. With a cry of anguish, she ran at Roland, her eyes apologizing even as she whipped the morningstar around on its chain, bringing the spiked ball down toward him. But Roland was a warrior like few others, trained by the Lord of the Hunt himself. He turned his axe blade and took the brunt of the spiked ball's impact broadside. Instead of the chain wrapping around the axe, the blow was harmlessly turned away.

The prince of the Hunt parried her attack and managed to move aside before his father could take advantage of the distraction.

"That's right, Slayer, kill him!" the Erl King said smugly. "Crush the ungrateful whelp's head for me."

Giles was a deft swordsman in his own right. The elfin Huntsman who attacked him now had the advantage of centuries of practice, however. There was no way Giles could beat him. He could only hope to hold out a while longer and hope for assistance.

Which came, quite suddenly, in the form of a broad curved sword, like a scimitar, which separated the Huntsman's head from his shoulder at the neck. The elf warrior went down, and Giles ran him through.

When he looked up, he expected Angel, or perhaps Oz.

It was Cordelia.

"Now, there's something you don't see every day," Xander said grimly.

"Yes," Giles agreed. "Quite."

Cordelia cried out, and Giles turned to see Buffy aiding the Erl King in his battle against Roland. She was struggling against the oath she had taken, he could see that. But it was only a matter of time before the young prince succumbed to the onslaught.

Giles ran toward them.

"Buffy!" Giles shouted.

Even as she brought the handle of the morningstar up to deflect Roland's blade, almost like bunting in baseball, she turned in response to Giles's voice. Roland's axe deflected off of her own weapon and sliced neatly through her shoulder. A superficial wound, but the pain helped her focus her thoughts.

"You've got to fight it!" the Watcher told her. "You're the Slayer. You aren't like other humans. You can fight."

Buffy frowned. Giles himself had as much as said the oath was unbreakable. Yet now he was saying it might be otherwise. Buffy was confused, but Giles was certainly right about one thing. She wasn't like other humans. She was the Slayer.

"We performed a ritual!" Giles added. "It's weakened them, you see?"

"Kill him now!" the Erl King roared. With Buffy distracted, Roland had turned his attention back to his father, and now the prince of the Hunt's axe dealt the Erl King a grievous wound to the left arm. Black mist escaped and the arm hung limply at the Erl King's side.

Buffy froze. She felt, more than anything, as though she was going to throw up. It was that moment of total body rictus just before she would start to puke her guts up. She began to hyperventilate, her breath coming too fast. She closed her eyes, heedless of the danger around her. She could hear blades clanging as her friends continued to war with the remaining Huntsmen.

Her muscles ached, pulled, seemed to tear as she fought them.

Slowly, she fought to slow her breathing. Then, suddenly, she opened her eyes.

Raised the morningstar.

The Erl King smiled broadly.

The spiked ball whipped through the air and crushed the left side of his face, flames shooting out past the iron.

"I'm the Slayer," she whispered, her throat tight. "I'm not like other girls."

With a roar of agony, the Erl King dropped his sword. He backhanded Buffy, sending her tumbling into the underbrush at the edge of the path. She climbed painfully to her knees, but Roland had already taken her place.

"Surrender, Father, or you will die here, so far from home. Not even your spirit will return to the Lodge," Roland said, his voice breaking with sorrow for a creature who had been nothing but cold and heartless to him.

The Erl King roared, all trace of sentience or humanity gone from him now. The fire in his eyes blazed high enough to singe his helmet, and trailed behind him as he bent his head and rushed at his son, horns aimed for Roland's gut.

Roland was exhausted and stunned by his father's ferocity. He brought his battleaxe up, but not in time. The Erl King's horns punched through his belly and lifted him up, and still, Hern the Hunter ran forward. Roland cried out in pain as he was lifted off his feet by the ragged wounds in his abdomen, and then the Erl King drove Roland into a wide tree, the horns driving deeper, goring him.

If Roland had been even remotely human, he would have been dead then.

Instead, he raised his axe over his father's head, grasped the handle in both hands, and brought it down with tremendous force, cleaving his father's skull in two. There was an ear-splitting roar, though from which of them Buffy could not tell, and then Roland's axe seemed to explode with flames. Fire jetted from the Erl King's skull as he died.

Fire that raced up Roland's arms to his face.

Roland roared and the fire reached inside him as if seeking shelter.

The prince of the Hunt threw his arms wide and his eyes exploded in a jet of viscous black mist.

Then the empty sockets began to burn.

"Roland, die in peace," Buffy whispered.

She closed her eyes and let a single, harsh sob escape her.

Then the wind whipped her hair. She felt the electrical charge of energy that had surged through her during her ride with the Hunt. Wailing stung her ears.

She opened her eyes.

Astride a jet-black horse sat the Erl King in all his majesty.

"Oh, God," Buffy groaned. She had failed miserably.

Roland was dead, but his father had somehow survived.

"Hern the Hunter is dead," the king said, his voice a guttural growl. His silhouette shimmered with black light that pulled in the colors of the forest and made the world around him gray and shadowed.

"Long life to the Erl King," chorused the four surviving riders of the Wild Hunt as they raised their weapons in gore-covered fists.

Three of them were elfin. The fourth was Connie DeMarco, known forever now as Treasure.

Buffy stared. It was Roland.

She tried to speak as four pointed horns sprouted from Roland's head and grew to a breadth unmatched by his father's. His skin was dark, and as she watched, hair grew on it. He became shaggy. Terrifying to look at.

He looked exactly like his father.

The flame that had coursed from father to son had been the passing of life, the passing of command from a king to his heir, the passing of all the power of the primeval forest, the first beasts to roam the land, from the Erl King to Roland, son of Hern the Hunter and Lucy Hanover, Chosen One.

He looked down at her and smiled. Dismounted. The girl, Connie, took the reins of his horse.

"How?" Buffy rasped.

"What was my body before, but a vessel?" he asked. "What is it now, but a shadow? The night cloaks me. She will always cover me."

"Roland," she whispered. "I—"

In his taloned hands he took her head, then bent—much taller than she now—and kissed her on the forehead.

"You swore an oath to obey the commands of the Erl King. I am king now, Buffy. Be free, Slayer, and be well," he said. "I fear that when next we meet, it will not be as friends."

Buffy frowned. "You could change things," she said. "It doesn't have to be this way."

"It does," Roland said simply, taking her hand, and she heard the growl in his wide chest, like the sound of animals lurking in shadows. "Oh, things will change. A little at a time. As much as I can manage. But the Wild Hunt will always ride, and the hopeless and foolish will always join us whether they wish it or not. We are part of the fabric of the night, Buffy. Neither the Lord of the Hunt nor the Slayer is powerful enough to alter that."

He kissed the back of her hand in a courtly gesture.

"I would ask you again to be my queen," he whispered, in a voice meant for her ears only, "but I already know your answer."

Buffy slowly pulled her hand away.

"Good luck, Roland," she said.

"And to you," he replied.

Then he turned and took Treasure's hand. He helped her mount her horse, and Buffy saw the way he looked at her. She would be Queen of the Hunt, of course. Giles tried to talk to her; so did Cordelia, in her way. But Treasure could not be convinced that there was any future for her in the world she had grown up in. Besides, she had already begun to die, to be resurrected into the life of the Hunt.

Even now, as Buffy looked at her, she thought that Treasure's eyes glowed just the tiniest bit.

The barrier that had held the Wild Hunt within the forest had slowly dissipated not long before Roland led the remaining Huntsmen back to the clearing and into the dark mist that still hung there. It would be gone by morning.

When they emerged from the forest, Oz returned completely to normal. It was cold, and he was shirtless, so Giles let Oz wear his tweed sportcoat. It had already been damaged beyond repair, so he saw no harm in it.

"Oh, man, I totally forgot," Oz groaned as they walked up the embankment toward Route 17. "They trashed my van."

"It'll be okay," Willow said confidently. "It might take a while, but I know you can fix it."

"Perhaps I could be of some assistance?" Giles suggested.

After a moment of silence, Oz said, "Really, I think it'll be all right."

"Okay, I'm technically sleeping at Willow's tonight, so I'm probably okay," Cordelia announced. "But I can't fit everyone into my car, so who's in the most trouble?"

"What time is it?" Willow asked, a little distracted as she looked at the night sky.

Angel glanced at the sky as well. "Almost three in the morning," he said with experience.

"I'm completely screwed," Xander said with a sigh, pleasantly resigned to his fate.

"I don't know if I'll have a home to go to, coming in this late," Willow said.

Buffy bit her lip at the sadness in both their voices. What they had just experienced was so horrible, so very real, and yet so completely surreal at the same time, that it was hard to readjust to the reality that the rest of the world knew. What was staying out all night compared to stopping a bunch of supernatural beings who preyed on the weak and hopeless and foolhardy?

But try telling that to a parent.

"All right, I'm staying with Buffy tonight," Cordelia announced.

Buffy blinked, then shrugged, realizing it was the only sensible plan.

"Xander and Willow, I'm taking you guys to the ER. You can tell your folks you were jumped or something, and let's face it, you need some medical attention anyway. Giles, you could use some too, but that's your business. You don't have parents waiting for you at home," Cordy went on. "Then I'll come back for the rest of you and get you to Giles's car."

"I can make my own way home," Angel said.

He moved to Buffy, whispered his goodbye, and when she looked for him again, he had gone. When he wanted to, Angel moved like the shadows, even harder to see the more you looked for him.

Oz went to Willow, kissed her lightly. "You going to be all right?" he asked.

"Yeah," she said. "They can't be mad at me for getting beaten up. And even if they don't buy it, they can only kill me once, right?"

They smiled together, but Willow was plainly worried.

Then Cordelia drove off, and it was just Buffy and Giles and Oz. They sat quietly on the side of the road.

Only one vehicle passed them, a tractor trailer, during the half hour they waited for Cordelia to return.

In the car on the way back to her own house, Buffy drifted off to sleep.

When Buffy woke the next morning, she didn't even remember waking up and going upstairs to bed.

It was just after eight o'clock on Friday night, and Joyce Summers was harried. The gallery hosted a number of events throughout the year, but only one or two as important as this.

This was a reception to introduce the new community liaison to the head of the police department's new runaway task force, Jamie Anderson. The policeman stood proudly with his son, who clearly had not fared well on the street.

Helping with the reception, a hollow-eyed Liz De-Marco continued to hope, and to pray, that her daughter would come home. She and her husband were divorcing.

Joyce bustled through the gallery, checking on the caterers, making certain her guests had enough wine, chatting with the security guards, and played the smiling diplomat for each and every person who might be able to help the troubled youth of Sunnydale.

It was going to be a long night, and the new black pumps she'd bought were killing her.

"Mom?"

Joyce turned, eyes wide with surprise, and saw Buffy standing behind her in a burgundy slip dress Joyce had never seen before. It was beautiful. She was beautiful.

"Buffy?" Joyce said. "What are you doing here?"

"You asked me to come, remember?" Buffy said wistfully. "Besides, you really look like you could use another pair of hands."

Joyce smiled, reached out and clasped Buffy's slender fingers in her own.

"I'm glad you're here, honey. I am so very, very glad."

Buffy grinned, rolled her eyes the way daughters do. Then she said, "Me, too."

About the Authors

Christopher Golden is the best-selling author of the epic dark fantasy series *The Shadow Saga,* as well as the X-Men trilogy *Mutant Empire* and the current hardcover *Codename Wolverine.* With Nancy Holder, he has written several other Buffy projects, including the upcoming *Gatekeeper Trilogy.* Please visit him at www.christophergolden.com.

Four-time Bram Stoker Award–winner Nancy Holder has sold thirty-six novels and over two hundred short stories, articles, and essays. She has also sold game-related fiction, and comic books and TV commercials in Japan. Her work has been translated into over two dozen languages. She and Christopher Golden have written four Buffy-related books together, the most recent of which was *Blooded.* She is the author of *Gambler's Star: The Six Families,* book one of a science fiction trilogy for Avon Books, due out in October of 1998. She lives in San Diego with her husband, Wayne, and their daughter, Belle.

BUFFY

THE VAMPIRE

SLAYER™

THE WATCHER'S GUIDE

The official companion guide to the hit
TV series, full of cast photos, interviews,
trivia, and behind the scenes photos!

By Christopher Golden and Nancy Holder

**POCKET
BOOKS**

Published by Pocket Books

1492-01

BUFFY

THE VAMPIRE

SLAYER™

As long as there have been vampires, there has been the Slayer.
One girl in all the world, to find them where they gather and
to stop the spread of their evil and the swell of their numbers

Child of the Hunt
By Christopher Golden and Nancy Holder

Return to Chaos
By Craig Shaw Gardner
(Coming in mid-November 1998)

The Watcher's Guide
(The Totally Pointy Guide for the Ultimate Fan!)
By Christopher Golden and Nancy Holder
(Coming in mid-October 1998)

Based on the hit TV series created by Joss Whedon

Published by Pocket Books

"Well, we could grind our enemies into powder with a sledgehammer, but gosh, we did that last night."
— *XANDER*

BUFFY
THE VAMPIRE
SLAYER™

As long as there have been vampires, there has been the Slayer. One girl in all the world, to find them where they gather and to stop the spread of their evil ... the swell of their numbers.

#1 THE HARVEST

#2 HALLOWEEN RAIN

#3 COYOTE MOON

#4 NIGHT OF THE LIVING RERUN

THE ANGEL CHRONICLES, VOL. 1

BLOODED

THE WATCHER'S GUIDE
(The Totally Pointy Guide for the Ultimate Fan!)

Based on the hit TV series created by Joss Whedon

  Published by Pocket Books